why birds sing

why birds sing

NINA BERKHOUT

Published by ECW Press
665 Gerrard Street East
Toronto, Ontario, Canada M4M 1Y2
416-694-3348 / info@ecwpress.com

Editor for the Press: Jennifer Knoch
Cover design: Jessica Albert
Cover artwork © Joey Gao / www.joey-gao.com
Author photo: Hans Berkhout

This is a work of fiction. Names, characters,
places, and incidents either are the product of the
author's imagination or are used fictitiously, and
any resemblance to actual persons, living or dead,
business establishments, events, or locales is entirely
coincidental.

LIBRARY AND ARCHIVES CANADA CATALOGUING
IN PUBLICATION

Title: Why birds sing : a novel / Nina Berkhout.

Names: Berkhout, Nina, 1975– author.

Identifiers: Canadiana (print) 20200235249
Canadiana (ebook) 20200235346

ISBN 978-1-77041-581-2 (softcover)
ISBN 978-1-77305-622-7 (PDF)
ISBN 978-1-77305-621-0 (EPUB)

Classification: LCC PS8553.E688 W59 2020
DDC C813/.6—dc23

The publication of *Why Birds Sing* has been generously supported by the Canada Council for the Arts which last year
invested $153 million to bring the arts to Canadians throughout the country and is funded in part by the Government
of Canada. *Nous remercions le Conseil des arts du Canada de son soutien. L'an dernier, le Conseil a investi 153 millions de dollars
pour mettre de l'art dans la vie des Canadiennes et des Canadiens de tout le pays. Ce livre est financé en partie par le gouvernement
du Canada.* We acknowledge the support of the Ontario Arts Council (OAC), an agency of the Government of Ontario,
which last year funded 1,737 individual artists and 1,095 organizations in 223 communities across Ontario for a total of $52.1
million. We also acknowledge the contribution of the Government of Ontario through the Ontario Book Publishing Tax
Credit, and through Ontario Creates for the marketing of this book.

MIX
Paper from
responsible sources
FSC
www.fsc.org   FSC® C103567

"Hope" is the thing with feathers —
That perches in the soul —
And sings the tune without the words —
And never stops — at all —

— EMILY DICKINSON (314)

1

On the morning of our anniversary, my husband took my hands in his like he had something meaningful to say. It had been a bad year. I thought a beach vacation might be on offer. "I'd like Tariq to come and live with us," he told me.

This was the brother who had declined our wedding invitation and left his own father's funeral early. The one who seldom wished Ashraf happy birthday or called to say hello. He lived just a few hours away but didn't visit. If ever Ash tried to see him, he would say he was out of town.

"Why?" I asked.

He wiped the inner corners of his eyes. "He has cancer."

I'd seen my husband cry only once, three years earlier when his father died. I now held him and we sat at the kitchen table in silence until I asked, "Doesn't your mom want to take care of him?"

Mina, who used to live in the suburbs, had recently bought a condo on our street. "We're not telling her," Ash said. "Not until he's better."

"What about his gashti, then?" That was Mina's nickname for Tariq's wife. It meant whore.

"He and Anabelle have separated," Ash replied.

I could count the instances I'd met Tariq on one hand.

The first was when Ash hosted a dinner party to introduce me to the Khans. We'd been together six months and the gathering did not go well. Instead of addressing me by my name, Ash's father kept calling me "the girl." I burned the cobbler and Mina mistook my quietness for arrogance. As for Tariq, he kept checking his flashy watch all night, and his wife never showed up. The second meeting was accidental. We bumped into one another at a country market. There I was presented to Anabelle, a statuesque blonde with high cheekbones. Ash and I were still newlyweds, overly protective of each other. I wanted to ask why they hadn't come to our wedding, but I could see how happy my husband was to see his brother, so I said nothing. Our next encounter was at Majid Khan's burial, where Tariq and Anabelle whisper-argued in the cemetery, leaving before the reception. And the last time I had seen him was a year ago at the hospital, when Mina was being treated for dizzy spells. After hugging his little brother, Tariq shook my hand without making eye contact. He had looked healthy.

"What kind of cancer?" I asked.

"He doesn't want to talk about it. I'm not going to push him."

"Is he getting treatment?"

"He's sorting it out."

"What does that mean?"

"I only know he wants to spend time with me. That's what he said. That's why I suggested he come here." He twisted the ring on his finger. "He has no one."

Well, he had his mother. But it seemed he didn't want her involved.

I asked Ash if his brother knew I wasn't singing. That I would be at home. "You'll hardly know he's here," he told me. "He'll stay downstairs."

Our house was old but big, the idea being that it would one day hold a family. There were four bedrooms upstairs and the basement was its own walkout with a sofa bed, a kitchenette, a bathroom, and French doors opening onto the backyard. Ash said we could rent it out if we ever needed money, but I knew the more likely scenario was that Mina would eventually move in.

My husband looked at me. He hadn't shaved and there were dark lines under his eyes. "Of course he can stay here," I told him.

We got up from the table and he wrapped his arms around me. "Poor Tariq," he said. "He wants to bring his bird, too."

I asked what kind of bird. He shrugged, gulped his coffee, and put his suit jacket on. "When will they come?" I added. "Your brother and his mystery bird?"

"Is tomorrow too soon?" he asked, scrolling through his phone.

My skin went cold at the thought of a near stranger in our home, disrupting my daily rituals.

Ash grabbed his keys, and I retrieved his gift from the cupboard. "Happy fifth," I told him, handing him a piece of driftwood tied with ribbon. We kissed, and he said he'd find a spot for the wood in the garden. Then he told me to reserve dinner anywhere I wanted, someplace fancy. I promised a home-cooked meal instead, although I hadn't used the oven in a long time. But I didn't feel like being around other people and convinced myself his forgetting our special occasion was fine.

The next day, I went downstairs, vacuumed, and opened the sofa. I pulled the wedding quilt my mother had made us from the closet. It looked like a burst of confetti on the bed. I cleaned the bathroom, putting out toothpaste, shampoo, towels, and a fresh bar of soap. I put tea and coffee, bread and milk in the kitchenette. Then I washed the French doors and opened them for the first time in months and stepped outside.

Summer was over. These were the last weeks of heat. The hum of crickets was growing faint, the green in the trees wasn't so green anymore, and the plants I used as remedies for throat aches choked each other out in tangles or died away. The patch of chamomile I usually dried for steam inhalations had withered untouched. A web of nettle grew over the sage, verbena, and mint. Only the rose bush still bloomed. The flowers had changed colour, though, the yellow of years past replaced by a deep orange. I snipped from it, went back inside, and dropped the stem into a vase on the nightstand. Then I lay down and stared at the ceiling and hummed "Musetta's Waltz," which I should have been performing at the House in two weeks, the first show of the season. Yet even without words, I couldn't control my vibrato. My range was gone and soon I was out of breath, so I got under the quilt and closed my eyes.

The bell woke me. I didn't know how much time had passed. I rushed to straighten the bed, pulled the French doors closed, ran upstairs, and splashed cold water on my face. After tying my knotted hair back, I opened the door.

Tariq stood at the bottom of the steps with a duffel bag. He appeared thinner and more dishevelled than the last time I'd seen him, like any recently divorced man in his early forties who wasn't taking care of himself. And he had the same stance I'd noticed on every occasion we met. Slightly stooped with his hands behind his back, like the elders of opera who paced around on stage in fur-lined robes but did not do much singing anymore.

His hair was as thick as Ashraf's, only shorter, and its black was flecked with grey. He was taller than his brother, his skin and eyes darker. I wanted to know how long he planned on staying and the details of his illness. At the same time, I was trying to recall the melody in the dream I'd been torn from.

I said hello. He nodded wordlessly, as though he were the one on vocal rest. Then I spotted a small carrier in the grass behind him. As I passed him to get a glimpse, he lowered his head and stepped aside.

I had expected a songbird, but this foot-tall feathered thing looked more like a pigeon with a raggedy tail and battered wings.

Part of its chest was bare, so I could see its belly moving in and out as it breathed. When I crouched down, it lunged and hissed.

"Who's this?" I asked, my voice hoarse.

"Her name is Tulip," Tariq said. "She's a Congo African grey parrot."

"Oh," I replied.

"It's good to see you, Dawn." He said it casually, as if we saw each other often. "She's normally more presentable," he added of his bird. "But she's been under stress. Since my illness."

I stood again. "How are you feeling?"

"Better now," he said with a half-smile.

Ash's brother walked back to his car and I watched him struggle to remove a large apparatus from his SUV. As he rolled it over, it made the sound of an empty shopping cart. The jumbo cage wouldn't fit through the front so I suggested we take it around back. He picked up the carrier, and I helped him steer the cage along the side of the house to the French doors.

Once inside, Tariq scanned the walkout, resting his gaze on my corner by the bay window. He moved my favourite red armchair and shelf of librettos out of the way and pushed the apparatus in place. Then he left again. When I approached the carrier containing his bird, she shrieked.

A few minutes later, Tariq returned with a flowered suitcase, a perch, and a baby playscape. He pulled a blanket from the suitcase and covered the back of the cage with it, unzipped the carrier door, and extended his hand.

"Step up," he said.

The bird poked her head out and assessed her surroundings before stepping onto Tariq's fingers. As they made their way to the bay window, she eyed me and peered into the larger enclosure, like she was trying to decide which fate was worse. Eventually she stepped onto a metal rung and from there, hopped onto a dead branch.

The cage contained several perches. Tattered toys lay on the floor, a swing hung down from the middle rung, and bells and baubles were clipped to the sides.

Tariq retrieved a bag the size of a sack of potatoes from the suitcase. He filled bowls with pellets and water and placed them on a tray. Then he saw the rose. He pulled the flower from the vase, plucked the petals, and fed them to his parrot.

He cleared his throat. "I'm sorry to hear you're not performing these days."

Ash's brother had never struck me as someone inclined to care for opera. "Do you follow the circuit?" I asked.

"A little," he replied, fiddling with the cage.

The veins in my neck began pulsating. My phone dinged. I told him to make himself at home and that Ashraf would be back from work soon. Tulip blinked and looked all over the place. Her head wouldn't stop moving around. When I told her goodbye, she narrowed her eyes and puffed her feathers out as I climbed the stairs to go.

"Don't stare at her straight on," Tariq said.

I turned back.

"Look at her from the side with one eye," he told me. "So she knows you're not a threat. As if you were a bird, too."

2

I hurried to the car, late for my course. Injured singers were always made to teach and I assumed I was leading a masterclass for the young artist program. My agent, Judith King, had sent me reminders that I deleted without reading. I hadn't prepared a thing.

The address was a community college on the other side of the city and it was rush hour. I couldn't understand why the class wasn't at the main building but figured the company was renting studios for lack of rehearsal space at the House.

Norwood College turned out to be a rundown place in an industrial neighbourhood. I bought a coffee from a machine-lined cafeteria and wandered past busy rooms with rows of adults wearing headsets and staring at screens. Finally I found the right wing and heard voices as I approached. The door was open a crack. I counted five heads in an otherwise empty lecture hall and stood and listened.

"Calm your horses, Reno. You'll be terrific," a woman with a close-cropped haircut was saying. Something on her shone. It was a tuning fork, hanging from a chain like a wishbone against her lumberjack shirt.

"Easy for you to say, Josephine," the bearded man a few seats down from her replied. He had a tattoo on his neck and was built like a wrestler. "You don't have a whole new routine to learn."

"It's thirty past. I don't know why we bothered," a sixtyish lady said, a swoosh of red hair twirled in a bun on top of her head. This one was all dressed up, but her lime wristbands didn't go with her outfit.

"Is this new teacher of ours the one who messed up on stage?" a teenager asked. He wore sunglasses and his sandy hair was in need of a cut. He slouched in his bucket seat.

"That's her," the redhead told him.

"We're paid up," an older man in a pressed shirt said. "Might as well give it a chance." He sat in the front row with a walker parked next to him. He shuffled to the table beside the lectern without it, picked up a cookie, and took a bite before putting it back on the paper plate. "These are stale."

"They were here when we got here," the wrestler mumbled.

"Hey, guys," the teenager said. "I finally got the cardinal down." He cupped his hands around his mouth and took a deep breath in. The sound that came out was loud and wobbly, several notes over and over. Everyone clapped.

The redhead stuck her tongue out. "I burned my mouth on clam chowder. I'm abstaining tonight."

"I bit mine. Actually my lady friend bit it," the wrestler said, nudging the older man who sat back down beside him. Then his face fell. "Yesterday at the grocery store, a fatty in a scooter said she'd run me over if I didn't shut it."

"You know the etiquette on doing it in public, Reno," the tuning fork woman told him. "Naturally you get glares. Now quit stalling and let's warm up." Striking her resonator on her shoe and putting it to her ear, she puckered her lips and made kissing sounds. They all followed along. Then they launched into their so-called music. The noise was awful.

There was a company brochure taped to the door. It advertised classes on Italian lyrics, German composers, Callas's life, set design, and anything else you could think of that got opera buffs worked up. But the course that was circled with a picture of the Seven Dwarfs and my name on it was Whistling Arias.

I tore it off, accidentally pushing the door open. The group stopped and stared. The teenager smiled and said, "Please announce yourself." When the wrestler stood, I saw that his shirt was patched with duct tape.

"You made it," the old man called out.

"That was weird," I heard another say, but by then I was walking away.

I drove straight to Judith's office and pulled up next to her electric car. After resting my head on the wheel for a breathing exercise, I entered the granite building and took the elevator to the twentieth floor.

Judith had negotiated my contract with the company. Normally singers were hired for roles, not seasons, but with her help I had landed a three-year job, with carte blanche to guest star with other opera houses when we weren't performing. By the end of the first year, my schedule was booked solid. I began receiving offers internationally, years ahead of time, at least until my last performance. Now those same offers had been retracted. The company had tried to cancel my contract, too. But Judith had negotiated an arrangement veiled in legal threats whereby they would retain me, albeit on extended leave, until they were satisfied that my voice had healed. Every time we met, my agent assured me that I would make it back to the stage again. Even though we both knew this reality grew dimmer with every passing month.

A glamorous woman in her fifties, Judith was worshipped by singers near and far. She favoured wrap dresses and braided updos, and always wore medallion necklaces around her neck that made me think of Nefertiti. Even the way she waved me into her office was grand.

"Dawn. What a surprise," she said. Then she glanced at her screen and frowned. "Why aren't you teaching? Why are you in sweats?"

I dropped the brochure on her desk. "This is insulting."

"What's the problem?" she asked. "You know how to whistle, don't you? Just put your lips together and —"

"That's not funny."

"It's not meant to be. This won't strain your vocal cords."

"Give me a masterclass," I told her.

She tsked. "You're supposed to be resting your voice. Not causing further damage. I sent you these details ages ago. You should have said something sooner."

"Cancel based on low attendance. There was nobody there."

"This is part of the company's outreach initiative," she replied. "Numbers don't matter. Only that it's on offer." She raised her chin a fraction. "Besides, done properly whistling is an art."

"That's ridiculous."

"It has no language barrier. And you don't need a good voice. In case you hadn't noticed, your profession's got to make itself more accessible and bring new audiences in, or all you big-mouth babies will be unemployed."

Opera was a superstitious world. One of the worst things a performer could do near a stage was whistle. I told Judith as much, but she only said it was a good thing the course didn't take place on stage.

Then her phone rang. "I'm so sorry. She had an emergency. How does an extra session sound? Perfect. And don't forget to use your registration discount on season tickets!"

"I won't do it," I told her after she hung up.

With a few keystrokes, she pulled up my contract, highlighting the part that read that while unable to perform, the vocalist was obligated to offer other relevant services determined by management and which did not hinder voice recovery. "Otherwise you won't get disability pay," she said. Then she shook her head and sighed. "I told you not to take it on," she added. "I told you it was suicide. All when your career was going so well."

"You're saying my career is over."

"What are you now, thirty-three? You could still peak. But you need to keep your distance until it's forgotten."

I asked for the syllabus. She said there was none and that it was my responsibility. When I turned to go, she came around her desk and squeezed my shoulders. "Exploring a new direction will be good for you."

I swallowed and straightened. "How is Svetlana working out?" Svetlana Minsk, my skinny replacement, was another one of her artists.

"Svetlana is doing fine," she replied, averting her gaze.

Then she told me she would be in touch with any updates. But I knew I wouldn't hear from her for a long time. There would be no offers, which was my fault, not hers. I had rushed into a role I wasn't ready for and this was the consequence.

My ponytail sagged. I combed a chunk of hair with my fingers.

"Try to look after yourself," Judith said, the corners of her glossy mouth lowering as she led me out and closed her door.

At home I found Ash and his brother in the yard. They sat under the apple tree with beer and nuts, the bird perched on Tariq's knee. As soon as I joined them, Ash asked how my class went.

"They're making me teach whistling," I told him. "To the public."

He raised an eyebrow the way Mina did when she mocked me. "You mean to people like us?" he asked.

I smiled, watching the bird.

Tariq offered his pet a pistachio. She brought the shell to her beak with her clawed foot, which worked like a hand. "Whistling is Tulip's favourite hobby," he said. He gave a two-note whistle but got no response.

While the brothers spoke, I studied the parrot. She had a black beak and yellow eyes with white patches around them. Aside from an unexpected flash of scarlet for her tail, the rest of her was a sooty grey. When she finished her nut, she used her feet and beak as grips to climb down Tariq's leg. Once in the grass, she unfolded her wings and they quivered like human arms stretching. Then she teetered around and gave a few half-hearted squawks before climbing back up to Tariq's knee.

"Why isn't she flying?" I asked.

Tariq opened and closed his hand several times. There was a square of gauze taped on it, and further up where his arm bent, another. "She doesn't go far," he said. "When I got her, she had muscle atrophy and improperly clipped wings. She had to grow her feathers back and learn to be a bird again." The breeze picked up and he stood with Tulip in the crook of his arm. "I'll bring her in," he said. "She hates drafts."

We asked if he wanted something to eat. He told us no and thanked us, and Ash and I went inside, too.

I warmed up the leftovers of our anniversary meal, a gloopy risotto. Then we watched some TV. Before going upstairs to our room, I listened at the door off the living room that led downstairs. Briefly I thought I heard the sound of violins, until Ash pulled me away.

In bed, my husband stayed sitting up in the darkness. "It's stomach," he finally said.

I turned the light on again.

"He's already had surgery and radiation," he continued. "It's early and totally curable. They found it when he went in for heartburn, or an ulcer, or something."

Tariq had taken a leave from his job and relocated to our city. He had a lot of connections who'd made his transfer to one of our hospitals possible. He would complete his treatment while living with us and return to work within the year. "He's calling it his sabbatical," Ash said.

"And your mom — who's five blocks away — doesn't know this?"

"It would kill her. She'd move in, too."

I asked about our weekly dinners. On Fridays Mina ate with us. First Ash picked her up, then they got takeout because my cooking didn't agree with her. Afterwards, at 8:45 sharp, my husband accompanied his mother home in time for her murder mystery program.

Ash replied that our dinners were nothing to worry about. Mina never ventured downstairs.

I turned off the light again and Ash lay down.

"That's the crankiest parrot I've ever met," I said to distract him.

"How many parrots have you met?" he asked. I said one, and he laughed. Minutes later he was snoring. I leaned in closer, curling my legs into his, wondering if I had made a poor choice. Tariq would probably find the wedding quilt too heavy.

3

When I woke up, Ash was gone. He always had breakfast with Mina before work, an arrangement predating our marriage that hadn't changed. Since Majid Khan died, he also ate supper with his mother on his way home from the office. Mostly it didn't bother me. I knew the division between households was temporary. Although with time, my mother-in-law's grief solidified rather than weakened her; she seemed to strengthen in its chokehold like a rhinoceros that would live forever.

I dragged a blanket to the living room. After listening at the downstairs door and hearing nothing, I made toast. Then I returned to the couch to review my final performance, analyzing for the umpteenth time how it all went wrong.

In hindsight, taking on a role at the last minute had been my first mistake. Everybody knew that *Tosca* was the *Macbeth* of the opera world. But when Judith phoned with the urgent request from the artistic director that I replace the lusty Aimée Guillou that same night, called away because her mother had died, I couldn't decline.

I'd just completed a demanding run of *Così* in San Francisco and was on my way to the airport for a few days off when Judith had called. Guillou's first cover, who was to step in for her, had the flu. We had fifteen minutes to decide before the company moved on. Without hesitation I told her to accept. I was eager to tackle Las Vegas, but Judith advised against it. This director's version took a lot of liberties. I hadn't seen the sets and I needed a break. Lastly, I was not a lyric-spinto and needed to stop taking leading roles for every type of soprano.

I argued that they wanted me for a reason. Judith claimed they were desperate, and everyone had declined. But I insisted, telling her that I knew Floria Tosca so intimately I could sing her backwards. Then I continued to the airport, changed my flight, and gave myself cortisone shots in the public bathroom.

And everything went well on opening night until the second act, when I lay sideways on the chaise longue for "Vissi d'arte," and the daybed gave way. I fell and rose quickly, stepping upstage closer to my enemy, Scarpia, and further away from the audience. But the next malfunction threw me off, when the curtain dropped and rose again. Through stunned gasps I kept going until the short rapid crescendo when I pushed my voice too far and felt it cracking as I finished to confused applause.

Then Spoletta, the police chief, arrived. The three of us discussed my lover Cavaradossi's mock execution in cantata, and our spectators were attentive again. A dog wandered on. No one had told me that was part of the production. It approached and sniffed my crotch, until Spoletta ushered it offstage to some audience murmuring.

Nevertheless I channelled Tosca's anguish at the thought of prostituting herself to Scarpia, as he drafted the papers for her safe passage out of Rome with her beloved. You could have heard a pin drop as Scarpia embraced me and I stabbed him, crying, "This is Tosca's kiss!" Then I knelt with a candelabrum to put a crucifix on his bloodied chest, leaning in with the famous "Now I forgive him."

Only when I blew the computerized candles out, they flickered on again. Snickers came from the audience as I left the stage. "You just exited through the fireplace," a stagehand told me. The lighting was dim. Everything was oversized, both the door and the fireplace were bricked rectangles, and I had only wanted to get away.

Clips were online for anyone to see. The theatre restricted phone use but a few attendees had managed to violate the rule, capturing my costumed self at different angles like mirrors in a funhouse.

Before I got to the worst of it, Mina showed up uninvited.

I recognized her hard repetitive knocking and quickly checked the backyard. Tariq and his bird were outside by the old lilac. I rapped on the window and ran downstairs, through the French doors. By the time I reached them, I could hear my mother-in-law coming around the side of the house.

"You are here, Done?" she called out.

"We have a visitor," I told Tariq.

Tulip squawked. He fed her and I followed them behind some trees, all of us avoiding Mina.

"Done!" my mother-in-law called again.

We retreated further against the fence, into a space smaller than Juliet's balcony. There we held our bodies still, while Tulip chewed her dehydrated fruit.

It started to rain. I could feel his breath on my temple and tried to concentrate on some branches while we waited for Mina to go. She didn't open the gate to the yard but she didn't leave either, instead rearranging her trousers over her waist, pulling them above her rolls of skin. Then she stared at a patch of crabgrass.

Through the trees, I considered the face I had long ago stopped trying to win over. Despite her angry eyebrows the nicest thing about Mina Khan's appearance was her wide-set eyes. She had a mild overbite and a sprinkling of freckles on her nose, her cheeks dipping in below the bone. I had seen photos of her younger, a laughing, handsome woman. Now she was overweight, slow, and short-tempered. She ate red meat daily and never smiled.

"Tulip is always up for a game of hide and seek," Tariq said.

I turned but found I couldn't look directly at him. Instead I broke branches off a low bough. "Then keep hidden until we're gone," I told him and stepped out into the open.

"What you are doing?" Mina asked when she saw me.

"Pruning," I said, tossing the cuttings in the grass. "How are you, Mrs. Khan?"

At our wedding, when I'd asked my mother-in-law what she wanted me to call her now that I was married to her son, she had lowered her gaze at me. "To you, I am Mrs. Khan," she'd replied, setting the tone of our relationship. From then on, in my mind I vowed to think of her only by her diminutive given name.

The rain came down harder. She tugged her bare ear while I led her inside by the elbow. "I lose my jhumka," she said.

"Did you tell Ashraf?"

"My son don't have time for this."

"If I find it, I'll drop it off."

She went through the living room into the kitchen where she dried her thinning, grey-black hair with a tea towel. "Please." She hugged herself. "This was gift by Majid."

While I searched for her earring under the furniture, she cut an orange, filled a jug with tap water, and dropped the slices in it.

"I'm actually on my way out," I told her. "To a rehearsal."

She placed the jug on the table. "Drink," she said and sat, pointing to my forehead. "These cracks in skin is no good."

I glanced outside but couldn't see Tariq or his bird. Mina slid her sandals off, crossing a leg over her knee. While trying not to stare at her bunions, a trace of gold in her cardigan's drooping pocket caught my eye. I reached in and held the bell-shaped antique earring out to her.

"Haanji. Here it is." She put the hook through her lobe. "First time I see Majid, I know he will be most important piece to my being. This is feeling like relieve." She rubbed the large dangling drops. "You feel this of my son? You are not liking him."

"Of course I like him."

"You are not alike with Ashraf."

"If you want to visit just say so." I finished my water. "You don't need an excuse."

She pulled her sandals back on and pushed herself up. Passing through the living room, she straightened piles of untouched opera scores and kicked aside a basket of unwashed laundry. "Aye haye," she said, shaking her head and closing the door with force.

After Mina left, I sat on the couch again for the end of my performance. Before act three, I had injected myself with another cortisone shot and re-entered Tosca's soul. Stepping back on stage, though, my mind went completely blank. It was all happening so fast. The conductor picked up on my memory lapse, and the orchestra saved me.

After my lover Cavaradossi was executed and I rushed toward him, realizing he was dead, I thought I could recover with my final task, a flying leap off the prison roof. I took a running start but tripped over my dress, sliding to my doom on my stomach instead. This was the audience's last look at Tosca, the suicidal heroine. By then the theatre was roaring.

Deep into my analysis, muffled voices interrupted my focus. Through the living room window, I observed Tariq and Anabelle outside, a taxi idling in front of the house. Clearly the Khans were not going to leave me alone.

Anabelle was draped in blue silks and kept raising her arms as if she was summoning the sea, while Tariq stood barefoot on the sidewalk. I tried reading their lips until she put her hand out and he dropped some keys in it. Then she sent her taxi away, got into his SUV, and drove off.

The door behind me creaked. I turned to see Tulip perched at the top of the steps.

"Hi," I said, looking away and back at her sideways.

She eyed my cold raisin toast.

I tore a chunk off, sat on the ground, and held it in my outstretched palm. For every step she took toward me, she did a backwards circle until she'd backed herself up against a wall.

I tried again.

After a few minutes of the shuffling dance, she was inches from my hand. From there she craned her neck out, snatched the bread, and retreated, dragging her prize to the foot of the couch, where she tore pieces off with her beak, making smacking sounds as she crunched.

When she finished, I approached with more toast. She lunged at my hand, bit me, and drew blood. I screamed with a ripping in my throat as Tariq appeared, looking from me to his growling bird.

He raised my hand to the light. "You don't need stitches. That was a warning nip." He turned his other palm out, revealing semi-circle scars on the padding beneath his thumb. Then he brought my wrist down but continued to hold it. A fluttering passed through my fingertips. Looking at his hand on mine, he let go and thanked me for sending his mother away.

"It's fine," I whispered, my vocal cords throbbing. "But why not tell her?"

He rubbed his forehead and I saw how his shaving was uneven. He'd missed patches and it looked like he'd recently attempted to trim his hair with the same lousy razor. "This is easier," he said, while Tulip pecked at the floor for crumbs.

I excused myself for the bathroom to tape my finger and gargle with saltwater, pausing at the sight of the half-empty box of pregnancy tests in the medicine cabinet. Since I'd stopped singing, we had been trying, without luck. Another failure. I turned off the light and lay down in my housecoat, pressing my face against the tiles.

The *toi toi toi* of singers backstage, lights dimming, the conductor raising his baton in that familiar nightmare turned into a *click click click*, and I could hear Tariq talking to his bird in a soft-spoken voice.

My scalp was so itchy that I decided to take a shower. The hot water loosened my chest and shoulders. I washed my hair. Then I washed it again.

Afterwards I went out to the yard.

There was only one bloom left on the rosebush and I clipped it. Through the French doors, I could see Tariq lying on the quilt with Tulip beside him. I watched them resting and left the flower on the entrance mat as a peace offering. Then I went back inside and upstairs to our bedroom, where I closed the blinds and slept.

4

I arrived at Norwood on time the following week. Once there, though, I stayed in the car, listening to recordings of arias I could no longer bring to life.

When I forced myself into the college lecture hall, the small group was sitting in their same places, as though they'd never left. I threw my belongings on the desk. "I'm Dawn Woodward," I told them.

"Are you —" the redhead began.

"Named after Dawn Upshaw? No." I had been compared to the American soprano once, early on in my career. The article was titled "Dawn of a New Era," and it called my multifaceted range "wondrous." I revered Upshaw for her interpretation of Górecki, but now I would never meet her.

"I was going to ask if you're related to Agnes Woodward," she said.

"Founder of the California School of Artistic Whistling," the old man offered. "Trainer of John Wayne and Pat Boone."

"I'm not related to anyone famous," I told them.

"We're the Warblers," the tuning fork woman said. She was wearing suspenders over her lumberjack shirt. She was probably often mistaken for a man until she spoke. Her stockiness didn't match her voice.

"Is that your band?" I asked.

The redhead stiffened and adjusted her lime cuffs, which glared brightly against her white arms. "We're a registered organization dating back to 1950. During our heyday, we had over two hundred members."

"We're what's left," the old man added, toasting a cookie at me. He ate from a box in his lap.

"Why whistling?" I asked.

They stared. I stared back.

"Because it feels good," the wrestler said. "And it's free." He gave a wide smile and shoved his hands under his armpits.

"Whistling's not my profession," I told them.

"We know you sang." The teenager grinned.

"I still do," I replied.

They shot each other knowing looks before turning back to me.

"We thought you could counsel us for our upcoming Biennial," the old man said.

I asked for clarification.

"There are local chapters like ours across the country." The redhead spoke slowly, as if I were a child. "We meet up every second year. There's a competition and we need help winning. Because Jojo here, despite her family connections, never pulls through."

"I thought you did this to feel good," I said.

The redhead folded her arms. "I want my trophy. Everyone steers clear of opera for the classical component of the contest. That's our in."

"Why would they avoid opera?" I asked.

"Well, it's so . . ."

"So what?"

"Loud," the teenager said.

"He means over the top," the old man added.

"It's the acting that's unfortunate," the redhead said. "Do they not equip you lot with lessons?"

They went on to call my vocation elitist, passé, self-indulgent, and impossible to understand. I banged my fist on the metal desk. It made the sound of stage thunder and the group went silent, their eyes fixed on me.

The tuning fork woman stood then. "I'm Josephine Wells, but you can call me Jo. I've been coaching these last few years. That's Georgie," she pointed to the redhead, and then to the wrestler, the old man, and the teenager. "And that's Reno, Walt, and Ben."

"Do you want to hear our stuff?" Ben asked.

Crossing over to the tiered seating, I stifled a yawn, while Josephine approached the lectern and turned on the microphone. Then she went back to her seat and said, "You're up, Reno."

The wrestler rolled his shoulders and cracked his neck before going to the mic. In place of his duct-tape shirt, he had on aqua blue scrubs. "I'm Reno Morrow," he spoke as if to a full audience. "Reno as in Nevada. I'm thirty-six and I've been whistling since I was two." He straightened his uniform.

"He wouldn't have had enough teeth at two," Georgie, the redhead, mumbled.

"Today I'll be performing 'American Pie.'"

"No, you won't," Jo called down. "It's a five-minute max and you know it."

Reno sighed. "Today I'll be performing 'Solitary Man.'"

Jo struck her fork against her temple and held the stem on the small desk above her knees. As the tines produced their hum, her whole large body relaxed.

"He's practically tone deaf," Georgie told her. "Your gadget won't help."

"These vibrations could heal your imbalances, Georgina." Jo hooked her fork back onto its chain and scrolled through a tablet. "And subdue your hysteria. If you'd just be open-minded." She nodded at Reno as music streamed from the device.

Hands clenched in fists at his side, Reno began. He had a certain musicality. But halfway through, his face turned red and his breathing became laboured between notes. He started sweating and licking his lips, eventually reining everything in with an unsteady ending.

"It's coming along," Jo told him.

He took a stiff bow and came and sat next to me. "So where's home?" he asked, wiping his forehead.

"Not this again. Leave her be," Georgie said.

"I'm only wondering, since you must travel a lot."

"I live here," I said.

He glanced back at the group like he'd proven a point. "You didn't call it home," he told me. "I've got the same problem, coming from a military family. I'm craving roots now, though. So I'm conducting a survey. About home."

Jo tapped him. "Let's not show all our cards at once," she said before turning to the teenager. "Ben, you're next."

He leaned to the side and ran a hand along the aisle chairs as he made his way to the lectern. "It's nine steps," Reno told him as Ben stretched an arm out to feel for the mic. He was blind.

"Hi," he said. "I'm Ben Tillett. I do bird sounds. In the woods, they sing back to me and fly closer." He whistled three notes over. "That's a brown thrasher. But since bird calls aren't allowed in the contest, I'll tell a story."

"We're working on getting that rule changed," Jo whispered to me.

"This is a tale about a venerable general," Ben continued. "One night he and his men were surrounded by troops of enemy cavalry who would kill them at first light. In the darkness, he went up a tower and whistled songs from the horse soldiers' faraway land, until they broke down and cried and left in the morning for home."

Everyone waited. Ben chewed on a cuticle.

"You're saying whistling defeated an army," Jo finally said.

"Bingo," Reno cut in. "The journey homeward matters most. Right, Benjamin?"

Ben nodded.

"Well done," Jo told him. "Now how about another song?"

The teenager cupped his hands and did a robin.

"Have you sent your audition package to the L.A. agents?" Jo asked. He gave her a thumbs-up and returned to his seat.

It was Walt's turn next. The old man took a puff off his inhaler and put on a beret before shuffling to the microphone. "Hi gang," he said. "My name is Walter Swift. I'm eighty-six and I'll be whistling 'White Christmas,' the Bing Crosby version."

"It's September," Georgie said.

He ignored her and adjusted the mic.

Walt's notes were long, low, and rich. He whistled without effort, leaving the rest of the group transfixed until he had a coughing fit a minute in. Struggling to unwrap a lozenge from his pocket, he apologized and tried again but couldn't finish.

"Do the lung capacity exercises we talked about," Jo told him as he headed for his walker. He dropped his beret into the basket and pulled a small cushion from it, setting it on his chair.

Then Georgie applied some lipstick, stood, and stretched. She tore open her wristbands and wrapped them tighter. She moved her head side to side, making a motor sound before she fluffed her ruffle blouse and went down to the podium.

"I am Georgina Bly and I will be whistling 'Ave Maria,'" she said. "Without accompaniment."

"That's risky," Jo told her. "Remember how whistling on its own makes people uncomfortable."

"Good," Georgie replied as she clasped her hands beneath her chest, the rings on her fingers gleaming like candies.

"Whenever you're ready, then," Jo said.

She stood there a long time with her eyes closed. When she finally began, the sound that came from her was powerful, then piercing.

Jo leaned over to me. "She's toned down the embellishments. That's her best yet."

The group gave Georgie a standing ovation. She stared above our heads, gave a theatrical bow, and strutted off.

Then they were all looking at me. The show was over and they wanted praise. I crossed back over to my desk.

"People will disrespect your craft if you have bad pitch and timing," I finally said. "Aside from Mr. Swift, you were all out of key and rushing. One reenactment in particular was deafening."

Georgie scowled down at her nails. The rest of the group nodded.

"You heard her," Jo said. "Class dismissed."

They gathered their things and I followed them out of the lecture hall.

"The one to beat at the convention will be Joop Nieuwendijk," Reno said.

"He's the reigning champion," Jo explained. "He comes from Holland to compete. He's got a recording contract and he even whistled in a car commercial."

"Don't forget Luella Starr with her harp," Walt added.

"Who's to say someone won't put hot pepper juice in their water," Georgie said.

"That won't change the fact that they're both in the Hall of Fame and you're not," Reno told her.

"Any tips before we meet next week?" Jo asked me at the building exit.

"Don't sit front row at the opera," I replied. "It spoils the illusion."

The Warblers said goodbye, chatting to each other and then, it seemed, to themselves as they headed their separate ways.

Alone back at my car, I lay on the hood and contemplated the impending darkness. Then I sat up and tried to sing. But the only sound that came from me was that of a dying animal. I was no better than the rotten whistlers.

5

Ash booked the morning off to attend an information session with his brother. When they returned from the hospital, he dropped a plastic bag on the counter and stared at it. He looked like he was going to be sick. "I can't go back," he said.

To the place where Majid Khan died, he meant.

I looked in the bag. It contained wet wipes, latex gloves, and boxes of nausea bags. We could hear Tariq downstairs on speakerphone. He'd left the dividing door open and was talking to someone from a health line.

"Your pet should be safe as long as you flush twice and disinfect," a woman was saying.

"And if she ingests my medications?" Tariq asked. "She's good with locks and lids."

"Call the Pet Poison Control Helpline," she replied. "But you shouldn't be scrubbing cages. Maybe have someone else care for your animal during treatment, so it doesn't transmit infection to you."

"Tulip has never caught a disease from bad hygiene," Tariq said. "She's obsessed with grooming."

"All right, sir. But wash your hands frequently if you touch your bird or feed it."

"She can feed herself. Thanks anyway." He hung up.

Ash knocked on the open door and I followed him downstairs, where Tulip was on the counter chewing a toilet paper roll. "She's going through a rough patch," Tariq told us. "She only recently recovered from chlamydia." Ash laughed, but his brother remained grim. "She could have died," he said. "It's a serious infection in birds."

He wiped the kitchenette sink clean. Then he ran the water, tested the temperature, and plugged the drain. Tulip dropped her roll and waddled over to inspect, then hopped in. Tariq kept the water going, draining it now and again so the level stayed below his bird's waist as she splashed around, dipping her beak beneath the faucet, lifting one foot then another under the jet.

The water trickled down her feathers, turning them a deeper grey. Her neck became long and thin, her wings transformed into little boomerangs. She shook the water off and puffed up to twice her size, and Tariq sprayed her with a misting bottle. When she was finished, he placed a cutting board in the sink, which she used as a ramp to climb out. Once on the ledge, she put her foot on the drain lever and pushed it down.

Tariq swaddled his bird with a towel and sat in my red chair, unwrapping her in his lap. She lay on her back, rolling to the left and right like a cat. He ran a finger down her belly and she wrapped her toes around it as he raised his arm high. She hung on, twisting around and flapping. Then he lowered her to his lap again and rubbed the sides of her head.

Ash gestured at the cage by the bay window and asked if she ever used it. Tariq said the cage was Tulip's roost. She went in at night to sleep because she felt safest there. Otherwise she roamed free.

He lay a placemat on the small kitchenette table and put his bird on it, offering her a banana. As we talked, Tulip mashed the soft fruit between her toes.

"Ami ka aj rat ka daura," Ash said. Mom's coming tonight.

Early on, I had tried to learn my husband's poetic language.

After all, I could sing in French, Italian, German, even Russian. Yet I still struggled with Urdu and only understood simple phrases.

They spoke on and lost me, although it was impossible not to notice how their tempos differed, Ash's electric charge clashing against Tariq's calmness. Hearing the brothers together was like mixing "Flight of the Bumblebee" with "Moonlight Sonata." It was my husband's lively enthusiasm that I had fallen in love with when we met. His energy buoyed and thrilled me, even if lately his quick rushes of excitement frayed my nerves.

I went upstairs. When they finished discussing, Ash followed, closed the door behind him, and said he had to get to the office. After he left, I noticed the hospital bag on the counter. I knocked and brought it down.

They were both still at the table, the banana replaced by a black hardback sketchbook. While Tariq drew, Tulip watched the crayon move along the page and kept trying to grab it. Then he presented her with her own crayon, and she settled next to him and got going.

"Mostly she mucks around with abstracts, then shreds them." He held a crayon out to me.

I drew the easiest thing I could, without thinking. Two curved lines to form a heart at the corner of the page. Tariq traced his fingers.

"As you can see our days are highly productive." He gave a small laugh.

"Can she eat it?" I asked of the paper.

"She prefers handmade sheets. You know, with berries and plants." Tulip scribbled over my drawing. "We were about to get some air," he added. "If you'd like to join us."

I hesitated. "I have a lot to do today."

"Another time, then." He took the crayon I handed back.

I returned upstairs and got organized in the living room with my blanket and Kleenex, but the couch was only a few feet away from the dividing door. I couldn't tell if they had left or not and worried he would hear. Part of me was also ashamed that Tulip's days were, in fact, richer than mine.

So I locked myself in the bathroom and studied my tongue and lips in the mirror. Then I tried to get them to make a sound.

No one knew I couldn't whistle.

It was crass and grating on the nerves, and it brought bad luck. But if I had nothing to offer this band of oddballs, they would tease me. *Not only can she no longer hit high notes, she can't whistle.* I couldn't face another humiliation.

I drank a glass of water and ran through the steps in my head. You only needed to position the lips and tongue and send air through. I said "two" and left my lips in their O shape. Then I said "eee" until I felt the sides of my tongue touching the inside edges of my teeth and the tip of my tongue touching below my lower teeth. Then I blew softly.

All that came out was a hissing. My tongue was too close to the roof of my mouth. I tried again. Another hissing sound came out. I was blowing too hard. I worked at it until my jaw tensed and my cheeks ached, still failing to produce a decent note. The aftermath of my fiasco rushed back to me then, when I'd received pity and hugs from the same caked faces who whispered behind my back, auditioning for my roles.

I gave up and returned to the couch, watching TV for the rest of the afternoon, then dozing, until a sharp-nailed claw dug into my arm.

When I opened my eyes, my mother-in-law stood above me. "Why you are all the time sleeping, Done?" she said and opened the blinds.

"Nice to see you, Mrs. Khan." I sat up.

Ash came in with bags of takeout. He kissed me and made his way to the kitchen while his mother scrutinized the dirty living room.

"How was the rest of your week?" I asked.

Mina ignored my question and called out to Ash, to go and

36

fetch it, son. I followed him to the garage where he popped the trunk. A large rug was stuffed inside it. "She wants us to have this," he said.

"But I love our wood floors," I told him.

Ash said the rug was a family heirloom. To not accept the gift would be unforgivable in Mina's eyes. When we pulled it from the car, the vehicle lifted. We dragged it inside and left it by the door like a body, while my mother-in-law watched on.

"Shukriya," I thanked her, and she nodded.

We sat down to our lukewarm meal and Mina asked after my parents. I said they were on a cruise. She commented that they were always on cruises. When I replied that they were simply enjoying their retirement, she turned to Ash and spoke at length, but all I could decipher was "Ebola" as she reached across the table and ran her fork through the dishes. "Let me get that for you, Amiji," Ash said, adding chicken and beef to his mother's heaping plate as a repetitive squawking came from downstairs.

"What is noise?" Mina asked.

"There's a vulture nesting in the yard," I said quickly.

The squawks got louder. I stood and helped myself to seconds while my mother-in-law looked me over. "You are pregnant?" she asked.

"I don't feel well," I explained. "I'll take this up and rest."

Ash glanced from my plate to the door off the living room. I left them and went around the corner, knocking lightly before going downstairs. As soon as I reached the landing, Tulip went mute on her perch, staring and blinking. Tariq apologized for the noise, explaining that sunset was her vocalization time.

"We thought you might be hungry," I told him, offering the plate.

He gestured to my red chair and I sat while he dropped a few vegetables into Tulip's bowl, then ate. "Normally she has oatmeal before bed," he said, turning to his bird. "You're going to get fat here."

They made an unusual pair, awkward yet close with each other. I asked how he had ended up with his parrot.

"Anabelle wanted a bird," he said. "But when I brought Tulip home, she said, 'Not that kind.' She made a mess and tore our place apart, and Anabelle wanted her gone, so I called the humane society. They said it would be a month before they could issue an appointment. They had a surplus of parrots because so many people bought them, got discouraged, and gave them up. They told me to talk with her and keep her challenged, and that I'd adopted one of the smartest animals on Earth."

The sun was low in the sky. Filtered light streamed through the garden and onto us, bringing out the topaz in Tulip's eyes.

I asked if she liked classical. Tariq said yes, so I played some Chopin nocturnes. As the music flowed through the basement, Tulip gazed out at the garden, lifting a foot then resting it on her perch and picking up the other foot, alternating every few minutes. Once the sky dimmed, she flitted to her roost and settled on a familiar-looking piece of driftwood, eyes half-closed. She tucked her right foot under her body, her silvery feathers slightly ruffled. Soon after, she made a soft grinding noise with her beak. Tariq clicked the door latch and pulled her cover down, and sat on the bed's edge near my chair.

Then we heard movement upstairs, and the sound of the garage door opening and closing. "How is she?" Tariq asked, nodding toward the ceiling.

"Impossible," I replied.

"Anabelle couldn't endure her. She likes you, though."

"Your mother will never like me."

"Well, you did steal her son. And you're white." He closed his eyes then and listened.

This was something I rarely did with Ash. Whenever I put a recording on, my husband's passionate exuberance translated into an inability to be still, so that he wound up talking or increasing the volume to the point of distortion.

There was a place in every composition where you went beyond it, to another dimension. Watching Tariq's fingers play an invisible instrument on the quilt, I wondered if he felt it, too.

When we heard the garage door again, he opened his eyes and stood. "Thanks for dinner," he said.

I collected his plate and went upstairs, closing the dividing door behind me.

Ash was already in the living room.

"Is he all right?" he asked, and I nodded as he walked around the perimeter, counting steps. He wanted to lay the rug out. We moved our furniture aside but it was too big for the space. Ash suggested tucking the edges under.

"Did you give your brother your driftwood?" I asked as we folded. It had taken me a month of walks along the riverbank to find the perfect piece.

He groaned, pulling at the bulky carpet. "He saw it in the garden. What could I do?" He stared up at me with red-rimmed eyes. He was under so much pressure.

"Hey —" I leaned over and kissed him. "Forget it."

He wiped his face with his shirt and glanced at the dividing door. "Infusions are scheduled for Friday nights. But my mom will get suspicious if I cancel weekly dinners."

The carpet looked terrible. We put the furniture back in place.

"I'll go with him," I said.

6

On the day of my third class, I took an afternoon nap and over-slept. When I reached Norwood the session was nearly over, yet the Warblers were still there, waiting. Even though I had nothing for them.

I told them to go about their business and that I would circu-late and listen. Then Ben had a sneezing fit. He wore a blue T-shirt covered in black velvety birds.

Walt pulled a handkerchief from his pocket and offered it. "Where did you get that shirt?" he asked. "Are those bats?"

Ben rubbed his chest. "They're swallows."

Jo passed paper cups around and poured everyone something from a Thermos. "Glycerine and rosewater, to regulate the water balance in our cells," she said. Then she turned to me. "What do you do?"

I said I didn't have dairy or eat spicy foods before performing, and I didn't smoke.

"Enrico Caruso chain-smoked." Georgie sipped from her cup. "It darkened his voice gorgeously."

"Who's that?" Ben asked.

"Italian tenor," Georgie replied. "A pillar fell on him in *Samson and Delilah*. Later he had a throat hemorrhage on stage. Then he died."

I leaned against the desk. Reno, in blue scrubs again, stared at my hand. "That is one big ring," he said. "Does your husband sing, too?"

I replied that Ash worked in finance.

He scratched his beard. "I'll bet he doesn't miss a single one of your shows."

Rather than explain that Ash hadn't been to a performance in a long time, and that he preferred sports, I simply nodded.

"I've caught a few operas myself," he added. "At the Cineplex."

Georgie snorted. "Hardly the same, is it."

"There were a couple nice songs," Reno continued, "but overall I found it unrealistic. I guess I couldn't relate."

"Opera is all about real life," I told him.

"How so?" Ben cut in. "Because the stories do seem kind of phony."

"It's about the human condition and universal truths," I told them. "It's about love and loss and passion." I couldn't believe I had to defend the world's greatest art form that contained it all — singing, theatre, drama, and dance — to such an uninformed party.

Ben wrinkled his nose and Georgie checked her watch, which rested over hot pink wristbands. Reno kicked his feet up onto the chair in front of his, while Walt jerked his head up like he was trying not to fall asleep.

"You have some convincing to do," Jo said.

"Ditto on your end," I told them.

"Anyone can whistle," Ben said. "It can't be taken away."

"Opera has been around for centuries," I retorted. "It's not going anywhere."

"But your voice did. Go somewhere," he replied.

"I beg your pardon?"

"We have a new mantra," Reno said then. "My lips are my magic flute. You ever do that one?"

I replied that I had starred in *The Magic Flute* many times. Then

I advised them to keep Mozart out of their repertoire because his operas contained arias insurmountable for novices.

"Our what?" Reno asked.

"Your selections. Don't you have that for your . . . whistling?"

"We like all music," Jo said.

"You need to narrow it down," I told them. "Or you'll never get anywhere."

Walt finished his drink in one gulp. "I got us a gig at the mall."

Georgie huffed. "Group whistling's a load of piffle."

"The shoppers won't be listening," he said. "And we've got to start practicing in front of people."

Georgie turned to me. "Tell him the mall's undignified."

"It depends who you want as your audience."

"Anybody," Walt said.

"Send us the details, Walter," Jo told him, and the old man nodded.

Reno asked to touch Ben's birds. Then they all started rubbing his chest and Ben had to slap their hands away.

I gave a loud clap to get their attention. "I thought we could discuss head voice versus chest voice," I told them. "You can start by —"

"Can you do the whistle register?" Ben interrupted. "Like Céline and Mariah?"

A timer went off, emitting the bright high ding of a triangle. Jo mouthed "sorry" and collected everyone's cups and put her Thermos away. "Seeing as none of you procrastinators want to work, we might as well wrap it up with Whittaker's 'Finnish Whistler.' So Dawn doesn't feel we're a lost cause."

At the mention of the name, they perked up.

Jo waved me over to their side of the room. "Roger Whittaker is the god of whistling," she said. Close up, I noticed thin scars on her face like lines from a blade. She caught me staring and shut her eyes, as if giving me permission to take it in.

The Warblers hovered around Ben as he pulled a tablet from his backpack. Its keyboard had eight large buttons plus a space bar. Ben tapped the keys and uttered commands to his device, which spoke back to him, until a video was rolling and a goateed man sat with his guitar before a quiet, wide-eyed crowd.

I had been taught by world-class vocalists and toured the globe, performing in famous opera houses, concert halls, and cathedrals. I had starred in complex, costly productions with dozens of singers, musicians, set designers, and choreographers. But I had never heard anything like what the Warblers played for me.

The melody was like a loon on water, slow and clear and pure. It floated on the air, soaring and spinning, while the whistler retained complete control. His face didn't contort and his cheeks barely went in or out. He even whistled on the intake breaths. His pitch rose without strain. It was total perfection when he hit high notes and sometimes he whistled two notes at once. This was sound stripped bare to its simplest form. This was something un-trainable.

When the song ended, Georgie sniffed. "Damn him."

"Stop comparing," Jo told her. "And remember what Henry van Dyke said."

Georgie twisted her wristbands around. "Well? What did that old ninny say?"

Jo looked at each of them in turn and they all looked at Ben, who opened his mouth and closed it without saying anything.

"How do you not know this?" she asked. "Van Dyke said, 'The woods would be very silent if no birds sang except those that sang best.'"

"Ahhhh," the Warblers reacted in unison.

"You're saying we're crap." Ben's shoulders slumped.

"I'm saying it takes all sorts," Jo told him.

She hit her fork on her elbow and pressed the stem to Reno's jaw, telling him to relax his clenching. Then she circulated it to everyone for their tension spots.

Georgie passed, handing the tuner back to Jo. "You're an intelligent woman, Josephine. But I've never understood why you swear by such mumbo jumbo."

Jo hit her knee and pressed the handle to her breastbone. "It calms and centres me."

"There's pot oil for that."

"The universe is made up of vibrational energy, Georgina. You could do worse than to listen."

"It's not even at pitch with our whistling."

"That's not the point. According to Buddhist philosophy, sound waves can treat all types of pain. Physical and otherwise."

"Those swollen mitts of yours would benefit from her therapy, Georgie," Walt said.

The Warblers bantered and played around with Jo's tuning fork, dipping it in water to witness the rapid splashing molecules. Reno's phone rang. He answered quickly, accidentally hitting speaker. "No more flowers, dumbass," a woman said. "How are we going to get a new flat screen if you keep wasting money?"

Reno's face went pale as he shut the phone off. "I have to go," he told us and rushed out.

"When's he going to get rid of that bitch?" Georgie said after he left.

"That's none of our business," Jo told her.

"Do you think she beats him?" Walt asked as they packed up their things.

Ben rolled out with Walt's walker and Walt put a hand on Ben's shoulder, shuffling behind him. Georgie and Jo trailed out after them. I turned off the lights and followed.

Outside, Ben shushed everyone. "Finches," he said.

"Which ones are those?" I asked.

"A singer who doesn't know her birds," Georgie commented. "Whoever heard of such a thing."

"Is it a chime of finches? Or a bevy?" Walt asked.

"A charm," Ben said. "Chime is wrens, and bevy is larks."

We listened to the sharp cheeps, the long score of jumbled short notes ending in upward slurs. In the distance, small brown bodies hopped along the cluster of trees lining the parking lot.

"That doesn't sound like the variation you gave us the other day," Georgie said.

"It's my interpretation," Ben replied.

"Right you are, young man," Walt told him with a pat on the back.

Then Ben turned and touched my arm lightly. I didn't know how he knew I was beside him. "Listen," he said, as the finches departed from the trees in a bouncing flight.

He removed his shades and kept his eyes closed, and I copied him as the birds flew above us, their tweets quieting down to a feathering in the sky, a near-silent concerto of overlapping sighs. "Ta-da!" Ben exclaimed as wingsong filled the air. "That's what I'm aiming for."

7

When I told Tariq that I would accompany him to chemotherapy, he insisted that he didn't need me there. His tumour had been removed with surgery. The added treatment was precautionary and not even necessary, in his opinion. I considered going to a movie or a bar instead. But I had promised Ash. So I said that I was only doing it to get out of Friday dinners with his mother, and he relented.

We hardly spoke on the drive. His thoughts seemed far away, and I didn't want to bother him. Once inside the hospital, we followed a path of yellow circles on the floor of the old main building, which smelled of disinfectant and was overcrowded with beds in the halls. The circles led to a glass overpass, which led to the cancer centre, a state-of-the-art facility, inviting in its brightness and clean, silent spaces.

The chemo unit was long and narrow like an airplane, with large vinyl chairs lined against a wall, interspersed with medical machinery. The chairs had little tray tables attached to their sides, and there were curtains that could be pulled for privacy. Directly across from the chairs was a wall with windows and framed pictures with mountains and lakes, forests and farms.

At the entrance was the nurse's station, and beside that was a kitchenette stocked with snacks and drinks. Tariq's nurse was Jenny, a chubby young woman with a bleached pixie cut, whose ears were adorned with emeralds. Most of the chairs were occupied and she directed him to the last one in the row. As he settled in, she pulled up a chair and offered it to me, saying, "If your husband falls asleep, we have magazines at the desk."

Then she took blood samples and asked Tariq if he wanted to try the cold cap. "I'll take an espresso," he said, and Jenny explained that a cold cap was an ice helmet you wore to prevent your hair from falling out. The unit had been donated machines that patients could try for free. Jenny said it had worked for half her clients and would add an hour to his treatment time.

Tariq looked at me. "You have good hair," I said.

"Why not," he told her.

She wet his hair and rubbed gobs of conditioner in it, then rolled the refrigeration machine over, and slipped a helmet on his head. She put a rubber cap on top of that and strapped it under his chin, and Tariq asked her where his plane was. Jenny giggled and said the cold would hurt until his scalp froze and then it would only feel numb.

"I'm doing this for my bird," Tariq told her. "She doesn't like change."

Jenny put a hand on mine. "Isn't he sweet, thinking of you."

Once the blood results were approved, Jenny studied his hand like a manicurist, then poked a short tube into his vein and administered several injections: a saline solution, a medicine to prevent an allergic reaction, a steroid, and an anti-sickness drug. Then she started his three-chemical treatment, said to drink a lot of water, pointed to the bathroom, and left us.

We watched the drugs enter Tariq's bloodstream, the clear liquid dripping from the plastic bag and into him with a metronomic beat. To our right sat an older lady. She wore a toque and her eyes were closed. A younger woman with similar features rushed in and shook her arm with "Mom . . . Mom!"

The lady opened her eyes and greeted her daughter, who said, "Hold on," until she finished texting. Then she went to the fridge and came back with a pudding and dug in with a plastic spoon. "So we went jogging this morning before breakfast." She sat down. "He loves running."

"Are you sure he's not running from you?" her mother asked.

"Joggers always look so miserable." Pudding oozed from the corners of her mouth. "Every one of them I passed this morning, miserable. But I guess I'll pretend for a while."

"Your father loved to jog. He wasn't miserable," the mother said.

The woman switched the subject to baseboards. She was tearing hers out because they weren't wide enough. When she pulled samples from her purse and pressed them into her mother's hand, the older woman fanned herself with them until her daughter insisted she choose her favourite.

The mother closed her eyes and wrapped her hand around a grey square. "This one."

Her daughter sighed. "You're not looking."

She opened her eyes again. "This one," she said, pointing to a greenish panel and handing the samples back.

"I'll probably go with hickory." The younger woman shoved them into her purse and got up. She was late for drinks with colleagues. "I won't bother asking if you want anything before I go," she said. "Since you always say no."

Her mother waved her away.

After her daughter kissed her on the cheek and left, she turned to us and introduced herself. Her name was Cherry. "That's my Laurel," she said, shaking her head. "The things that consume that poor girl." She pulled her blanket up over her chest. Then she pointed to Tariq's cold cap and said, "I tried that, too."

Hers was breast cancer. When I asked how many sessions she'd had, she raised three fingers, saying she was on her third course of six cycles. Then she asked where we were from and if we had children.

"I have an African grey who's my joy and my torment," Tariq told her. "Like a child."

Cherry asked if that was the parrot with the red tail and Tariq replied that not many people knew that. She said she loved birds, especially seagulls, which she found beautiful for their wingtips. She asked Tariq if he'd ever touched a gull and told him it was a fantasy of hers, to get close enough that she could pet one because they looked so damned soft, softer than a cloud. Then she closed her eyes again and rested. When her infusion was over, she wished Tariq luck. They were on the same schedule so she would see him again.

After Cherry had gone, Tariq spent his time dozing and using the bathroom. Whenever he got up, he had to unplug his ice cap and roll his IV pole back and forth with him but declined my assistance.

While he slept, I looked out the window. We were on the third floor, and you could see treetops and crows passing. Then I studied one of the pictures on the wall: a red barn before snow-capped mountains and a full moon on a ruby sky. The place seemed impossible, a cut and paste of landscapes. I stared at the image for a long time, until Jenny arrived to unhook Tariq and he woke up. "You're all done, Mr. Khan," she said. "How are you feeling?"

He pointed to the ice cap and said, "I've been to the future. They don't find a cure after all." Jenny tut-tutted him. Then he told her he felt fine and reached for his coat.

On our way out, we stopped at the counter where there were baskets of different coloured ribbons. The colour for stomach cancer was lavender blue. Tariq dropped a bill into the box and took a fistful, and on the drive home he removed the pins and glue from the ribbons and put them back in his pocket.

It was past nine when we got to the house. All the lights were out. Ash would be getting Mina settled in at the condo with tea and her mystery. We went in through the front and I followed my husband's brother down to the walkout. At the bottom of the stairs, I was surprised to hear *Trout Quintet* playing quietly, Tulip hanging upside-down from her roost swing, swaying to the melody.

"We love Schubert," Tariq said.

The few times I had aspired to learn the composer's songs for voice and piano, I had failed. Since then I had avoided Schubert's Lieder, which I told myself contained too much melancholy and too little dramatic power.

I sat in my chair while Tariq prepared oatmeal for his bird and brought her to the kitchen table. There, she ate on a placemat adorned with a cartoon car and her name. Then he wiped what she'd spilled and they came and sat by me, in the bay window.

Jenny had told Tariq he might feel off after each session. That some people had a lot of side effects and others, none. When I asked if he felt queasy, he gave me a curious look. I wondered if he was having trouble understanding from the drugs, until he said, "I feel lucky."

Then he bent his knees and cradled Tulip so she was on her back, her legs sticking up in the air. Studying the undersides of her scaly feet, in particular a toe on her left foot, he told me that she was developing a pressure point. This was the foot she stood on most. He said it happened sometimes, even though he tried to vary the sizes and materials of her perches. He had a special cream from her avian vet and hoped it was only a tenderness, not the beginning of something else.

I asked why she didn't talk.

"Not all parrots do," he said, pulling a ribbon from his pocket and tying it in a bow before offering it to her. "She has a good vocabulary. She's just lazy."

Still on her back, Tulip undid the bow. Then he flipped her upright and stretched his legs out, and she walked down them. When he wriggled his toes, she chewed on his sock.

"She needs distraction," he added. "Last year she got kicked out of parrot club for disobedience. So we joined a birdwatching group. But the birders said she was too noisy on hikes." He pulled another ribbon out and tied it into knots, which took longer for his bird to undo. "She could attend that class of yours."

I raised my finger at him. The bite had healed but still.

As if she'd caught our conversation, Tulip snapped her beak in my direction.

"She'll whistle," Tariq said. "If she finds inspiration again."

His bird manoeuvred her way to a cement perch and ran her nails along it, filing them before drawing each one through her beak. Then she raised her foot of needle-fine points, swiping the air.

The garage door opened and closed.

"Bring her yourself," I told him.

"I would. But Anabelle took the car," he replied, as Ash came down the stairs with chips and drinks.

"How'd it go?" he asked, his tie loose and his shirt untucked. "Give me the play by play, brother."

"We had a ball," Tariq said, glancing briefly in my direction.

I left them to talk and went upstairs.

When Ash came to the room later, he asked if I'd washed up since the hospital. I said no. We undressed and he pulled me into the shower with a grin, his lovemaking ravenous under the too-hot water.

"Anything yet?" he looked at me expectantly afterwards.

I shook my head. "Not yet," I told him.

Ash had wanted children as soon as we married. I had been the one to put it off, worried about a growing baby crowding my lungs and diaphragm for nine months, not to mention the impact of morning sickness and hormones on my voice.

Now that we were both ready, we couldn't seem to conceive. My body was betraying me again. Taking away the only other thing I'd ever wanted. And I had no one but myself to blame, for having waited too long.

Ash pulled me close again. "We'll just have to keep trying." His mouth twisted around. He was chewing the inside of his cheeks, which he did when he was nervous or rethinking something. Then he asked if I wanted to go to Tokyo. It would be his third trip there in under a year, but we could turn it into a holiday.

On his urging, I'd travelled with my husband on business before. Despite promises of romance and adventure, chances were that Ash wouldn't leave the financial district, and I'd be on my own the whole time.

I had also been to Tokyo myself once to perform *Aida*, and the place wouldn't bring back fond memories. The production had two choruses, a brigade of horses, plus lions and a cheetah. I argued with the artistic director about their inhumane use of animals, and on the night of the last show I got a stomach bug. After my final duet with Radamès, I silently vomited all over my colleague as we lay dying in our tomb. I had no desire to return there.

"What about your brother?" I asked Ash.

"He says he's fine."

I turned the water off and handed him a towel. "I have to teach," I told him.

He pulled me back and kissed my shoulder. "Come on. Don't degrade yourself."

I hesitated, running a hand along his wet arm. "I think there's something to this. That's worth exploring."

He stopped kissing me, put his sweats on, and brushed his teeth. "Sure thing," he replied. The way he kept glancing at me I knew there was something else.

"What?" I asked, drying my hair.

He spat into the sink. If I stayed, I would need to look in on his mother.

8

My first whistled note came out in the bath.

I'd been trying to hum the Queen of the Night's vengeance aria, but my voice broke and my throat hurt. I wasn't ready. So I chose to whistle a nursery rhyme instead. Placing my tongue behind my bottom teeth, I formed an O with my lips and blew lightly until a faint sound travelled through the steamy room. When I increased my breath flow, it became louder, stronger, like the wind picking up speed as it passed through certain objects. I moved my tongue slightly to change notes and kept going, stopping only to inhale.

I hadn't reached the end of a song in months. Once I finished "Twinkle, Twinkle, Little Star," I did "Row, Row, Row Your Boat" in every key, perfecting my pitch until the water ran cold.

After that, I dressed and found a recording of the Biennial online. Most of the performances were inharmonic and jarring. But a few participants sounded like flutes and theremins and castratos. And the virtuosos and flops all shared one stage, and none seemed to care, so focused were they on their craft.

I was taking notes when Tariq knocked on the dividing door. Even though Ash told him to come and go as he pleased, he still always knocked before entering our living space. I looked up. Tulip was in her carrier.

"We're ready," he said.

I rushed to gather my things and we went out to the car. Tariq slid Tulip into the back seat, strapping her in. On the drive, he wanted to know about the lives of my students. I told him I had no idea, and that such information had nothing to do with making music.

"Of course it does," he replied. "How can they reach their potential if you don't know their histories? How can you connect?"

I had no response and gave a tight-lipped smile as we pulled into the lot. Then Tariq went around to unstrap his bird, giving her words of encouragement, and I left them there without waiting. Walking into Norwood, I couldn't shake my anger. I had studied with the most revered vocal masters in the country and trained internationally as an artist-in-residence and on exchange programs. Who did he think he was with his insipid tips on teaching?

To make matters worse, the Warblers were talking noisily when I reached the lecture hall and barely acknowledged my arrival. I slammed my bag down on the desk. "Why aren't you studying scores?" I asked.

Georgie shook a finger at the group. "Because these cretins can't read notes."

"We were just chatting about tongues," Jo said.

The room's fluorescent lighting made my head throb. "Tension in your tongues means tension in your tones," I told them. "I noticed none of you can trill aside from Ben. That means tension."

"Jo was telling us how every person's tongue print is unique," Reno said. "Like our fingertips. Researchers are working on tongue databases to identify humans."

Ben asked Jo if they took tongue prints from criminals in prison, and she replied that she didn't want to talk about what they did in prison.

I looked at Jo. "Were you incarcerated?"

"She's a guard." Reno studied my mouth. "Your lips have individual marks, too," he added. "No one else has the same lines and wrinkles as you do."

I put my reading glasses on. "How do you expect to improve when all you do is sit around talking?" I asked them.

"She's got a point," Walt said.

Reno was still staring at my mouth. As I sucked my lips in, Tariq entered with Tulip tucked into his coat. He put her carrier down and the Warblers gawked as he waved. "I'm Tariq," he said, checking his chest. "And this is Tulip. Ms. Woodward suggested we join your class."

"We're not a freak show." Georgie yanked her wristbands. "It's a no pets policy here."

Tariq unzipped his coat and Tulip stepped onto his hand. When she shook out her feathers, the small bell he'd secured around her neck chimed. "She likes to wander," he told everyone.

"Wait," Ben said. "Is that a bird? Does she whistle?"

Tariq replied that, as a matter of fact, she did. Georgie sat back and crossed her arms behind her head, waiting for proof. Reno gave Tariq the once-over. "Who are you to Dawn?" he asked.

Tariq glanced at me. "Her husband's brother."

I looked away, adding, "He's staying with us temporarily."

Tariq took a seat off to the side. As soon as Ben chirped, Tulip flew to him and landed on his knee. He pet her like it was the most natural thing in the world. "Hey there, pretty bird," he said.

"Ben is our Saint Francis," Walt told Tariq and off they went again, this time about pets and Georgie's canary, Luciano, who had kept her awake all night with his singing back in the day, so she never got another bird. Jo said the prison had a pet program that included a cockatoo named Bubba, and inmates who'd earned privileges got supervised time with him, and the bird danced and told dirty jokes.

I said "Can I have your attention?" twice. I waited. But they kept up their racket until I switched the lights on and off with "What do you people want to *sing*?" which startled them into silence.

Tulip gave a hawkish squawk in my direction.

"What's your hurry?" Georgie asked.

"How about introductions?" Tariq looked my way again.

"Fine," I said, my jaw tightening. "I'm Dawn Woodward, no relation to —" I turned to Walt.

"Agnes," he said.

"Right. No relation to Agnes Woodward. Profession, lyric soprano. Ben, your biography please."

Facing Walt, Georgie moved her head and arms robotically, and he replicated her movements. They were like children. I told them to cut it out.

"This year I graduate," Ben said. "Then I'm moving to L.A. to whistle professionally. And maybe get a record deal. Also, I know trees by their — whatchamacallits, Georgie?"

"Susurrations," Georgie replied. "You recognize species by their rustling leaf voices, like Thomas Hardy did. Have you read *Under the Greenwood Tree* yet? It took me a damned long time to find that in braille, Benny."

"I'll just listen on tape."

"Audio's not the same," Georgie told him, "as a book."

Georgie was a librarian. When machines had replaced her work, she took a package but was left with bad arthritis from years of heavy lifting. "You probably thought my compression wraps were high fashion." She undid her bands and rotated her wrists. "I found whistling when I was searching for a hobby that didn't involve my hands. Then I realized that I was uncommonly gifted."

Walt was a retired schoolteacher. Before his wife died, they travelled around in a caravan, teaching youth the lost skill of pucker whistling. And Jo was taught everything she knew of whistling by her grandfather, who'd performed with the great siffleur Ronnie Ronalde in the music halls of London. Her tuning fork came from him, an original from the Ragg manufacturer in Sheffield. She couldn't whistle herself anymore, on account of heart disease causing shortness of breath. She liked to coach, though.

As for Reno, he worked night shifts in a long-term care facility. He was saving up to buy his first home in the form of a highway motel, where he would offer guests free breakfasts and a twenty-four-hour coffee bar. He hadn't told his girlfriend, Desiree, about the dream yet, which would require a large loan.

"And you, sir?" Walt asked Tariq.

"Engineer," he replied.

"Of what?" Ben asked.

"I used to assess big buildings. Now I work on animal crossings."

Ash never mentioned that his brother had changed specialties.

Tariq described how he helped build structures over roads and waterways for wildlife to cross safely. Ben asked what kinds of animals and Tariq said elk and bears and deer. Georgie said she'd heard those crossings didn't work and Tariq agreed that sometimes they didn't.

Tulip hopped off Ben's knee and headed toward me.

You could hear a *click click click* as she walked, her long nails causing her to skitter and slide along the floor. I froze, her bell dinging as she stepped onto my boot. But she didn't try to bite me. Instead she craned her neck in Tariq's direction and he connected his thumb and index into a circle, giving her the A-OK.

"How old's your bird?" Ben asked.

"Seven," Tariq replied.

"A baby," Ben said, and Tariq told him yes, if she was well taken care of she would live another fifty or sixty years.

Then the Warblers wanted to hear them whistle. So Tariq approached the podium and Tulip flew up to the mic handle, and I moved over to the front row. He had a bottle of water and sipped from it, apologizing for his dry mouth caused by medication. Then he leaned in and said, "Here's the King."

His melody, deep and honeyed, was slower than the original. He closed his eyes for a couple of stanzas, then opened them, his gaze falling on me at the "Take my hand, take my whole life, too" part. I felt myself redden. Jo fanned her face with her fork and Georgie said, "Oh my." Then Tulip tapped the head of the mic with her beak and it went *thump thump thump*, drowning out the rest of the song.

Even so, the Warblers admitted that Tariq had skill enough to join them. They also wanted to hear Tulip, but Tariq said she was shy and needed time. That seemed to satisfy them.

When she pooped and it landed on his sneaker, he pulled a tissue from his pocket and bent down to wipe it off. He wobbled as he bent over but managed. Then Tulip stepped onto his hand and they came and sat with the group.

Everyone wanted to find a solution for Tariq's dry mouth. They debated what was better for lubrication — egg rolls, fried chicken, or pierogies — and they agreed that he should start his days off with sausages. Then came shouted recipes.

I stood behind the lectern again and attempted a wolf whistle. It came out loud and clear. "Discuss your greasy snacks later," I told them, dimming the lights and screening the Biennial video.

That shut them up. They surveyed the competing whistlers and when Joop Nieuwendijk went on, there were some groans. I hit pause. "He takes it to another level with his grace notes and portamento," I said. "Can you hear the subtlety in those mordents and turns?"

"He's a piccolo player," Reno said. "It's easy for him."

"You don't need a musical background," I replied. "What you need is to *become* the flute. *Become* the violin or the piano."

We watched the footage up until Joop and Yu-Lin Chen from China had a whistle-off for first place. After Joop won, I turned the lights on.

I thought the Warblers would be motivated, but the mood was sullen. Everyone including Ben stared at the ground. "You're going to swap songs with one another," I told them.

They all looked up.

Jo approached the podium and quietly said, "They've been practicing their own ones for months."

I told her I didn't care and turned back to the group. "Repeat it until you get it," I told them. "Then insert yourselves into it. You need to leave your comfort zones."

"What about you, boss lady?" Georgie said. "You've shown us squat."

My stomach tightened. I said I would perform when we reconvened the following week, then demanded that everyone practice an hour minimum daily. They nodded and turned their backs on me, cooing around Tulip.

On the drive home, Tariq looked out his window, suppressing laughter. "You're a tyrant," he said.

"Those whistlers are slackers," I replied. "They need discipline."

"I think they just want to have a good time." He kept an arm over his abdomen, as if trying to prevent his organs from falling out.

"That's not what I was hired for," I said.

"Do you think you had your mishap because —"

I took a corner too fast. The tires squeaked and Tulip squawked. "Because what?" I asked.

He glanced back at Tulip in her carrier. "Because you weren't enjoying yourself?"

"That's absurd." I sped up and ran two yellow lights.

How could I expect him to understand that voices aged and broke like instruments. I wanted to tell him to jump off one of his bridges. Instead I asked that he mind his own business. "Some of us are too busy to live it up," I added, thinking about his mother. "We can't all dump our responsibilities on others like you did."

As we turned another corner, a full moon appeared before us. There was a pale ring around it, saturating the sky with light.

"All I mean is, we think we'll leave a mark but we won't," Tariq said, staring up through the windshield. "Most of us will be forgotten. So you might as well have fun."

9

We had our first killing frost. With it came the arrival of hazy days, cooler nights, and the departure of my husband. Before leaving, Ash spent time in the backyard with Tariq. I opened the kitchen window, listening to him ask about recent tests and scans, slapping him on the back and saying, "It's all good, brother. I'll take care of you."

Then a company SUV pulled up. I followed Ash outside and stood in the middle of the street, barefoot like Tariq had been when Anabelle drove off, only my husband stuck his arm out and waved, and he would return.

Afterwards I went to the kitchen window again and stood at the sink, rewashing clean dishes. Tariq was still out there. He did lunges and push-ups in the grass with Tulip on his shoulder. He did arm circles with Tulip on his wrist. He did leg lifts and Tulip gripped onto his toes, his body an amusement park of rides. Then he tugged at her tail and squirted bottled water into a bowl before drinking some himself. Pulling an apricot from a plastic bag in his pocket, he divided it into pieces and held his hand out until she ate. When she moved on to chew some nearby weeds, he picked her up and they disappeared out of sight through the French doors.

We hadn't spoken since my outburst in the car. I went to the dividing door and listened to him speaking gently to his bird. It was Friday. A few minutes later, I heard Ash's car starting in the driveway.

He had opted to go to his treatment alone.

I phoned Mina and suggested Thai, one of her favourite foods, plus it made her drowsy. An hour later, she opened her door and took the hefty takeout bag from me with "After Tokyo, my son will come more to me."

I didn't know how more than two daily visits would be possible. I hung up my coat and removed my shoes, walking across rugs that fit perfectly on the floor.

Mina pointed to the dining table and told me to sit. I asked if she'd had a nice day. She gave a loud exhale, replying that she hadn't slept. "Lately I am all the time worried," she said.

As she brought plates and glasses over, I noticed she'd gone to some trouble with her hair and clothes. Her blouse was ironed and she'd put on extra jewellery. This could only have been for me. Aside from her son and sister, she had no visitors or friends, no hobbies or pastimes. It unnerved me that without singing, my life was starting to resemble hers. Except I didn't spend my days gossiping with relatives overseas.

Once when I asked my mother-in-law about her homeland, telling her I hoped to go someday with her son, she'd thrown her hands in the air and said, "Bewakoof." Fool. "Pakistan is hard country. You cannot understand."

Mina sat and ate. When I complimented her on her necklace, she pointed at my wrist with her knife. "Why you wear all the time silver? Gold is best."

I slid my bracelet up the sleeve of my green dress. I'd made an effort for her, too, but she still found things to criticize. "This is from Mexico City," I told her. "I sang there. At the Palacio de Bellas Artes."

She pushed her plate away. "Oh choro, Done. Better to sing to babies than strangers."

When I asked if she wanted to lie down, she only smoothed the tablecloth, picking up rice and dropping the grains into her napkin. Her hands were tiny compared to the rest of her, like the wrong pieces had been clicked into the wrists of a big doll.

A photo collage decorated the wall behind her. There were old black-and-white shots of Mina and Majid in Lahore, in front of water fountains and palaces, and with their boys on picnics, flying kites. There were group photos at family gatherings with their sons and other relatives and spouses. Anabelle and I were the only ones absent from these.

Looking at a picture of Tariq in graduation attire, I recognized the campus as the one where I'd met my husband. That day, I had been practicing in the grass under a tree, and Ash liked to recount how at first he thought I was praying. When I felt someone there, I had rushed to stand. The man before me had light brown skin and his eyes were the grey-blue of dusk. He wore his hair in a ponytail and his lips were full like a heart. That we had little in common hadn't mattered. He charmed me before we even spoke.

I asked Mina if Tariq had graduated from our university. She nodded, adding that he'd taught there, too. "After Majid get layoff, he finish paying our mortgage," she said. "Then come that stupid beauty, and we don't see him no more."

My mother-in-law sized me up. She did not find me beautiful. In the past, I'd overheard her refer to me as "moon face" and "cow eyes" to her son. Although I had been told my large features were good for the stage, her nicknames stung.

"If Tariq paid your mortgage, how did Mister Khan help us?" I asked.

Mina folded her hands over her stomach. "This was Tariq."

As soon as he'd become an analyst, I'd encouraged Ash to invest our savings. As a result we had little to put toward our home. Ash had told me that his father contributed to our down payment as a wedding gift. More than once I had thanked him for it myself.

I checked the time. "I have to go," I told her.

She switched on the TV. As I put on my coat, she said, "Why you are keeping him from me?"

I turned back from the door.

"Once a week is no good." She stared hard at the screen and poured her chai. "I come for you here to this place. And still I cannot see him."

"What about every morning and after work?"

"Sometimes he come. Not a lot."

"You're saying Ashraf doesn't eat with you?"

She sucked on a sugar cube. "Go," she said and drank and flipped channels.

Jenny greeted me at the outpatient unit. She pointed to the end of the line of brown chairs and told me that my timing was good: they were behind and she was about to start Tariq's session.

I walked down the row of cancer patients. Some slept. Some looked fit and others like they came from a labour camp. Some had carry-ons full of distractions and supplies, others wore pyjamas and a couple were in suits, working on laptops. Some had visitors but many sat alone. Some had their curtain drawn.

Tariq was stationed across from the fantasy farm picture. I pulled up a chair and asked why he wasn't wearing the ice cap. When he opened his eyes, he told me my dress looked like a forest, and that the steroids would save his hair.

Then Jenny arrived with infusion number one. But it was harder to insert the tube into Tariq's vein this time around. His hand was swollen, so she tried his arm and had to rifle around under his skin before taping the catheter in place. When I asked her where Cherry was, she said that her treatment had been post-poned. Then she told Tariq to let her know if anything didn't feel right and moved on to her next patient.

Tariq closed his eyes again and asked if I'd come to apologize. I told him no. "In that case, how about some music?" he said. When I asked what he wanted to hear, he replied, "Nadir's aria."

The Pearl Fishers was a story about two men who loved the same woman. It caught me off guard that he knew Bizet's famous opera. I told him it was a tenor aria and therefore impossible for my voice. Not to mention the nodules on my vocal cords.

"So whistle it," he said, his lips slightly parted.

I steadied my breathing and began, noticing right away how my tone and pitch were improving. Impressed with my sound, I continued, focusing on the photo of the bright barn and its ornamental wind vane, until Tariq moaned.

He didn't look right. His skin was turning red and his body was stiffening. I called for help and three nurses came running. One stopped his infusion and checked his blood pressure, the other rushed over with a new bag, which was injected into the IV, while Jenny told him to hang in there and that he'd feel better soon.

Once his colour and breathing were back to normal, Jenny took my hand and put it on Tariq's, and the nurses went to their desk to confer. We watched Jenny make a call, his hand burning hot under mine. Then she came back to us while the other nurses returned to their clients.

"We're going to start over," she said.

She had spoken with the doctor and would administer the infusion at a slower rate and lesser dose.

This time there was no small talk as she rigged Tariq up. The drugs started dripping down the long line, into his vein, and would take four hours instead of two. After ten minutes, Jenny left but kept glancing over. Then it happened again. Tariq puffed up like he'd been stung by bees and he put a hand to his chest. The nurses rushed back with an EKG machine, checking his heart, removing the drip, and repeating the same routine until he stabilized.

Other patients looked on, alarmed by the commotion. Orderlies arrived with a stretcher and rolled him to a room in another wing. I followed with Jenny, who said that the doctor would be by soon, and left us.

In the new room, a new nurse gave him a mild tranquilizer. The space was cubicle-sized, and I squeezed in by his head while he slept.

Unlike Ash, whose hair was beginning to thin at his temples, revealing a forehead lined with worry, Tariq's most prominent lines were around his mouth and eyes. His eyelashes were longer than mine, his lips cracking dry. I pulled a tube of moisturizer from my bag, pressed some onto my finger, and ran it over his skin. He didn't wake.

I went for a walk to clear my head and wound up in the cafeteria, where I phoned Ash. "Should I fly back?" he asked after I told him what happened. He was still in transit. I said there was no need yet, but that I would let him know if things changed. We spoke a few more minutes. Before hanging up, I told him I'd seen Mina. "Did your brother help with our down payment?" I asked.

He blew into the receiver, making static. "I'll pay him back. It's just . . . everything's tied up now. For the future."

"It's not right," I said. A wedding gift from his parents was one thing. But a loan from his brother felt wrong.

"What's the difference?" Ash asked. "He was doing corporate stuff then. Making hand over fist. He probably did it for a tax break. I helped him out."

"Your mom also says she doesn't see you," I went on. "Even though you stop in every morning. And every night."

He didn't respond.

"Can you hear me?" I asked.

"Sometimes I go to the gym instead," he finally said.

"Since when?"

"Since she drives me crazy."

With my leave from the stage, I was beginning to realize that my husband and I had not actually spent a great deal of time together, both of us preoccupied with our careers, which often required late hours and travel.

"Maybe I could work out with you," I told him.

"You wouldn't like it," he replied. "People don't clean the machines." Then his voice softened. "Let's figure it out when I'm back. I'll check in tomorrow."

After we hung up, I ate an oily piece of carrot cake and returned to Tariq's room. By then the doctor was there and Tariq was sitting up in the bed. When the doctor asked how he felt, Tariq told him he was ready to try again. But the doctor shook his head. He could not try again. His second allergic reaction had been more severe than the first. His body wasn't tolerating the drugs.

"What first reaction?" I asked.

Tariq explained that he'd returned to the hospital after his initial infusion, with an erratic heart rate. I asked if Ash was aware and he said yes. No one had told me because, Tariq said, it was nothing.

"Please stop leaving me," I said, my mouth dry, "out of so much."

Tariq offered me water. As it travelled behind my heart, through my diaphragm, I felt better. I handed the cup back and he took the last sip.

Then we turned to the doctor, an older man with a British accent who introduced himself as Clarence Horne. His head was closely shaved, I wondered if out of delicacy for his patients. Dr. Horne asked if I was the one providing care at home. I nodded. He told Tariq to rest and drink fluids, and that they would recon-vene in a week to discuss next steps. "Your body needs to recuperate before we start on a new plan," he said.

In the hall, I pulled the doctor aside. "What if it comes back?" I asked.

"There are plenty of options." He glanced into the room. "Try not to worry. Go home and get some sleep."

It was past midnight when Tariq was discharged. At the house, I helped him out of the car and we went around back and through the garden, to avoid the stairs.

The moon had waned to a crescent but there were stars, and geese flying over the neighbourhood. There must have been dozens of them. We saw their aerial formations in silhouettes as they passed and heard the creaking pump of their wings between their flight calls.

"It's not a honking at all," Tariq said as we stood in the shadowy darkness. And it was true. Their sound was more like a drawn-out, mournful note that broke midway into a high, near-shrill wail. We listened to the plaintive cries awhile longer then went inside, where Tulip was asleep in her roost.

Tariq swayed as he drew the cover over her cage and had to lean on the chair. "There's a pomegranate," he nodded toward the counter, "for her breakfast."

I split the fruit open over the sink, staining my fingers as I peeled the seeds from their husk and dropped them into a bowl. I turned to offer him a cluster, but he had fallen asleep in my red chair.

Walking around the small apartment I noticed how he had bird-proofed it, hiding cords and adding plastic locks to the drawers. I had expected the space to start smelling but it hadn't. Tulip smelled of air or something faintly sweeter, I thought, on the rare occasion I'd gotten close enough to sniff her.

She even seemed to be litter trained. Mostly, that mess was near her play stand, a three-tiered contraption with ladders and a beaded hoop swing. There was also a fine white film everywhere. I'd observed it coming off in Tariq's hands when he stroked her, and she appeared to produce it when she preened or flapped her wings.

Toys, ropes, and stuffed animals lay on the ground in organized piles. Had she done this? The sides of her cardboard boxes were chewed up, her suitcase emptied out. On the kitchenette's vinyl floor, a half-completed puzzle lay scattered.

I sat on the ground and worked on the picture of a rainforest, until Tariq woke up again. "Why are you still here?" he asked when he saw me.

I looked out the French doors then, but there was nothing to see. The sky had clouded to a profound blackness, as if we were on the edge of a stage with an extinguished ghost light.

"I'm sorry you're sick," I told him.

He rubbed his jaw and came over and knelt down, locking a few pieces of the jigsaw in place. "Things don't ever turn out the way you think they will," he said. "The sooner you accept it and move on, the sooner you save yourself from grief." He shook his IV arm. "Tulip's a jealous bird," he added. "She'll be mad if you're here when she wakes up."

I linked another shard of greenery in the puzzle, then took my cue and left.

Upstairs was lonely, though. The night geese were my only company and when I finally fell asleep, I dreamt of their inconsolable bodies propelling forward, navigating the dark. Their lament stayed with me for days.

10

The dividing door remained closed most of the week. When I knocked to ask if he needed anything, my husband's brother only called up with "We're fine." Sometimes he left in the car with his bird. Other times in the early morning, he went jogging and I would watch him disappear down our street, a body diminishing to a point in the predawn.

When I sent directions to the Warblers for our next practice, I didn't think he would come. But as I locked the front door, he appeared from around the side of the house with Tulip, her little foot scratching at the netting of her carrier.

"Shouldn't you be resting?" I asked.

"There's no poison coursing through me," he replied. "I feel great."

While we drove, Tariq told me he often lay awake thinking how Tulip wasn't living the right life. But even if he wanted to release her, she could never fly back into nature. She wouldn't know how to find food or defend herself and wasn't used to being around other birds. Her first day would be her last in the wilderness.

"She seems happy enough with you," I said.

He glanced over his shoulder. "Believe me, there are bleak periods." Tulip screeched as we pulled up to the parkade.

The air was crisp and the reds and golds on the changing trees stood out against the overcast sky. We joined the Warblers, who were gathered at the metal door of the multilevel building.

"This better be good," Georgie said, blowing into her hands.

The elevator was broken. Walt had Reno carry his walker, insisting he could climb the stairs. At each level I popped my head out the door, looking for a rehearsal spot free of cars and taking breaks until Walt was ready to continue. Once we reached a high floor with few vehicles, I led the group to the centre of the concrete space.

When Tariq released Tulip, her feet stayed gripped around his fingers as she bobbed her head around.

"Is this the Woodward method?" Walt asked.

"Pretend you're in a mountain range," I suggested.

Ben did a test trill and it reverberated back at us.

Georgie covered her nose. "These mountains stink like exhaust."

"There are certainly no distractions here," Jo said, while Reno let out a yodel.

Scouting for spots with good acoustics was something I had done as a student, before I had access to state of the art facilities. For years, I had practiced in marble bathrooms, cement tunnels, and even shipping containers. Such places made my voice larger than it was. Once I drew out my strengths and weaknesses, I moved on to rooms where the sound was dampened, so I could hear myself without added resonance.

I told the Warblers to scatter around and concentrate on their technique.

Georgie raised her collar and leaned against a pillar. "You first," she said, and they waited.

My pulse quickened as I walked to a corner where I knew the sound would carry. Turning my back to the group, I whistled the signature song that had helped me make my name. It had taken me years of arduous training to perfect Mozart's staggeringly difficult Queen of the Night aria. I could sing it on any stage in any country with any air quality, within an hour's notice. My timbre and coloratura had been called "sparkling" by critics, my dramatization "star-blazing."

Learning to whistle something of such fast pacing and varied range proved almost as challenging. But the Warblers didn't need to know that I'd been practicing in the bath and in the garden and in bed, barely able to catch my breath between phrases. To overcome the speed issue, I'd developed an exercise whereby I submerged my head in the tub until I got dizzy, increasing my lung capacity more in a week than I had with five months of voice therapy. But they didn't need to know that either. Or that this was my first performance since my last performance, a half year prior.

Channelling my rage into my role, my notes didn't fall flat and I didn't get winded. I knew it was my most phenomenal interpretation yet.

Reno gave a whoo-hoo. Georgie did a slow-motion clap and said, "Not bad." Walt and Jo just stood there smiling. Then my melody came again, from the far corner where Tulip was perched on Tariq's hand.

Everyone's attention turned to her, my triumph forgotten. In perfect pitch, she repeated the hardest and highest phrase from the aria, her body rising at each top F.

When she finished, Tariq pulled an almond from his pocket.

"That was exquisite," I said, astonished. "How long has she been doing Moz—"

"She just picked it up," Tariq said, his eyes steady on me. "I think you've inspired her."

My pulse quickened. I waited for more from his bird, but she was busy with her nut, her little black tongue jutting into the cracked shell.

Tariq suggested we not give her too much attention or she'd take advantage. So after a few minutes of everyone unsuccessfully trying to hit their high Fs, the group shifted focus to their own songs while I circulated.

Georgie had already mastered Neil Diamond. She'd chosen a low register and it worked. The sound came from deep inside her body and it carried through the cool, dank space. I told her to go easy on her vibrato, it would be more powerful that way, and she told me to take a hike.

At the next column over, Reno was getting frustrated with Bing while I explained that his tone would change depending on his mood. Some days would be tougher than others. I recommended he try the song in a slightly lower key and he did, then said, "For the record, I think you're great."

There was something different about him. "Your beard," I said. He blushed. "Like it?"

"Are you whistling better without it?"

"So far I only feel naked." He zipped his hoodie up over his scrubs. "I may have found a place with fishing. Do you fish?" He described a property he was looking at outside the city and how the Big Dipper looked bigger out there. Then he whistled a tune I didn't know. When I asked what it was, he said, "Take Me Home, Country Roads," and I told him it sounded peaceful.

I crossed the parkade to Ben. He'd decided on "Suspicious Minds" because, he said, Tariq's Elvis song was hokey. His sound was buttery and I said so, which pleased him. Then we discussed birding versus opera binoculars, and I wondered if this meant he might see again but didn't ask.

When I went over to Walt, he said he would be imitating backyard birds. The ones that wintered with us, like juncos and waxwings. He attempted some double trills and leaned on his walker to catch his breath. Then Jo came over, pulling a book from her bag and handing it to me. The book was the autobiography of Ronnie Ronalde, titled *Around the World on a Whistle*. She opened the flap and pointed to his autograph, and I assured her I would treat it carefully.

I went over to Tariq last.

He was watching Tulip rush around on the concrete. She moved surprisingly fast but never strayed far. He said he hadn't worked on "Ave Maria" and wanted to focus on another song. When I asked what, he said, "Flower Duet. It's a two-person job."

"I'm well aware," I replied, while Tulip grappled with my shoelace.

"Let's give it a whirl." He smiled.

I swallowed and licked my lips.

"Would someone get the girl a Chapstick," Georgie called out.

Then I imagined we were in the Himalayas and launched off. A few seconds later, Tariq joined in. It felt good and we pressed on.

The Lakmé opera took place in India. It was a story about the daughter of a Brahmin priest falling in love with a British soldier, who chooses duty over her. In the end, she kills herself by eating the leaf of a poisonous, blooming plant.

I had always believed that Lakmé knew what was coming and tried to convey this when singing the role. The trick was to sing it like she realized there was little chance of her living out any future with the man she would soon come to love. You had to sing it with a broken heart.

When I looked up, Ben and Georgie were covering their ears.

"You two need fine tuning," Jo said.

Walt approached and offered Tariq a Werther's. "That was pasty," he told him.

"It's the drugs," Tariq said. "My tongue feels like old bread."

"Is it cancer you've got?" Walt asked.

Tariq gave a few vague details and the group quietly nodded.

"Well. Whatever we can do," Jo said, and everyone reiterated the sentiment, then Ben asked, "Do you two want to do it?"

"Pipe down, Benjamin." Walt pulled him away.

"Do you want to do it again," Ben repeated. "To redeem yourselves."

I told Tariq to continue with his mezzo part because he'd shifted up to my soprano part. "Stick to your harmony or it won't sound right," I said. We tried again, but he couldn't hold his own. "Maybe we should switch roles," I suggested. "You go first." He began and I joined in. Then he slowed and couldn't catch up.

"Keep going," he said. "Don't wait for me."

11

Not long after Tulip's breakout performance, Tariq and his bird came upstairs. I was reading on the couch. When Tulip saw Jo's book, she clamped onto it, and I had to wrestle it from her vise grip until Tariq slid it under the cushions and sat next to me with "It's time to file her nails."

First he inspected Tulip's feet and determined that her wound was still there, but no worse. And he didn't see sores developing elsewhere. "It's important to monitor closely. To make sure it doesn't turn into bumblefoot," he said.

Then he offered her a sunflower seed and when she stepped up, he pulled an emery board from his pocket. As soon as Tulip saw it, she squawked, but Tariq held her toes down with his thumb and gave her another seed.

While he filed the sharp points, she flapped and flapped. She tucked her pinky under her other toes so Tariq couldn't get to it. Then she gripped tighter around his finger so he couldn't reach those toes either. "She hates it if you accidentally hit the skin," he explained.

He did the back toes as fast as possible while Tulip growled and nipped. When he finished, he took her to the kitchen and offered her a piece of pepper, and she wiped her beak on his shirt after eating. Returning to the couch, he put her down on the rug and held a toy out to her, and told me he had to have surgery again.

"I thought this was unnecessary therapy," I said, confused.

"Apparently once it spreads, it's not easy to control. Like her dander." He nodded at his bird. "Things change quickly, I guess." Tulip worked away at dislodging a peg from a wood cone. "There are new growths that need to be removed," he added. "Then I'll take a course of pills. I should be all right after that."

When he stretched out on the floor, Tulip scaled his chest. "Who needs acupuncture when you've got talons!" He ruffled her. Then she marched down his leg, hopped off, and rushed around the living room like a pinball.

Tariq rolled over and studied the rug, running his hand along the diamond motifs and vibrant crimson-blues. "Did you find the mistake yet?" he asked. In every rug, he said, was a deliberate flaw woven into the patterning, because only a higher power was perfect. Usually the imperfection was in something hard to see.

I said I hadn't noticed anything.

He got up and walked around, looking down. Then he crouched, pointing to a tiny petal of a slightly different shade than the rest. "There it is." He sat again. "She's given you her favourite of all our rugs."

"You should tell her," I said. It was too strange that Mina was just up the street, unaware of anything.

But Tariq only rubbed at the petal with his thumb. Trying to stand, he laughed and said his feet had gone numb. He stretched his legs out and shook them. It took several tries and Tulip became unusually still. Then she sneezed. "Bless you," he told her and leaned against the living room window. "I worry she'll think I deserted her, when I'm in the hospital. Greys are sensitive and can be unforgiving. Their love isn't unconditional like a dog's."

Outside, a long white cloud was forming. It looked like a spine. "I'll watch over her," I said. "But I'm not doing her nails."

Tulip climbed his pant leg, and once she reached his waist, he unlatched her and she repositioned herself on his hand. "Deal," he said, adding, "I go in tomorrow. I'll catch a lift from Reno. So you two can nest." His bird twisted her neck away from me, and they went downstairs again.

Later on I deadheaded, shearing away the tops of old plants and pulling dried flowers off stems. I thought he might come out through the French doors and I raked a long while, leaves falling around me like yellow feathers. When the air cooled and the sky dimmed, I went back in.

The next morning, he was gone.

He had left a binder on the kitchen table. A homemade manual divided by subject, containing information on all things Tulip, including notes on healthy foods and favourite snacks, sleep and nap cycles, safe temperatures and outdoor activities, bath times and water toys, stimulating games and tricks, and vocalization and song lists.

I made my way down to the walkout.

Tariq's bird was still waking and squawked angrily as I unlatched her door. I sat in the bay window and pretended to ignore her, while she shuffled left and right on her perch, spread her wings, and shook her body. This went on for ten minutes until she finally pushed the door open.

From the cage ledge, she hopped onto her play stand, climbed the ladders to the top, and pooped on the metal surface lined with flyers. I gave her a minute, then half turned to her and said, "Good morning, Tulip."

She flitted to the ground, rushed at my chair, and tried to climb it. It took a while, but once she settled on the headrest, I placed a grape a few inches away. She nabbed it and gave me the stink eye. Then she jabbed at the chair's red fabric with her beak.

"That's a prop from Madame Butterfly," I told her and got up to put on Puccini.

Once in a while, we studied each other when we thought the other wasn't looking. While she remained fixated by my fingers tapping to "Bimba, bimba, non piangere," her feet were what fascinated me. Her black nails arced into tiny scythes and her skin seemed ancient like an elephant's. Each foot had four toes, the first and last facing back and the two middle ones facing forward. Unless she was flying, she was always on them. She stood day and night, even to sleep, and I thought how tiring it must be.

As Tulip looked out at the squirrels and birds in the fading garden, "Un bel di vedremo" began.

"This is the part where Cio-Cio-San pictures Pinkerton's return," I told her.

Her body sank a little.

"Too depressing?" I asked. Her wings drooped so I played Roger Whittaker instead. But Tulip would not speak or sing to me.

As I climbed the stairs, I thought I heard a sigh. Some shuffling around. Another sigh. "Have a nice day," I called down and left the door open a crack.

Then I phoned Ash. "Your brother is having another surgery," I told him. "You should come home."

"We talked," he replied. "He says it's nothing to worry about."

It was difficult to hear him. There was jangly music and loud beeps and chimes in the background. "This is serious," I said. "He's still sick. And I'm not equipped to babysit a parrot."

"Just keep it in the cage." He was almost yelling. "How hard can it be?"

Tulip flew across the living room then, and I jumped and dropped the phone. When I picked it up, there was cheering and Ash was saying, "I'll take one more," then, "Stand."

"Where are you?" I asked.

"Casino," he said. "Also, Mom's at Aunt Roya's. You don't have to go. We're almost done here, babe. Another ten days max. You know how it is. Like when your tours got extended."

"But . . . I'm ovulating this week."

"And you will be again next month." There was a note of irritation in his voice.

"Where were you when I phoned yesterday?"

"In a factory without reception."

"What else have you been doing?"

"Mhmm." I could hear the clinking of ice.

"*Ashraf.* Did you get to a fish spa like I told you?" I asked. "To have the dead skin eaten off your feet?" This had been the only part of Tokyo I enjoyed, after my ill-fated performance there.

Ash exhaled like he was smoking. "Not yet," he said. "I haven't made it there yet."

After we said goodbye, I tossed the phone. It bounced from the couch to the carpet and Tulip rushed over to it but lost interest quickly. I studied the dividing door handle a minute before turning on the TV, while she kept her distance and watched me flip channels.

At a nature show, her eyes darted to a scene of lush vegetation with monkeys and flocks of bright birds. As the camera panned the jungle, she climbed the stand up to the TV to *tap tap tap* her beak on the screen. Then she tapped forcibly, and when nothing happened, she charged at it. She was going to hurt herself. I turned it off.

"It's probably not as great as it looks there," I told her.

She gave a few more half-hearted raps before dismounting. Then she trudged over to the curtains and started chewing them.

"How about a walk," I suggested and approached with four fingers extended horizontally, like I'd seen Tariq do. Then I bent my top two fingers and folded in the bottom two and said, "Step up!"

She leaned forward and bit me. But it wasn't a fierce bite like the first time. Instead of carrying on with the assault, she just turned her red behind at me and got going on the curtains again.

And then she spoke.

"Ben."

I gasped. "Did you just say Ben? Do you want Benjamin?" I asked but got no reaction.

Ben was surprised to hear from us. I explained that Tulip was requesting his presence, and he said he wasn't busy and didn't live far and could meet us at the park.

As soon as I hung up, Tulip waddled to the front door and waited.

I grabbed an old backpack and her carrier. There were loops on the pack and I attached the carrier to the loops with twine and clicked the water dispenser in place, adding a bowl of chopped apples. As I tried to guide her in, she climbed the exterior until I put a donut hole in there, and she hopped in after it. Then I put the straps over my shoulders and we stepped outside.

It was a mild and sunny day. There weren't too many birds around, but those that remained stood out in the leafless trees like tiny messiahs trading ecstasies. People stared as we walked the river path toward the park. Joggers passed with barking dogs, but they were small and didn't seem to bother Tulip. Neither did the babies squealing and pointing from strollers.

"This is where I found the driftwood you've been shitting on," I told her, as brown birds called back and forth over the creek.

Then the same sound came from behind me. I paused and looked in the other direction down the path, before realizing the chirps came from my back. When I commented over my shoulder that she was a good mimic, the singing stopped.

Ben was waiting at the entrance to the park.

He wore his sunglasses and had a white cane. As we approached, I greeted him and he saluted us, and ran his fingers along the carrier. "What's happening, Tulip."

We walked to a nearby bench. As soon as I unstrapped the pack and put it down, Ben felt for the zipper and opened the door, and Tulip stepped onto his fingers.

"You really have a way with her," I told him.

"What can I say." He smiled and pulled a blanket from his bag, folding it on his lap. Tulip nestled into it as a slight breeze moved the fine, sparse feathers around her nostrils and eyes.

I asked Ben how he'd come to know birds so well.

"When I was small, I had a speech impediment," he explained. "So my mom said, 'Talk to the trees.'" He removed his sunglasses then, and his eyes flitted back in a constant, flicking motion. He rubbed his eyelids and put the glasses back on. "Can I touch your face?" he asked.

"Are your hands clean?"

He raised his palms. I told him to make it quick. He ran his hands up my shoulders and along my neck and jawline, taking his time. He touched my collarbone and my hair, running his thumbs over my eyebrows, cheekbones, and ears, eventually resting his arms back around Tulip.

"It doesn't help me know what you look like," he said. "I just take advantage if I think someone's hot."

"What makes you think I'm hot?"

"Your raspy voice."

"That's from nodules on my vocal cords."

"Silver lining." Ben grinned, and his dimples made him seem more innocent than he was.

When I asked if he'd been born blind, he said it had been brought on by a childhood disease. He could still distinguish shadows and differentiate between light and dark. "Because I used to see, I remember," he said. When I asked if that made it harder, he shrugged. "Shit happens. We adapt. Right, Tutu?" He scratched Tulip's neck, adding, "I pick things up in sounds. For instance, vibes and tensions between people. Often it's in pauses, not words. Like with you and your dude. Describe Tariq to me."

"He's not my dude. And I will do no such thing."

"Gotcha. Tell me something cool about why you became a singer, then."

"I was good at it."

"That's it?"

"What did you expect?"

"Like, that you beat all odds and lived in a car or whatever."

I told Ben that although I loved singing as a child, I still needed a lot of training. I did well as a student, and from then on, I had tried to please others, listening to what professionals told me to do. I explained that most of the singers I knew had uneventful lives occupied with auditioning, rehearsing, and performing. Which left room for little else.

"Huh," he said. "So you got more joy from it when you were no good."

My story hadn't impressed him. Apparently the Warblers were all born with symphonies inside them, unlike us professionals.

"What do you and your showbiz pals do for laughs?" he pressed on.

It was easier to be rivals than to forge lasting relationships in opera. Especially when you were always on the road, prioritizing singing above all else. I had done it for so long that the void of people in my life felt normal.

"There's a joke about that," I told him. "Why don't opera singers have friends?"

"Who knows."

"It's always about mi mi mi."

Ben cringed. "No posse, no life. Sounds great." He fed Tulip a piece of apple and asked me if sopranos could sing normally. I sang "Unchained Melody" in a low key. Partway through, I forgot the lyrics and my voice broke, so I switched to singing just *la la la*.

"Please stop," he said. "I have my answer."

I offered Tulip some apple. She turned away. "Tariq's in the hospital for surgery."

Ben straightened on the bench. "So why aren't you with him?"

"He asked me to stay home with you-know-who." I ate the apple, adding, "I hardly know him."

"Liar." Tulip nuzzled Ben's armpit. "Are you sure she said my name?"

I told him that it was the one and only word she had ever spoken to me.

"Cool." He got up with her. "Let's try a free fly."

"I don't think so," I said, but he was already walking with Tariq's bird to the green space behind our bench. Once a ways into the field, Ben tilted his body forward and extended his arm. Tulip sidestepped up to his shoulder, hesitating a moment before taking flight.

She didn't really glide or go all that high. Her wings moved more like a butterfly's, fast fast fast, and her red tail rose and fluttered like the tail of a kite. Before long, she seemed to tire and began circling lower. Ben raised his arm and she touched down on it as if he were a tree.

"How did you do that without seeing her?" I asked, approaching.

He pet Tulip, perched on his fingers. "My imagination sees her."

"But . . . how did you know she was coming?"

"Intuition. Same as you with singing."

"Well, yes, but there are technical and scientific aspects —"

"Blah blah. Don't you ever wanna defy science?" His free hand reached out, straightening my arm. "Hold still."

Tulip wasn't small, yet when he placed her on my wrist, I felt no extra weight. I was stunned by her lightness. The bones of birds were hollow, Ben explained. Tulip's feathers outweighed her skeleton.

He bribed her up to my shoulder with sunflower seeds and I leaned forward for her takeoff, but she stayed put.

"Give her a minute," Ben said, asking if the field was clear behind him before distancing himself from us, until we were about twenty feet apart.

When he nodded, I tried again, and Tulip flew, and something in me went up with her while my feet remained on the ground.

I worried we might lose her. But whenever Tulip neared Ben, he reached for the air. With his guidance, she flew back and forth, never straying far. "Beautiful!" he exclaimed each time she landed on his outstretched arm.

Afterwards we returned to the bench and gathered our things, and Ben led Tulip back into her carrier without issue. "How many songs do you think've been composed about flight?" he asked.

I'd never thought about it. Probably too many to count, I told him. Then I asked if his mom had dropped him off and he laughed, saying he got around fine on his own, and that he'd even found himself an agent in La La Land. After graduating, he would go.

"Have you booked auditions?" I asked.

"Not yet," he replied. "But I'm not worried."

I asked if there were many bird species in L.A., despite the smog.

Ben said they had hummingbirds, and did I know they only hummed because they'd forgotten their words. "Like you," he added with a titter.

"Touché."

"Birds see colours we never will," he went on. "They see tints in polarized light and glimmers that humans can't."

I asked if hummingbirds sang. If they did, I hadn't ever heard their song.

"A couple species make scratchy calls," Ben said. "But most sing through the feathers. And we don't hear it."

He thanked Tulip for the excursion. As he left us, I watched him head down the sidewalk. He went slowly at first, stopping once or twice to adjust his direction. Then he picked up his pace. People moved aside as he went by, or they went wide around him to pass. Which really wasn't necessary, because he walked a pretty straight line.

12

At the hospital, Tariq was sucking on ice chips, his body a tangle of wires. He had a morphine drip and a tube in his arm for fluids, a tube going through his nose to his stomach for nutrition, a tube near his incision to drain his bladder, and other tubes draining the liquids coming out of his incision.

"You're not supposed to be here," he said. I sat down anyway.

He asked about Tulip and I reported on her activities, including pushing through doors and free flying. Then Dr. Horne came in and pulled up a chair. He told Tariq he'd removed two tumours and all the cancer he could see. His other organs and lymph nodes were clear. But there could still be traces of the disease remaining, he added, which the chemo pill was meant to eradicate.

I got up and walked over to the window. The room looked onto the hospital's massive pay lot and a line of cars was forming at the exit. The front car was stuck at the machine, holding everyone up. Drivers leaned out their windows and honked. Then a man in coveralls got out of his truck and a woman in a suit exited her BMW. An elderly man emerged from the stuck car. He handed them his ticket and they took turns inspecting it and feeding the machine. Finally, the man in coveralls forced the toll bar up and all the vehicles passed through, rushing away from illness and death.

As he stood to go, Dr. Horne asked Tariq if he had any questions.

Tariq wanted to know how much longer he would feel so thirsty, and Dr. H. said another few days. Then Tariq asked me to pass him his jeans from a bag at the foot of the bed and pulled one of Tulip's tail feathers from the pocket, offering it to the doctor.

"Bookmark," he told him.

Dr. H. ran it through his fingers. "Extraordinary."

He patted Tariq's shoulder and told him to get rest. When he slipped the feather in his breast pocket, it looked like a splash of blood against his white coat.

After the doctor left, I took his chair and Tariq asked to see my hands. I held them out and he studied each finger, then the insides of my palms. I asked if I needed a nail trim, and he said he was glad to see that Tulip hadn't bit me. Then another hospital employee came by, a silver-haired lady in a floral jacket. She reminded Tariq that he had access to a social worker, a nutritionist, and information sessions on self-care. It could also be arranged for him to speak with a survivor buddy. He accepted her card, and when she left, he let it fall to the floor and closed his eyes.

I shut mine, too, but it was impossible to rest with the noise of staff and machines, elevator bells dinging, carts rolling, intercom voices, and neighbouring TVs. So I hummed the Habanera and realized that my laryngeal muscles no longer felt knotted up.

When I opened my eyes, Tariq was watching me. Then the Warblers were spilling through the door, making a racket as they gathered around the bed.

Ben had set up the visit. They presented Tariq with an African violet, which he asked me to feed to Tulip, and they admired his lips, pink and puffy from drugs.

Tariq asked Jo for a shot of vibration. She looked unsure, but then unhooked her fork and quickly struck the back of Reno's head with it. When she pressed the stem to Tariq's shoulder, he told her he could feel the frequency travelling all through his body.

Georgie promised to throw a pool party when his ordeal was over with, at her apartment complex. Walt brought a bag of Werther's, which Reno tucked into right away, only to complain that they weren't the ones with soft centres. And Ben brought everyone coloured whistles shaped like birds.

Jo filled the whistles with water from the jug on Tariq's bedside table and passed them around, and we blew on the tails, but only Ben was able to get music from his instrument.

The plastic birds led to a discussion about a computer program that could whistle anything. It could do exactly what any human could do and it could sing like birds, only better. Jo found a demo online and we listened. The sound was pitch perfect.

"There's no soul," I told them, adding that it was like the fairy tale Hans Christian Andersen wrote for his unrequited love, the opera singer Jenny Lind, about an emperor who preferred a lavish mechanical bird to a real nightingale, but then when he lay dying, only the true nightingale's song could revive him.

We asked Ben to do a nightingale. He said that was impossible because they weren't native to North America and he needed to hear their live song, not recordings. He'd tried studying caged ones and Northern mockingbirds and whippoorwills, which came close, but none sang in the same way as the free bird.

Georgie told him he'd have to go to Romania for the real thing. She'd travelled there as a young woman and still remembered the bird's haunting music, which she'd heard from a terrace along the Danube Delta with the man she was engaged to, briefly. Her lower lip shook and her chest blotched above her scoop-neck sweater until Dr. Horne, who was still doing rounds, popped his head back in.

"Is this your notorious club?" he asked.

After Tariq apologized for the noise, Dr. H. suggested an impromptu performance in the lobby. There was someone out there with a therapy dog attracting a lot of attention.

Walt elbowed Jo and said, "I told you we should get into these places," and Georgie said, "Because the audience can't escape? We might as well do prisons, too," and Jo said, "Whistling's not allowed in prisons. What do you want to perform, everyone?"

Georgie said she'd been practicing Bocelli and Brightman's "Time to Say Goodbye," but Jo told her that was inappropriate. Reno wanted to do "Stairway to Heaven," which Jo also shut down. Ben voted for "Heigh-Ho," and Walt suggested "Joy to the World." They just could not agree on a song and started arguing until Jo cut them off. "How about we let Tariq decide?"

Tariq told the group that one of Tulip's favourite songs was "Here Comes the Sun." They shuffled out with his request, whispering conspiratorially about harmonies and who should do what verse.

The lobby was a few doors down from Tariq's room. I asked if he wanted to go in a wheelchair, but he couldn't with all the tubes and said he'd listen lying down. Then a nurse arrived to change his dressing, so I went out into the hall to give them privacy.

The Warblers' take on the song was pretty. They kept their whistling soft and respectful of their environment, and the music carried down the hall like water lapping.

"Da da da daaaaa." I could hear the nurse singing quietly. "It's all right. It's all right." I felt unsteady as she came out and had to lean against the wall. "Oh honey," she said. "It's going to be okay." Her name was Marina, meaning of the sea, and she rubbed my back and said she would return later.

There was clapping and requests for more songs. They did "Sittin' on the Dock of the Bay," and I heard Dr. Horne ask if they knew "I'm a Believer" by the Monkees. Then the volunteer the Warblers had ousted from the lobby passed by, with her furry little caterpillar of a dog. The volunteer wasn't allowed to enter rooms so she stood at Tariq's doorway while her dog snuffled around, its hair dragging on the ground.

"I'm Laverne and this is Abel," she said.

Abel collapsed into a heap, rested his chin on his paws, and looked up sorrowfully.

"Do you come here a lot?" Tariq asked Laverne.

"We did when Mom was sick. Then after she died, we kept coming. Abel cheers folks up."

Tariq told Laverne about Tulip, saying that once she'd ridden on a dog's back and the dog had looked a lot like Abel.

Laverne said maybe they could meet someday. "Must be hard being apart," she added. Then she hesitated and asked, "Are you going to pull through?"

"Absolutely," Tariq told her.

She looked right and left, scooped Abel up, and snuck him over to the bed for a quick pet. Tariq scratched him behind the ears. "You two take care," he said. Laverne fed Abel a biscuit before they moved along down the hall.

When the Warblers came back, Marina followed them in and said Tariq needed to rest. Then I told them to have their arias chosen for our next class, because it was time to buckle down, and they gave me dismissive looks before turning back to Tariq to say goodbye.

I left soon after but returned over the next few days.

Each day, the nurses helped Tariq move around and do leg exercises. They helped him get up and walk, and they helped him go to the bathroom, removing one tube after another. The duty nurse told him that if he climbed a small flight of stairs, he could go home. At a practice staircase, Tariq lined up behind others undergoing the same test. There were a lot of bodies in gowns looking up those steps as though they were ascending Everest, going into the clouds and the great unknown.

Once Tariq went up all six steps, taking more time to come down them, the nurse clapped her hands and turned to me with a radiant smile, saying, "You can come and fetch your hubby tomorrow."

13

"Do you know Plutarch's story of the Spartan child?" he asked, his voice quiet and close. I'd fumbled to answer the phone in the dark and thought it was Ash calling. Until I remembered he was in the air flying home, and it was the middle of the night, and my husband did not know Plutarch.

I sat up and turned on the bedside lamp. "Vaguely," I told Tariq.

"He stole a fox and hid it under his cloak. Then the fox tore out his guts and he let it, rather than get caught."

"That's horrific."

"In the wild if a bird is unwell, it masks its symptoms," he went on. "If it shows signs of sickness, its flock ostracizes it to avoid predators attacking the group. Pet birds hide their suffering until they die, too. So their human flock won't abandon them."

I lay down again. "Are you asking me to check on Tulip's bumblefoot?"

"I don't want my illness impacting her spirit. I need your help keeping things normal for her."

"I'll try."

"It's snowing."

I turned the lamp off, drew the curtains open, and watched large white flakes fall over the garden. Then Tariq suggested taking Tulip outside in the morning. He'd been acclimatizing her to the changing weather. She had built up a down coat and would be fine to play outdoors for fifteen minutes, if the day was mild. "Is she in her roost?" he asked. "Are you giving her oatmeal before bed?"

I told him yes. Then I asked if she was allowed donuts and he said he supposed one hole would do no harm, so long as it wasn't chocolate, which was toxic, as I would know from the binder. Had I browsed the reference guide yet?

"It's on my to-do list."

"So do it," he replied, and said goodnight.

In the morning when I unlatched Tulip's door, she came out right away.

After she climbed the play stand to poop, she looked out the French doors. When she saw snow, her whole body shook, and she ate her raisin toast so fast that most of it landed on the floor.

I was beginning to understand that if I ignored her, she would follow. I went upstairs, checked the temperature, and dressed, all with the tapping of her talons close by. "I'll clear the way," I told her, and she held her beak wide open, almost panting.

In the cold air, my energy went up. I shovelled the front steps and Tulip waited there as I made a path to the driveway, keeping an eye out for dogs. Nobody was out: it was a school day and a workday. At a small mound, she stretched her foot and pulled it back. Then she stretched her leg behind her and spread her wings, and her tail fanned out like Carmen's red dress before she bunched her body up again.

"Step up and we'll go for donuts," I said, and she stared at my gloved hand. I held it at her chest level but she wouldn't budge. Before she could object, I swaddled her with my scarf and tucked her into my parka like Tariq did because, he said, parrots nested in tree holes.

She hardly weighed a pound. I recalled what Cherry had said about the softness of gulls and lowered my chin to feel her feathery being, which was like a balm. But she started to squirm when I touched her, so I pulled back.

My coat was warm, and she seemed comfortable in her nook as we made the short walk to the shopping complex a few blocks away. When we got to the near-empty donut store and I ordered, the man at the counter said, "You can't have that thing in here."

I looked down at the grey head poking from my parka, then handed him a five. "Four honey dips and two old-fashioned holes, please."

"We can't serve you, lady," he said. "Read the sign."

My nose ran. I took a napkin from the dispenser. The man peeled his plastic gloves off, tossed them, and Tulip clicked her tongue. I had to wrap my arms around my chest to contain her. She was trying her best to get out.

The man pointed to the door again. We left.

Then I walked around the building to the drive-thru and spoke into the order board. As we approached the service window, a girl peered out and said, "Oh, you're on foot. You have to go inside. Holy cow, is that a . . ."

She held our bag of holes. Cradling Tulip against my chest, I reached into the window with my free hand, but she pulled back. "I'll get fired," she said. "It's motorized vehicles only."

Tulip tucked her head under her wing. She was getting cold. "I need to take her home," I said. "I'm not leaving until you give us our donuts."

She reached a hand out, then bit her lip and moved back. "It's a liability thing," she said. "You could rob us."

I laughed. "A robbery would be more effective with a getaway vehicle."

"Or get hit by a car," she continued.

I looked over my shoulder. There was no one. Blowing into my coat, I pulled a twenty from my pocket and reached into the window for our bag again, but the girl was already talking into her headset and the man who wouldn't serve us reappeared. "If you don't leave, we'll call security," he said.

There was a person sifting through the trash in the parking

lot. I covered the top of my parka and offered him the twenty for some donuts. He went inside and we waited. But he didn't come out again.

When I approached the storefront one last time, I saw Mina. She was alone, settling in at a table in a corner. I uncovered Tulip and we watched my mother-in-law remove her coat and hang her purse on her chair. Once she sat down, she stared at the pink box before her like it contained treasure. Then she opened it and ate three sprinkled donuts in a row, and Tulip made a *tch-tch-tch!* sound on seeing what Mina consumed.

The fourth donut pulled from the box my mother-in-law tore to pieces as if at the edge of a pond, feeding ducks. When she finished, she pushed the box aside, tilted her head down, and placed both hands in front of her face. Then she wrapped her well-worn sweater around her large frame and stared off into space, drinking her tea.

Tulip had stopped trying to escape and I could feel her shivering. "How about coconut milk instead," I told her and we turned to go, sliding through the parking lot and along the sidewalk, trying not to fall as we rushed back to the house.

Once inside, I turned up the heat and let her down on the table, spreading a puzzle out to distract her. But she latched onto my coat again and tried to climb back inside. I was overcome with a feeling then, not unlike the joy I experienced on discovering a new colour in a note I didn't know I could produce. Only there was something more, even, than that. I wondered if this was what it felt like, to have a child.

"I'm not a kangaroo," I told her, carrying her to the linen closet and leaning into a shelf of towels. She unlatched and worked her way onto them, settling in.

I went back to the kitchen and prepared her drink and cherries, which I cut into small pieces. Then I went downstairs and dragged her playscape up, and a perch. "Snack time," I called out, and she flew from the closet to the table where she ate and slurped, using her tongue like a paddle to drink while I busied myself washing piled-up dishes.

By the time I finished, she'd migrated to the living room window and was gazing at the snow like she wanted to go out again. When I went to change her linings and bowls, though, I noticed blood on her playscape. Looking around, I saw it splattered on the floor and kitchen chairs. I tried to examine her but she hopped off the sill, and every time I approached, she ran away like we were playing tag.

I called Tariq in a panic. "She's bleeding," I told him. "There's blood all over the place."

He calmly said that if she broke a feather it could be dangerous, and I needed to check her wings and tail. With a teaspoon of peanut butter, I was able to pick her up. But when I lifted her into the air, she struggled out of my grasp, nipping at my hands until I put her down.

"I can't see anything," I said.

"Where is the blood coming from?" Tariq asked. "Is it spraying?"

"There's none on her."

"Then where is it?"

"On her perch. Around the floor."

Tariq asked what she had eaten. I told him and he exhaled. "I hope you removed the pits," he said. "She'll be fine after she finishes digesting."

Tulip waddled back to the linen closet. Once she tucked herself safely into the shelf, I went back to the living room.

"We saw your mom earlier," I said. "I thought she was at your aunt's."

"She probably made that up."

"Why would she do that?"

"To save you from stopping in. She's scared of becoming a burden. What did she say?"

"I didn't want to put her on the spot."

"I'll help. When this is done. It's my turn."

I looked at the mess Tulip and I had created. "Please come home," I told him.

It took him a long time to respond. I thought he had hung up. "Soon, Dawnjaan," he finally said.

Outside I watched a lone cardinal in a tree, this flash of red against the bare branches. His chest went in and out like it was going to burst as he hopped from bough to bough.

"Ashraf will pick you up when he lands," I told him. "He insisted on it."

"No problem," Tariq said. A nurse interrupted our conversation then. I heard her ask him about pain control, and he said he had to go.

14

Ash smelled different when he returned. And with his brother there, instead of our usual embrace, he only drew me in and kissed my forehead. Then his phone was ringing. "It's my mom. Again." He shook his head and stepped outside to take the call.

As for Tariq, he moved stiffly when he came through the door. Like old times, he uttered a hello without looking at me. From her perch in the living room, Tulip eyed him suspiciously before turning to the window.

Tariq approached her with "Do you want to talk about it?"

But his bird kept her tail to him and continued her staring contest with the cat on the sill in the house across the street.

He cleaned and refilled her dishes and attempted to greet her again. When he reached his hand out, Tulip assessed it from all angles. Then she stepped carefully over a bandage and came to rest on his forearm, and Tariq tilted his head back and mouthed "thank you." There would be no grudge after all. She studied his bruised hands for a long time and kept glancing up at him.

"It doesn't hurt," he told her as he tried to sit on the couch.

I offered my arm and he clutched it to lower himself, exhaling after he sank into the cushions. When Tulip bowed her head, he rubbed it and kissed her black beak. "What did the swan say when

she bought lipstick?" he asked. Tulip waited. "Put it on my bill!"
He laughed then winced, and Tulip emitted a little "Ah! Ah!"

When Ash came in again, he asked why the bird was upstairs.
"I couldn't keep running down there," I told him. "She can't stay
locked in a cage all day long."

Tariq watched on with a faint smile.

"Take it easy," Ash said. "I'm only asking why you've turned
the place into a jungle."

In the last week, I had installed every one of my humidifiers
and hung ropes, swings, and bells from the ceiling for Tulip to play
with. I'd also bought tropical plants she could chew.

Ash grabbed two beers out of the fridge and offered one to
his brother, but Tariq declined. My husband toasted him and put
the second bottle on the mantle, next to my bird whistle. Then
he picked the whistle up, blew into it, and said, "Doesn't work."
I took it from him and set it back down while he drank. "Missed
you, beautiful," he said, tucking my hair behind my ears. But his
mind was elsewhere. He kept checking his phone, and when I
asked about his trip, he told us there was nothing to tell. They'd
made the deal and he was tired.

"What was the best part about Tokyo?" Tariq asked.

"The nightlife," Ash said. "And the Fragment Room."

"Is that a museum?"

"It's a room where they give you a bat and a mask and you
smash things."

"What kinds of things?" I asked.

"Fragile things. Crates of ceramics. Plates, cups, stuff like that."
He kissed me on the forehead again. "I better go. Mom needs
groceries." Then he turned to Tariq. "Hamari ma ko fon karo,
bhsijan. She's threatening to get on a bus and visit you because you
aren't returning her calls."

Tariq rubbed his temples. "Preshan na hon. I'll phone her,
brother."

Ash added that he'd been researching experimental drugs and wanted to discuss his findings. "Tomorrow," Tariq said, and Ash nodded and left.

I stared after him at the front door, the back of my neck going tight.

"He could never relax," Tariq told me.

Nowhere was this more evident than in a concert hall, where Ash couldn't sit without fidgeting. Then the leg twitching would begin, and the incessant clearing of the throat. Sometimes he cracked his knuckles. Once, he got up before intermission. People glared. It was embarrassing. We argued about it and he stopped coming. He just couldn't quiet his thoughts long enough for the euphoria of music to set in.

I asked Tariq if he wanted to eat something. I could make pasta. He replied that Tulip would not say no to noodles. Looking down at his bird, he asked if she'd been troublesome. I told him we'd had bonding moments and that we had graduated from bites to nips. He thanked me for taking care of her and got up with difficulty, saying they would keep out of our way.

"You're not in the way," I told him.

But he was already descending the staircase.

I boiled the pasta and brought bowls down on a tray, and the three of us sat at the kitchenette table, looking out the French doors to the white yard.

During Tariq's stay in the hospital, I had set up a winter feeder with suet cakes and seeds, so Tulip would have something to watch. I was learning my birds and beginning to recognize their calls and colourings. Their individual habits and traits. While we ate, nuthatches, finches, and chickadees appeared. Then came the jays, scaring the others away. Even when I rapped on the glass, they returned. It was useless to try to get rid of them.

Tulip flung noodles across the room and yawned. Then she hopped off the table and climbed my red chair, and out of nowhere, she started whistling, her head nodding at each end phrase, and I recognized the melody . . . *is falling down, my fair lady* . . .

Her tone carried a warm, bouncing quality, and Tariq finished the tune with her, then turned to me. "We enjoy songs about bridges," he said.

I wondered out loud who the fair lady was. Tariq replied that she was probably the River Lea. Then I asked what had drawn him to engineering these structures, and he told me he'd always been fond of overpasses.

"We realize a lot standing on them," he said. "For some reason when you're in the middle of one and you look out . . ." His thought trailed off. He wiped Tulip's placemat with the side of his hand. "Sometimes it's the only path to a place," he said. "Or to a person. It's a passage over something you couldn't otherwise cross."

I wanted to say I understood. That bridges lived in every melody and got you from one part of a song to the other. I wanted to tell him that his description was how I felt about the effect of music on the soul, only I'd never had the words for it. But instead I just nodded.

He swallowed some pills and lay on my mother's quilt. Tulip climbed up the bed, and they played peek-a-boo and one potato two potato under the blankets. Then Tariq pulled a hand mirror from under a pillow and raised it at different angles, while his bird observed herself in the glass. When he moved it, she followed the dancing prisms of light on the wall. Then he laid the mirror flat on the bed, and she took guarded steps onto the surface, bending over and sticking her red behind in the air like a duck diving into water.

They finished with a waving game. Tariq waved his foot, and Tulip raised a leg and waved back. When she did so, he held her steady with one hand and caught her foot with the other, to investigate her pressure point. After he let go, she settled into her preening and Tariq asked me to pass him a libretto from my shelf.

"Which one?" I asked.

"A favourite."

I chose *Tristan und Isolde*. Whose love, it had been said, was so great that it could only be fulfilled through death. Some also said that Wagner's tour de force contained the meaning of life. While he read, I sat on the edge of the bed near Tulip, who'd returned to ignoring me since her companion had come home. Then Tariq handed the book over.

"The perfect tragedy," he told me.

So he had seen it. "Was Anabelle an opera enthusiast?" I asked. He pulled a bandage off his hand. "She prefers New Age." His face remained emotionless. Whenever Tariq spoke of Anabelle he seemed completely unphased.

"Don't you miss your wife?"

He watched Tulip raise a wing to pick at some feathers. "An earlier me would have," he finally replied. "Before my father died and before my cancer. Anabelle wanted nothing to do with these things. But I had to enter into them. To understand them. And that changed everything between us. Besides," he hesitated, "it wasn't love that brought us together."

"What did?"

"Dashed hopes." Tulip rubbed her beak against his arm to clean her face. "We were both in bad places when we met," Tariq continued. "I ignored it until I got sick."

It was getting dark out. The squirrels had chased away the jays, all the birds were gone, and through the French doors, the shadows of trees cast a blue light against the snow.

When I asked about his treatment and things to come, he studied the patterning on the wedding quilt and ran his hand across it. "All I need to do now is take drugs. Easy peasy."

I ran my hand near his across the padded squares of stitching. "My mother is a perfectionist," I told him. "You won't find a flaw."

"I don't doubt it."

As he looked up, a feeling like scintillating quills washed over my body. I gathered our bowls and hurriedly said goodnight. But as I climbed the stairs, I sensed parts of our conversation drifting unspoken in the air, a Wagnerian feather neither of us could grasp.

I made my way up to the bedroom to watch Birgit Nilsson sing her final, climactic "Liebestod." But my laptop wouldn't charge so I retrieved Ash's from his carry-on.

Opening it, You've Won a Free Spin blinked on the page. I clicked to get rid of the ad and behind it a browser window showed my husband's name and a ledger of wins and losses, and his history revealed several similar sites. Ash's penchant for online penny slots was a habit he'd hidden from me. A harmless one, when the wagers even on multiple pay lines amounted to under ten dollars. But a secret nonetheless, and I found myself thinking, *Who is this man?*

I went through his files and trash bin. I searched deleted conversations, then his bag and suitcase and clothes' pockets. In one pair of pants, I found foiled candies. He wasn't one for sweets. This led to a search through the house. I looked in every cabinet and drawer for a hidden phone or letter, a strand of hair not mine, a new scent or stain. I stuck my hand in shoes, emptied his desk and dresser and toolbox, his cereal boxes and designer watch boxes and his baseball card collection. I checked his bookshelves, too, until I came across our wedding album and stopped.

Returning to bed, I opened his laptop again, scanning each folder until my eyes couldn't focus. Then I set the screen aside and lay down.

When he got home and came upstairs, I sat up and turned on the light. "How is your mother?" I asked.

"She seems well," he said, removing his tie.

"A lot happened while you were gone," I told him. "You should have come back sooner. This is your family, not mine."

He pulled something from his jacket before removing it. "Souvenir," he said, handing me a kabuki facemask and a rum raisin Kit Kat. They sold these everywhere in Tokyo. You could buy them from vending machines. "I'm doing my best," he added, undressing. "It's going to be fine."

"You didn't see what I saw." I sensed my voice rising. "His body is rejecting treatment."

"Allergic reactions are common. They'll use other drugs. I'm on it."

"This isn't a merger, Ashraf."

He stared at his laptop on the nightstand, then got into bed.

"Are you smoking again?" I asked.

"What do you expect. With all this."

"Is there anything else?"

"Like what?" He reached for my hand, but I pulled away, lay down, and turned my back to him. Then he leaned over me for the laptop and opened it, and I heard a quick succession of clicks. Our discussion was over. Later, he brushed my hair aside and kissed my ear, but I pretended to be sleeping.

When I got up in the morning, I noticed the toilet seat was lowered in the bathroom. In our five years of marriage, my husband had never closed the lid. Or folded the hand towel so neatly.

15

Without asking me, Tariq volunteered us to host Aria Night, when the Warblers would commit to a sole piece of music for the remainder of our sessions. After the parkade outing, a lesson in the subway, and a government building with a domed sound chamber, they refused to return to Norwood. They preferred exploring new venues, Ben said, when he phoned to ask what he could bring.

Ash and Tariq were out with Tulip and I was alone in the house, worrying about my larynx, which felt inflamed again. After hanging up with Ben, I phoned Ash twice, and he asked with impatience if I was checking up on him. I invented excuses. When I heard Tariq in the background, I told myself to calm down. Then I called Mina.

"Has your son been visiting?" I asked.

"He give me Tokyo hair clip, very expensive. You?"

"I got a chocolate bar. Mrs. Khan, has Ashraf stopped in this week?"

"Yes. He is good son."

"Does he stay long?"

"We eat strudel. Every morning he bring it for me."

"What time does he leave?"

"Work time."

"And he stops in at the end of the day?"

"Haanji, yes. Go away, Done."

"You should have fruit with your breakfast. Not just pastry."

"Oyye fitteh mooh tera!" She used the saying with me often. It meant may your mouth burn in hell.

Reassured, I said goodbye to my mother-in-law and went from room to room, thinking about singing. But I was scared of straining any muscle or nerve above my collarbone, so sat in silence instead.

Then there was cleaning to do.

In the laundry room, I emptied Ash's pockets of more foiled candies, to mask his smoking, I guessed. There were also cancer ribbons scattered on the floor. A forgotten T-shirt with the Golden Gate on it, soft from wearing, lay atop our own clothes like a flag. Smelling it left me with an unfamiliar ache. I threw it into the wash with Ash's collared shirts and closed the lid.

While I was vacuuming traces of Tulip from the furniture, the bell rang.

When I opened the door, Walt lifted his walker over the threshold and pulled a bear from the basket, the word Chemo-bearapy stitched across its chest. "That was Mae's," he said. "I thought Tariq could use a laugh."

I put the stuffed animal on the front bench and helped him with his coat, then led him into the living room. He asked where the crew was. I said they would arrive in an hour and he cursed Georgie for giving him the wrong time. Dragging the vacuum out of the way, I told him it didn't matter. He offered to help, but I encouraged him to unwind. So he picked up Jo's book while I went to the kitchen to prepare snacks.

When I heard him yawning I returned and sat with him.

Walt slapped his knees. "Mind if I pick your brain before the troops invade? I'm thinking 'Nessun dorma' would be a humdinger for the Biennial."

He pulled a notepad and pencil from his bag. I suggested he go with a less clichéd number.

"If Pavarotti sang it at the World Cup, it's good enough for me," he replied. "I visited the school where my wife and I taught yesterday. To show the kids how it's done. The invitation was last minute. Their performance clown cancelled."

"How did it go?"

He rubbed the bridge of his nose with his finger. "I wore a chicken costume to get their attention."

When I asked if his strategy worked, he shrugged. "It was hot. There was a lot of talking and bodies huddled over screens. Then I gave them 'Finnish Whistler.'"

"And?"

"They found it hysterical. I had a kid come up and I told him, 'Once you've got it, you won't stop. It's contagious that way,' and someone yelled, 'Like STDs!,' and all hell broke loose. They didn't hear a thing after that."

"Then what happened?"

"I left."

"You just walked out in your chicken suit?"

"Yes, ma'am. I had my dignity."

Walt cracked up. So did I. We laughed until there were tears streaming down our faces. Then his smile vanished and he took a puff off his inhaler. "I wanted them to be the ambassadors of whistling. Before it dies out. They were too old is the problem. We've got to start with the kindergarteners." He drew a treble clef in his notepad.

"Some people find it annoying," I told him. "Like opera."

"My theory is the haters are the ones who can't do it." He removed his glasses and cleaned them. "There was one kid watching me like a hawk, though. I bet he's practicing right this minute."

I agreed that he probably was, and therefore his visit had been worthwhile. Then I went to the kitchen to boil water, adding lemon and honey to our mugs. When I came back and sat with Walt, he looked hunched over and very old.

"Was Mae your wife?" I asked.

He shaped his hands into a steeple and nodded.

"And she had cancer?"

He nodded again. "It started with her routines changing," he said. "She'd go for groceries at nine at night instead of on Saturday mornings. And she packed strange things in our lunches. Canned gravy. Bags of uncooked lentils. She got headaches and dropped things." He glanced at the bear then back at his hands. "My wife had the prettiest eyes. An under-the-sea kind of blue. But they darkened like they'd lost their oxygen, and her personality changed. They ran tests and told us she had the type of brain tumour with spreader tentacles like an octopus. Our kids, Beth and Adam, flew out for a family meeting. The medical team said they could use all measures to try and cure her, or make her comfortable. Mae insisted they do everything. So they sawed her head open and scooped out what they could before stapling her skull back together. Then she got an infection. They gave her antibiotics that downed her immune system, and she contracted one of those superbugs and was quarantined for a month. We had to wear gowns and masks to see her. Then the seizures started."

"I'm so sorry," I told him.

"That was the beginning," Walt replied. "She lived seven more months in a facility where they left her in soiled diapers and rarely bathed her. There were too many complications for her to come home. I tried to care for her there, but sometimes I had to get back to the house, just a few hours here and there, you know? Meantime, they brought her trays of food but didn't help her eat. They didn't massage her limbs or turn her body to prevent sores. A ceiling vent blew cold air on her, but they wouldn't move the bed. Not that she complained. Do you know what she said the week before she died?" He looked at me, eyebrows raised like he was still in shock. "She told me, 'This was a mistake. We could have had nice moments.'"

His gaze fell to the ground. "I was on the john when they phoned early one morning. After fifty years, that was our ending."

He got up and took stiff, short steps to the window. "A trembling," he said. I approached and he pointed. "You've got a trembling of nuthatches in your tree."

We watched the scrambling whitish-blue bodies disappear in collective flight. After they were gone came the echo of their persistent, simple call.

Helping him back to the couch, I asked when Mae died. He said it had been ten years. "I didn't whistle for a long time after," he added, "and when I did start back, I'd just gotten dentures. Every time I blew, my teeth slid out. It took me a year to relearn everything." He patted my hand the way my father did. "People think whistling is for happy folks. When actually it's a solitary occupation." Suddenly he jolted back like he remembered something. "I bought a tux for the convention," he said. "It's wrinkle-free so I can pack it any which way and scrunch it into a ball. Beth's remarrying next summer, so I'll wear it then, too."

I said his tux sounded handy but if he was really going to play Calaf in *Turandot*, he should consider a kimono and sash.

He sketched the prince in his notebook, a tiny lone figurine. "Nessun dorma indeed," he said, rubbing his chin.

"It means none shall sleep."

"Don't I know it," Walt replied.

We heard something then and turned to find Tariq leaning against the dividing door with his bird. I wondered how long he'd been there. He offered Tulip a slice of cucumber, which she nibbled at unenthusiastically.

"Where's Ash?" I asked.

"Office," Tariq replied. Then he turned to Walt. "I'm sorry about your wife," he said, and Walt nodded.

"I may not be far behind her. I fell twice this month at home," Walt told us. "My body's going."

"Your whistling's not," Tariq said.

"That's what I tried demonstrating to those kids," Walt replied. "I said, 'One day you'll grow old. So will your voice. But your whistling won't age. It's your instrument to take along wherever you go. You'll always have it with you.'"

The others arrived through the front door, which I'd forgotten to lock. "This year someone better *explain* to those cub reporters that 'Canon in D Major' is not by K'naan," Georgie was telling Jo. They carried a piñata and a cake, and I went over to help them.

While Georgie led Ben around to get a sense of the space, Reno went up to Tariq. "How're you feeling, man?" he asked.

"Pretty good, thanks," Tariq said.

The piñata was a donkey. Jo hung it from one of Tulip's ropes and Reno handed Tariq a broomstick and said, "Have at 'er."

Tariq passed Tulip to Ben, raised the stick, and whacked the piñata until a rainbow of candies spilled from the animal's backend and onto the floor, Tulip crash-landing into them.

Then Jo set the cake out on the table. She said they'd chosen periwinkle because it was his cancer's colour. The cake was shaped like a raised fist, and in white icing was written TARIQ TOGETHER WE FIGHT YOU!

"It's supposed to be fight *with*," Georgie said. "The bakery messed up."

Tariq stood tall. "You shouldn't have," he told them.

I cut and distributed pieces. While we ate, Ben said he had a surprise and pulled a stack of swallow T-shirts from his backpack. Everyone put them on right away. Then he said he had another surprise and whistled the call of the Missouri skylark, also known as Sprague's pipit.

No one knew the bird. Ben said they were small and plain-looking and that they spiralled high in the sky to make their music, lost to our view, so it seemed like the song came from the air itself. His rendition was spectacular. It had taken him months to refine. While he emitted the call, Tulip's bottom bobbed tunefully from her perch, and Walt was excited to hear the melody clearly. His new hearing aid gave no feedback, and his doctor had removed the wax build-up from his ears. At the mention of this, Jo inspected everyone's ears and urged cleanings before the convention to gain a competitive edge.

"Swanky rug," Reno said, looking down at the floor.

Tariq invited the Warblers to take their socks off, and they walked around the living room barefoot, wriggling their toes into the wool. Then everyone closed their eyes as if they stood on something magical that would elevate and take them away, until I told them enough silliness. It was time to for them to announce their song choices, so we could start honing their selections. "Firstly, what's an aria?" I asked.

"A loud howl." Ben pulled his socks back on.

I explained that aria meant air, and that arias were all about breath control.

Walt declared that he had dibs on "Nessun dorma." Georgie told the group that she'd decided on "O mio babbino caro." When Reno asked how it went, she hummed a few bars.

"Woodstock whistles that in the Charlie Brown Christmas special," he told her.

"I hardly think so," Georgie replied. "And what have you got that's any better?"

Reno turned to me. "'When I See You Smile' by Bad English."

"I don't know why you're looking at Dawn," Georgie said. "She never smiles."

"Unfortunately that's not an aria, Reno," Jo told him.

"Rock ballads are the arias of our era," he replied.

"They'll laugh you off stage," Georgie said.

"Don't care." He reached for another piece of cake.

"How about you, Ben?" I asked.

Ben took a step forward and put a hand to his heart. "The great tit from Bruckner's fourth."

"Also not an aria," Georgie said.

"And I don't care either," Ben replied.

I returned Jo's book to her and said I had enjoyed it, especially the part where Ronnie Ronalde toured Australia. Then I turned to Tariq.

"Nadir's aria," he said without hesitation. Tulip was on his shoulder, and after he spoke, the white around her eyes acquired a pinkish hue.

"Is she blushing?" I asked.

"Birds can't blush," Georgie said.

"Can, too," Ben told her. "Look it up."

"And what has our resident expert chosen?" Tariq asked.

"'Casta diva,'" I said, and he nodded like he knew it.

"Just don't do your eyebrow thing," Georgie said.

"What thing?"

"Where you raise and lower your eyebrows while you sing. It looks idiotic."

"I can't help it."

"Rubbish. Do we look like blowfish when we whistle?"

I waited for someone to interject, but no one did. So I told them to get practicing and went around listening. When I got to Ben, I quietly asked if he knew what it meant if someone's smell had changed.

"It means the way they feel has changed," he replied.

Walt leaned over with "Or they're dying."

Reno called out to Ben across the room. "Would tintabulation be related to the tit?"

"It's tintinnabulation and it's a word made up by Poe," Georgie said.

"What does it mean?" Reno asked her.

"It's the sound of a ringing bell after the bell's been struck."

"Like tinnitus," Walt said. "Or Georgie's voice after she stops talking."

"Got a gong, Dawn?" Ben asked.

Jo tapped her palm with her fork and pressed the stem against the coffee table, and we listened to the undying flow of sound waves.

Since we wouldn't see each other again before the holidays, I suggested finishing the evening off with a carol, and "Silver Bells" won the vote. But the Warblers' rendition was the pits. They rushed it, even though Jo and I told them to slow down. It was one of those hard songs to perform because you always wanted to speed it up, which ruined it.

When they tried again, they were smooth and steady, swinging to and fro like a carillon, their mouths aimed upward. Then the music swelled until it felt as though they were announcing an important event, like most bell songs did. But whether a sad or happy one, who knew.

16

Over the next several days, I studied scores and hummed, parts of my voice returning in waves that advanced, then receded. When my nodules and tension blocked my range, I told myself to relax so my cords would vibrate freely. It was uplifting to be singing again. Before long, I felt so energized that I decided to tone my body, too. But the morning I dug up my workout clothes to join Ash at the gym, he wasn't there.

I called and left a message and he replied a half hour later. *In early today. Tight deadline*, he wrote. Yet even when I drove to his downtown office and saw his car there, I didn't believe him and waited across the street. At noon he emerged like I knew he would. My husband could never skip a meal. Two steps behind him came Julia, the rich associate he'd once described as stuck-up. I had met her at their Christmas banquet the year prior; she'd worn a dress trimmed with fur. A decade older than us, she stood out like Salome among Ash's tame colleagues.

They got into his car together. I followed them to a residential area, past century-old mansions interspersed with modern buildings that floated above wide white lawns. Eventually they pulled up in front of the kind of glass house you would see in a magazine.

After they went in, I counted to fifty while snow fell in perfect disorder. Then I approached the door and pushed. It wasn't locked.

There was no dog or alarm. I stood there, staring for a second, then pulled the door shut and turned to leave. But I stopped again after a few steps. I had to find out what was going on. I turned back, took a breath, and pushed the door back open.

I went inside unnoticed, down a hallway to the bedroom. Nobody was in it. The bedspread was satin and the vanity was decorated with brushes, scarves, and sea sponges. Soon enough I heard murmuring. I found them in the main living area on a mossy couch, Julia's head resting on Ash's shoulder. The scene hurt to watch. I'd expected something less tender and more graphic.

Then my husband rubbed her abdomen and put his ear to it.

Disoriented, I couldn't retrace my steps and instead ran through the dining room opening onto the yard to get out. Only I couldn't tell where the room ended, and there was a thunk and a stinging. I fell down, my eyes watering until I couldn't see.

Ash rushed over. I pushed him away while Julia stood by, a coral blot. "You can't be here," she said. "This is private property."

I stood to face her. "So was our marriage."

She turned to Ash with "She might have broken her nose," and then she was gone. When Ash approached again, I kicked him. Then I kicked the plate glass. Suddenly I was like Tulip, using my feet for everything.

My face felt wet and slimy. I wiped it with my coat.

"Take this," Ash said and pressed a tissue against my lip.

I tilted my head back. There was a chandelier made from antlers suspended above the dining table. I couldn't take my eyes off it. "She's too old to have a baby," I said.

Ash clasped his hands behind his head and paced. "I wanted to tell you," he started. "I was waiting until you got through your depression."

I pounded the glass with my fist. "I'm *not* depressed!"

"You're better lately. But last spring, after what happened —"

"All your trips," I said. I sensed my neck muscles constricting, my voice leaving again. "Did she go, too?"

"Every time I asked you to come, you said no."

"So you took your slut." Spit flew as I spoke. I sounded like Mina. Who, I now realized, had never had daily visits from her son. He stopped pacing and looked away. "We want to try things out in Japan," he said. "The office has offered me a contract. I'll stay until Tariq's finished treatment. He's agreed to take care of Mom after that."

"Where is our money, Ashraf?"

"What do you mean?"

"You work in finance. Why have we had so little for so long?"

He gripped the chair in front of him. "I made a few bad investments."

"You're a gambler."

He looked up, his chest rising and falling rapidly. "I can triple what's left. It'll come back. It always does."

I'd bitten my tongue. I could feel it swelling up, the blood pooling in my mouth.

Julia returned with a bag of ice, extending it to me. I flung it from her hand and it flew through the air and landed on an antler. I kicked the glass again but no matter how hard I struck it, it wouldn't break.

Facing my husband one last time, unable to articulate my thoughts, I stole from Verdi. "È un monte di lardo," I screamed, each syllable ripping through my throat.

Then I found my way out and downtown again, past high rises and lines of traffic slithering toward intersections like yellow-eyed snakes. The snow fell harder, bringing with it a fractured sound as it hit the windshield. I could see the tip of the opera house rising into the air like an icicle. And then the hospital, a giant glowing cube.

Once home I trudged to the backyard. There in that barren whiteness, I thought about Ash and our first happy years. I thought about my career. And the children we had talked about having, and put off having, and now it was too late.

It hurt to breathe in. I couldn't feel my feet. Snow came into my boots and burned my ankles. I stared at the glinting stone on my hand, removed my ring and looked for a spot to lie down. Closing my eyes, I saw waterfalls, then felt warmth and a voice saying, "Come, now."

When I looked up, Tariq blocked the sky.

I pushed myself up and left him there. Inside, I packed as much of Ash away as I could until I heard his brother climb the stairs and stand at the bedroom door. He had never come upstairs before.

"What happened to your face?" he asked.

"I walked in on my husband and his gashti. You know the one."

He said nothing as I continued filling garbage bags. When I passed him to get downstairs, he followed. "Please go," I said, piling the bags at the door. "And drop these off to him."

"I was on my way to visit friends," he said. "But there's been a derailment. Trains are cancelled and flights are oversold."

I threw my keys and told him to take the car. My tongue was throbbing, my words thick. I tried not to panic about how it would affect my singing while my phone lit up with messages from Ash, and the lights in the house flickered.

Outside looked like a blizzard. I sat on the couch as swaths of snow hit the window. Only then did I notice Tulip next to me in a nest of blankets, a radio on low beside her.

I kept my eyes on the storm as Tariq took the black bags out to the car. Then he came in and went downstairs and returned with his duffel and Tulip's carrier, before sitting across from me. He didn't look well. He wore a toque and his fingernails were yellow like old glue. Around his mouth were tiny ulcers.

When "Bridge over Troubled Water" came on the radio, Tulip migrated from her spot to my lap, her feathered body swaying with each note. As the song progressed, I struggled to contain my emotions and the bird looked up, then climbed my shirt to my shoulder. There, she stretched and pumped her neck, oblivious to me. Her head kept bobbing until I felt something else and convulsed on seeing a partially digested blob on my collarbone.

"She's regurgitated on you," Tariq said. "I've never seen her do this in winter."

I reached my hand up but Tulip nudged it away.

"It's an expression of affection," he went on. "As if she gave you her last summer rose. Or something."

"How do you know that song?" I asked.

"What song?"

"'The Last Rose of Summer.'"

"I was referring to your garden."

I felt my neck go hot as Tulip climbed down my arm and back into my lap.

"Pretend to eat it," Tariq said.

"You can't be serious."

He nodded. "Or she'll be devastated."

I sighed and looked at Tulip. "Thanks for the gift," I told her. She monitored my every move as I pulled a tissue from my pocket and wiped off the warm, wet offering, bringing it to my mouth with a prolonged *Mmmmm*.

"Your nostrils are flaring," Tariq said. Then he rushed to stand and ran downstairs and threw up.

I hummed to try and keep Tulip calm but with the dividing door open, we heard everything. I heard him gasping for air, throwing up again and again, taking a swig from a bottle and spitting. I heard him coughing and brushing his teeth twice over. When he came back to the living room, his toque was off and I saw that his head was shaved.

"Did you start the new pills?" I asked, and he said yes.

We watched as drifts smudged the outside world like a cold production of *Onegin*, a story I despised for its pointless ending where the lovers, both still alive, did not wind up together. After some time, Tariq said, "I'm sorry for what's happened. I didn't feel it was my place —"

"It's got nothing to do with you," I told him.

He checked the time, reached for Tulip's carrier, and coaxed her in.

"It isn't safe out there," I said.

"We'll be fine," he replied. "I move slowly these days."

"Are you going to see Anabelle?"

He nodded. "Our last meeting didn't end on a good note. I want to wish her well. I'll drive my mom home after. She's visiting Aunt Roya."

I said I admired his deception, adding that it must run in their family.

We looked at each other a long time then. I could hear Tulip trying to escape, her little toes tugging on the zipper.

"May peace be with you, Dawnjaan," Tariq finally said.

"And you as well," I replied.

He wrapped a blanket around the carrier, got his bag, and closed the door. When he walked away, I waited for him to look back as he disappeared with his bird behind the wall of falling snow. Instead he raised his free hand and waved, then moved it through the air like a conductor before an orchestra I couldn't see.

17

Night and day came and went. Thoughts of my married life and stage life came and went. Songs drifted in and out of my mind. But dreams did not come. And my husband did not come.

Then one morning I heard the front door open, a hesitant shuffling in, and the sound of my parents assessing the disarray, discussing what could be wrong with me. My father suggested a midlife crisis. My mother wondered if I'd finally deafened myself with the sound of my voice. "Shame on you, Alice," my father told her as they climbed the stairs.

"For years she's been belting out tunes too close to her own eardrums. It was bound to have an impact." My mother sat on the edge of the bed and shook me. "Come and have breakfast, Dawnie. You've got to eat."

My father gave my knee a firm shake and went back downstairs to the kitchen, where he struggled with the espresso machine and cursed.

I turned my face into the pillow.

"Should I move in for a while?" my mother asked.

I sat up quickly. "Everything's fine. What are you doing here?"

"Tariq said you needed us and told us where to find the spare key. We made it in just before the road closures."

"How do you know Tariq?"

"We don't *know* him know him. He phoned us." She offered me water. "What's happened?"

"It's nothing." I set the glass down and put my hand on hers.

"Did someone strike you?" She reached out to touch my face. "Should we call the police?"

I laughed and told her no.

She stood and gathered dishes from the floor. "Did you flub on stage again? Is that all?"

My academic, unmusical parents had always been supportive of my profession. But they had also warned me that it would be short-lived, like an athlete's. The career of a soprano was briefer than a pursuit of the mind.

"I shouldn't have married Ash," I eventually said.

She nodded.

"You agree?"

She wanted to know if it was over. I told her yes.

"Then I agree," she replied. "So does your father."

I got out of bed and put my robe on. "Why didn't you ever say anything?"

My mother sighed. "You never asked."

There was a music box on the dresser. I opened it and a blue-bird popped up, turning to Beethoven's pastoral symphony. "I'm teaching whistling," I said.

My father stood at the door again. "You know a piece has made it in the annals of history when someone whistles it," he said, then, "Silbo Gomero."

My mother turned to him. "What are you going on about, Howard?"

"The whistled language of the Canary Islands," my father, the linguist, replied. "Nine different whistled sounds make four vowels and five consonants. Children learn it in school. It's how they hear each other across ravines."

"How remarkable." The raised eyebrow indicated that my mother wanted to learn more. Then she remembered the task at

hand and turned back to me. "Your gran was a sublime whistler."
She started on a Henry Mancini song. "Whistled in the garden,
my mum. When she was planting turnips and beans."

"People don't whistle anymore," my father said. "I guess they
have no time. Even though they should have more time now than
they did then. That's what technology is for, right? To give us
more time."

"The world's too noisy now." My mother closed her eyes. "You
needed silence for that sort of thing. How is your hearing, by the
way, sweetheart?"

I asked if they had heard of Roger Whittaker. "Of course!"
they replied simultaneously.

"We saw him in concert." My father gave my mother a sly
look. "Quite the night," he added, and she reddened.

"Did he perform 'Finnish Whistler'?" I asked.

"Brought the house down with it." My father started singing
a song called "The Last Farewell." He whistled half the stanzas,
the words, I assumed, forgotten. Then he knelt for my mother's
hand but couldn't get back up. I helped him to stand. "Flapjacks
are on," he said.

When I joined my parents at the table I noticed a turkey on the
counter, and realized it was Christmas Day. I ate a pancake, then
another. "I don't know what to do," I told them.

"Start over. Get divorced," my mother said. "It's not like you
have cancer."

I tried to swallow and choked. They slapped my back. "It's
Tariq," I finally said.

My mother, professor of literature, poked my father. "I told
you he was a Heathcliff."

"We met at your wedding," my father explained.

I blew my nose. "He wasn't at our wedding."

"We had a wonderful chat about Urdu phonetics," he went on.
"Remember, Alice?"

"I remember discussing *The Bridges of Madison County* with him. A guilty pleasure for both of us."

"Was he with a tall blonde?" I asked.

"He was alone." My mother frowned. "Honestly, Dawn. This is disappointing. Mina will chop you to pieces."

My father went to a shelf and came back with a reference book. "Tariq, Tariq, Tariq," he said, licking his finger and turning the pages. "Ah. Nightcomer. Morning star. He who knocks at the door."

"Dawn and morning star. That's a bit much," my mother said.

"They're equals," my father replied. "Could be fate."

"Enough," I told them. "I'm not having an affair. Tariq has cancer. He's staying with us."

Their faces fell.

"Whatever you do, don't let him stop with the treatments," my mother said. "Remember Joanie Boggs? Why, she got an extra year with triple chemo, shark cartilage, and yams."

"It's his choice, Alice," my father said. "Not Dawn's or Ashraf's or yours or anyone's. Not even bully Mina's."

"Mina doesn't know," I said.

My mother's hand covered her mouth. "That poor woman."

"How is Tulip managing?" my father asked.

I gave him a blank stare.

"He talked about her when we met him." He glanced toward the living room. "And I'm guessing from all the doodads, she's here, too."

"She regurgitated on me," I told him. "That's how she's doing."

Then I started laughing. I couldn't stop, thinking how Mina now had two gashtis. It was going to get confusing. Unless she named them gashti one and two.

"Are you having another episode?" my mother asked. "Breathe deeply, honey. I'll run you a bath."

"You do that," my father said. "I'll take a quick snooze."

"Shouldn't you be in Hawaii?" I asked.

"We sail tomorrow. Why not come, Dawnie."

"I have a Biennial to prepare for."

"All these trials you put yourself through." My mother wrapped an arm around me.

"This one's not demanding. It's . . . nice."

"Well now. There's a first."

I helped her in the kitchen with the turkey, and when my father woke up, we sat in the living room with eggnogs and turned on the news. Reporters talked about world trade deals and shopping deals, and the holiday forecast. After that, the anchor said, "Let's visit the airport where Colleen is standing by."

Travellers were still stuck in transit because of the whiteout. As the camera zoomed in on the scene, I spotted the Warblers in Santa hats, standing in a semicircle among the chaos of luggage and lineups.

Most people rushed past with headphones on or stared at their phones. But the group had a small gathering before them. The reporter's face brightened when she heard the hand-held sleigh bells jingling. She rushed over just as Walt was saying, "This last one is for our friends, if they're watching. Joyeux Noël, Dawn, Tariq, and Tulip!"

My father leaned forward. "Well I'll be —"

"You haven't had friends in ages, Dawnie," my mother said. "This is the best news story of the year."

The song was "I'll Be Home for Christmas." Intercom voices droned overheard, but the Warblers tuned it out. They performed without rushing and their interpretation contained nostalgia and yearning, as if none of them would ever get home again. When they finished, the reporter wiped her eyes before she looked at the camera and said, "How about that. I may have to make learning to whistle my new year's resolution. Over to you, Donna."

"Are those your pupils?" my mother asked.

I said they were the Warblers and that they had existed long before me.

My father asked me for a song, but I couldn't just then. So my parents whistled "Santa Baby" to each other instead. But I wasn't really listening, too caught up with the Warblers' airport masterpiece. And how easily they had offered themselves entirely, taking us to a lyrical place we'd never been.

My parents stayed the night, and in the morning, I persuaded them to leave for their cruise. After they had gone, I walked through the absence of Ash's belongings. In the front closet was a gap where his coat should have been. There were more dark spaces in the bedroom where his clothing normally hung. And the jammed toiletries drawer we shared slid open easily, half-emptied. Even without his things, I knew my husband would adapt to his new life quickly, like a stagehand switching scenes at intermission.

Out of habit, I knocked on the door before going down to the walkout. Prescription bags and information pamphlets littered the countertop. I pulled the quilt off the bed and sat in my chair with the brochures. Only they were too difficult to read, so I opened the French doors and stepped outside in my robe and slippers.

The storm had passed. It was early morning, and a dull sun hung behind a whitish skin of cloud. I listened to the air but there was no sign of any bird, the feeders empty. I was on my own again. Looking at the immaculate, untouched snow, something slipped away from me, a pressure released in the stillness.

18

While families gathered to celebrate the holidays, I reverted to the couch for a marathon review of my blunders, adding wedding footage to my analysis until a heavy fatigue overcame me.

For days I slept a wakeful sleep of low consciousness, eating only toast. Eventually, hunger cramps forced me up. I had soup and went through reams of tissue, heading downstairs for more once I ran out. But as I passed through the kitchenette, I slipped on Tulip's puzzle, a now-permanent fixture on the floor.

My bare toes had undone a chunk of the image. I sat and tore the whole dense rainforest apart. Piecing the puzzle together again, I felt the fine pointillism of Tulip's nails over her lost land. She had walked the jungle, trying to re-enter it until she understood, probably, that she couldn't. And so she had moved on.

I finished the scene, loosening a cluster of orchids for when she got home. Then I returned upstairs and deleted every bookmarked link to my stage clips. I boxed up my memories with Ash and threw them into the garage and did the same with what remained of his things. Finally, I gave the house and myself a scrub down.

The next day, I messaged the Warblers for an impromptu practice. Then I went to the grocery store, came home, and baked. After they arrived, I passed around plates of crumble. The unscheduled get-together bewildered everyone.

"What's the big idea, calling us over the break?" Georgie asked. She'd glued rhinestones to her wristbands and her eyeshadow matched the stones.

"Your airport performance was decent, but there's still work to do," I explained.

Reno brought gifts. We unwrapped our mugs, which said I Love Tits on one side and had the outline of a tufted titmouse on the other. The image was supposed to turn colourful when a hot beverage was added. He poured in cider and we watched the bird's feathers glitter. A patch of rust appeared beneath each wing, then a black patch between the eyes and a grey crest on the head. Reno described the transformation to Ben, who did the call, which sounded like *peter peter peter*, and Georgie requested a mug with I Love Cock and a rooster on it the next time around.

It was New Year's Eve and everyone was distracted. Ben told the group he had a date later, and the Warblers complimented him on his bow tie. Reno was fired up because he'd put in an offer on a motel, and Georgie was torn between dresses for the convention. Walt, dapper in his beret, was preoccupied with his upcoming move. Even Jo was unfocused, saying she was nervous about a visit with her son the next day.

"Does he live here?" I asked her.

"Yes," she said. "But I don't see him often." Then she asked where my husband was and what our plans were for the night.

"We're separating," I said.

"No wonder you're puffy," Georgie said. "I thought you were expecting."

Reno put an arm around me. "Des and I split, too," he said. "If ever you want to talk."

I felt my tongue with my fingers. It had been so painful and swollen. Yet it was almost back to normal already, as if walking into glass and ending my marriage were no big thing. I told the Warblers that the evening was to be dedicated to our tongues, the only muscle in the human body incapable of tiring. "Unlike the heart, the tongue never gets worn down," I lectured. "Without it, we'd taste nothing. We wouldn't speak or sing."

"Or kiss properly, Daybreak." Reno grabbed my hand. "I've got the biggest heart on earth."

"I believe that belongs to the elephant," Jo said.

"The giraffe's is bigger," Walt replied.

"The blue whale heart," Ben cut in, "weighs over four hundred pounds. Their tongues weigh as much as elephants." He raised a finger. "Fact. They sing quieter now because of the acidity in the ocean, so their song can't be heard by other pods. It's a problem." He smoothed his hair back. "The smallest belongs to the fairyfly. You'd need a microscope to see it."

"Are we talking hearts or tongues now?" Walt asked.

"Hearts," Ben told him.

"Although they're interconnected," Jo said.

Reno agreed. "The heart commands the tongue."

"I mean you can tell what condition your heart's in by your tongue." Jo checked her pulse. "If your tongue's red, your heart's okay. If it's pale, there's not enough blood in your heart."

"What quack says that?" Georgie asked.

"It's Chinese holistic," Jo told her.

We drank champagne and Jo discussed travel logistics for the Biennial in spring. The convention always took place in a different city and this one was in historic Quebec, a five-hour drive away. As coordinator for the central provinces, Jo was in touch with the heads of the other regions, and all were rounding up their siffleurs.

"Any indication on the number of registrants so far?" Walt asked.

"Eight," she said.

Walt scratched his chin. "Eight dozen?"

"Just eight," she replied. "But it's still early. On the other hand, most of our population is over seventy now. This may be too far for the Westerners to travel."

"Any news from Joop?" Georgie asked.

126

"Joop Nieuwendijk and Luella Starr were the first to sign up," Jo told her.

Georgie swore.

"How about the Wetaskiwin Pipers Club?" Walt asked. "I wouldn't mind seeing those fellas again."

"I think they died," Jo said.

"Hélas." Walt shook his head and adjusted his beret. "On a happier note" — he emptied his mug with a small burp — "I look forward to exploring la vieille ville with you all."

Then Jo proposed that the Warblers create a display as a means of introducing the group to the other participants. Objects that could be set up on a table. Everyone liked the idea. "What should we include in our mini museum?" she asked.

"Georgie's mouth," Walt said.

Georgie smacked her lips. "Better than that ratty beret."

"I've got a tin whistle," Reno offered.

"I'll bet you do," Georgie replied.

"How about just our sound," Ben suggested. "You press a button and hear it for all eternity."

"Avant garde," Georgie said. "I like it."

"You like it because it requires no effort," Jo told her. "You work on that recording, Ben, but let's put tangibles in. Everyone pick something meaningful. Think of this as our time capsule. We'll bury it afterwards."

Georgie bit the head off a gingerbread man. "What are we, in kindergarten?"

"It's fine if you don't want to be part of this, Georgina," Jo told her.

"Of course I should be part of it."

The walkout stairs creaked with someone's steps. Tariq opened the dividing door and put Tulip down. "What did we miss?" he asked.

I stood and my chair fell backwards.

"Easy, Maestro," Ben said.

He looked rested. He came and sat with us, and Tulip rushed over to Ben, climbing his leg and scooping and swallowing from his plate.

Everyone asked Tariq how he was feeling and he told them never better. He had dined with his mother and aunt, escaping when his brother stopped in.

I blocked the thought of Ash by helping Walt drag a cardboard box over, which he'd left at the door with his walker. The box contained things he had to part with before his move. He was in the process of selling his home and going to a residence. At Birchwood Village, he told us, there was a reception lodge and dining hall and gym that reminded him of college. You could see he was trying to talk himself into it. He said there was another building there that would eventually come in handy, too. Situated on the river near the property's grove of birch trees, the hospice lay at a distance from the other structures. "So I won't have far to go." He chuckled.

"Sounds pretty," Tariq said. "Is there a waiting list?"

Walt nodded. "Dying involves a lot of paperwork."

Georgie took a blender, Reno a handsaw, Ben a ukulele, and Jo a painted plate of an old man teaching a young boy how to play the accordion. Jo ran her hand across the boy's face while I picked a yellow scarf from the bottom of the box. "That was Mae's," Walt said. Then Tariq pulled out something hairy. "And that was her halo hairpiece," he told Tariq. "She got a kick out of that."

When Tariq put the ring of hair on, everyone roared. He looked like a monk, bald on top with a bowl cut. I made a skullcap with the scarf, reached over, and slipped it on his head. When he put his hand up to feel it, I saw that one of his nails had fallen off, and his eyes had a sunken quality. I'd been mistaken in thinking he looked better, and the others saw what I saw and went quiet, until Ben blew raspberries on Tulip's belly and she emitted a sound like *how! how! how!* and we all laughed again.

After that, things got silly fast. I tried to get the Warblers to practice, but a second bottle of champagne had been opened. By the end of the night, they were harmonizing "How Much Is That Doggie in the Window?" and Ben was barking but not at the right parts, until he realized he was going to be late for his date.

"I'll drop you off," Jo said. Everyone else got up because she was their ride, and Reno had a night shift. So they put on their parkas and disappeared together into the cold air, like the tufted titmouse vanishing from our empty mugs.

Once the Warblers had gone, Tariq pulled the wig off and Tulip lunged at it. "Are there any Popsicles left?" he asked.

I went to the freezer, came back with one, and asked how he was really feeling.

"There's a tingling in my hands and feet," he said. "Like when you're waiting outside in winter, for a bus that's not coming."

He finished the Popsicle and offered the wooden stick to Tulip, while I retrieved the brochures and held them out to him. "Have you looked at these?"

"Reading a boatload of printouts won't alter anything."

I decided not to push it. "How was your visit? Did you reconcile?"

He unwrapped his mug and smiled. "We said goodbye. Then she went skiing."

I rubbed my neck, feeling tired and a little sick from the champagne. "Were you at our wedding?" I finally asked.

Tariq watched Tulip raise the stick with her foot, moving it this way and that like a wand. "No," he said. "No, I wasn't." He glanced up, then back down at his bird, adding, "She wants to see the sea."

"Who does?"

"Tulip. When I asked her what she wanted to see, she said the sea. Have you seen it?"

"Seen her talk?"

"Seen the sea."

"I've seen the ocean and the sea."

"While on tour?"

"Yes."

"So you haven't really seen it."

We heard explosions then, and yelling and laughter coming from outside.

"Midnight," Tariq said.

We stood and approached each other, and when we hugged, my ear ended up pressed against his chest. Through his sweater, I felt his heart's quick pace, most likely from medication. He smelled salty, like he'd been swimming, and a strange desire overcame me to lick his neck.

Then the bell rang.

When I opened the door, Mina stood there shivering.

"Happy new year, Mrs. Khan," I said, taking her coat. "That's a beautiful sari."

She charged straight to her son and slapped him. Of the words flying through the room like fireworks, all I could extract was Ashraf and old gashti. Even Tulip who normally attacked strangers, stayed perched on my foot, and the more they argued, the more her claws dug into my toes through my sock.

"And you!" She finally pointed at me and started to weep. "How you are not telling me of troubles?"

I passed her a box of Kleenex.

"I will not go to Tokyo," she said, shaking her head. "I will not see this baby girl."

"They have pearls there," Tariq told her. "You can take a shopping trip with Roya."

Julia wasn't even showing. It had to be too soon to tell. My hand went to my throat. "They're having a girl?"

"Is girl. I know it." Mina stared hard at her son, the black around her eyes running down her cheeks. "What is this sickness?" she asked. "Why I must hear it from Ashraf?"

Tariq rubbed her arms. "I didn't want to worry you for no reason."

She pressed his cheeks and forced his jaw open.

Tariq pulled her hand away. "Those are just mouth sores. From the pills, Amiji."

"How long you take?"

Tariq sat with his mother on the couch and rested his chin in his palm. "A few more months," he said. "Then I'm finished."

Mina cried some more and blew her nose. "You are so ugly," she told her son, rubbing his head. Then she turned back to me. "Done," she said, "go and get my things."

19

Mina took over the would-be baby's room. She took over the kitchen with vats of spicy food and the bathroom with strong-smelling lotions, and she played mystical music loud around the house, tunelessly humming for hours.

Tariq ignored his mother. His mother ignored Tulip. And the grey bird watched Mina from afar as if she were a queen. Then one day, my mother-in-law handed me a grocery list and pushed me out the door before I had my coat on. I knew it meant Ashraf was coming. He was the last person I wanted to see.

Once in the car, though, I didn't feel like going to the grocery store. So I phoned Jo, who had asked for help selecting the Biennial trophies. As a longstanding committee member, she was in charge of acquiring them. She'd just finished her shift, but Reno had borrowed her car for his motel inspection and it was a two-hour wait until the next bus.

I told her I would pick her up.

When I reached city limits, I could see the central watchtower of the correctional facility in the distance, the razor-wire fence around its perimeter shimmering. As I approached, the cellblocks expanded out from it like the long hard arms of a star.

From the parking lot, the fence was higher than it had looked from the highway, and double-layered. I parked as far away from the main building as possible. It was quiet outside. I'd expected drill bells and the loud cries of inmates. But there was no indication of any life there, aside from the sound of my breathing.

Inside the visitor and staff entrance was a waiting room containing rows of chairs, old magazines, and a plastic plant. A female officer sat behind a reception counter. "Wells will be out soon," she told me when I approached, looking me up and down.

While I waited, a young woman came in. The officer asked for identification, told her to stand against the wall, pulled a camera arm from the computer, and took her picture. "Cell, keys, bag. Whatever else you've got on you," she said.

The young woman emptied her purse and pockets out on a metal table. "None of this is allowed," the officer told her and pointed to a wall of lockers.

"Not even my apple?" she asked.

The officer said no. The young woman put her belongings in the locker. She looked like she was going to cry as she passed through a body scanner and some metal doors. A side door clicked open then, and Jo came out. The officer called her over, and they talked and grinned in my direction before Jo joined me.

"What did your cohort say?" I asked as we walked out.

"Nothing," Jo replied.

"I'd like to know."

"You worry too much what others think," Jo said. "Nobody's thinking about you. They're thinking about themselves." She glanced at me again.

"You're holding out."

She paused until I gave her a little push. "Okay, okay. She said you were smoking."

"I was not."

"She means attractive, Dawn."

"What else?"

"She asked if you're the Warblers' new drillmaster. I said yes, and that you're stricter than our warden." She grinned. "She said you can punish her anytime."

Crossing the lot, I asked Jo what she did exactly, aside from goofing off.

"I'm in Block C." She led me to the fence, pointing at a low building in the distance, and said the men there were incarcerated without possibility of parole. Then she pointed beyond the cellblocks to a hill by the tree line, dotted white. "That's the cemetery," she said.

"What are your days like?" I asked.

"There's only one day on repeat," she replied. "At zero five hundred hours, we do a headcount and unlock doors. After breakfast, those fit to work have jobs. Shifts start at zero six hundred hours and last eight hours. Lunch is at eleven hundred hours, in the same chow hall serving breakfast and supper. There are always complaints that the food's not edible but it tastes fine to me. And so many of them are fat, they can't hate it that much. At fourteen hundred hours, work shifts end."

"And you go home?"

"I try to get overtime," she said. "Usually I stay through the afternoons when inmates head outside or sleep or get up to their violent acts. Dinner's at seventeen hundred hours. After that, they read or make calls or watch TV. Others go to chapel, or classes. A lot get high in their cells." She paused, adding, "Some write. I think these guys are the last people on Earth to write letters."

"Do you wear a gun?"

She felt at her waist. "All I have is a panic button."

When she saw that I was studying her face, she put a hand to her scars. "Job hazard," she said and continued looking through the fence. Then she told me that her son was in a facility a few hours away. Legally, she couldn't be stationed there. But she'd become a guard to understand the system and make connections, since inmates were often moved.

"What did he do?" I asked.

Her head sank into her shoulders. "Something very foolish," she said, "when he was young."

Along the far end of the fence was a row of small houses, each one contained in its own cage. Jo said they were for family visits, and inmates stayed in them with loved ones for seventy-two hours. The wait list was three years long. Under the snow were plots of grass. There were barbecues and they could even cook their own food.

"Does your son's place have those?" I asked.

"Our visits are non-contact," she replied, kicking at the snow as we walked to the car. "We talk with Plexiglas between us."

When I asked if she taught whistling to the men, she laughed, explaining that it wasn't permitted since it was used for signalling and riots. "No one wants to hear it inside anyway," she added. "It reminds them of the freedom they don't have. And the birds they can't see."

We got into the car and I followed Jo's gaze up to the barbed wire. "What's your son's name?" I asked.

She took her tuning fork from her bag and put it around her neck. "DC 70261," she said. "But his real name is Everett." She rubbed at her prongs. "Is it lunacy," she asked, "that a cold piece of metal's kept me from the precipice?"

I extended an arm. She hit her fork on the door and pressed it to my exposed wrist, and I felt the pure tone resonate up to my shoulder.

"I get it," I told her. "It's soothing."

As we pulled out onto the highway, she lifted one of Tulip's stray feathers from the seat and ran her fingers along it. When I suggested practicing scales as we drove back into the city, she kept staring out at the white fields. "You go ahead," she told me.

Instead I played a compilation, quietly vocalizing when "Coro a bocca chiusa" from *Butterfly* came on. The interlude was one of my favourite moments in opera. It took place between the second and third acts when the still hopeful Butterfly, accompanied by the wordless melody of an offstage chorus, waited calmly through the night for her man.

"I like your voice like that," Jo said.

I turned the music down. "Like what?"

"Without the pyrotechnics." She glanced over her shoulder, the prison no longer in view. "They've had all sorts of performers," she said. "But never an opera singer. I bet you'd drive them to tears."

I thought about the audiences I had sung to night after night in the darkness, most of them probably half-asleep or thinking about money. "I was never able to do that," I told her.

"Maybe you have to suffer first."

"Does divorce count?"

"Sometimes. Death and heartbreak top the list."

We arrived at the address she'd given me, a place that looked about to be torn down.

"Here?" I asked.

"Best we can do with our budget," Jo replied and got out.

Inside the awards store, the salesperson showed us their so-called whistling trophy, which was a field day decoration with a coaching whistle. We picked up the cups and columns adorned with figurines and instruments, and Jo stood back and told me to pretend to hand each one out, while she commented that the piece of plastic was too small, too tall, or too shiny.

Then Mina called to ask me to buy bananas for her low potassium and to say I could come home. "My mother-in-law," I told Jo after hanging up. "I seem to be stuck with her."

"Take what you can," she replied. "How's Tariq?"

"I think he's all right," I said.

"You don't sound sure." She tucked her thumbs into her belt loops and widened her stance. I could see how her manner could be intimidating to inmates.

"Ash went to the house today," I continued. "Probably to spend time with him. And Mina has taken over."

She stepped in closer, waiting.

"It's not my place to help anymore. I was doing that for my husband." I looked down at the cup I was white-knuckling, adding, "These look cheap."

She turned and scanned the wall of awards.

"I have silver and gold ones, and some carved in stone," I told her. "You'd only need to change the plates." I pulled out my phone again and sent a note to my parents to ship the trophies.

"What if you want them back after we hand them out?" she asked.

"I won't."

We re-shelved the awards and left. Jo said she could get home from there, but I insisted on dropping her off. Ten minutes later, we pulled up to a soot-stained complex near the bus depot and a high-rise construction site, and she invited me in for tea.

I couldn't imagine prison cells to be much smaller than her basement apartment. If you reached out from the futon, you could touch the fridge. From the fridge, it was five steps to the bathroom. There was a rectangular window with bars on it and she folded her futon and draped a throw over it. We sat down and watched feet go by to the sound of diesel buses and garbage trucks, and workers throwing slats off flatbeds, cracking jokes, and swearing.

"How do you sleep?" I asked.

"I could move," she said. "But I'm saving for Everett's release."

"When will that be?"

"I don't know. But it'll be there for him." She picked some lint off her shirt. "He's a philosopher, that boy. The other day he said he'd come to a conclusion. That the summer we want to relive and the summer we live to regret lead to the same reflecting pool."

There was no photo of her son around that I could see. The only thing on the wall was a faded print depicting a man on the edge of a field with his dog, watching a bird soar into an early morning sky. The sun radiated behind some hills and to the left, a cottage was visible.

"I'd like a new one," she told me after I stood to look more closely. "But the museum says they're not reproducing it anymore." Beneath the etching was printed *The Skylark* by Samuel Palmer. "It's from England, 1850," she added. "Ben says skylarks can sing an unbroken song for twenty minutes. Isn't that something?"

I sat down with her again. The tea was good. "What flavour is this?"

"Licorice," she said. "Helps with digestion."

"Thank you, Josephine," I told her.

"Don't mention it," she said.

20

One late afternoon Mina had a hair appointment so she instructed me on Tariq's dinner. Holding the eye charm from her necklace and rubbing it, she warned me that it had to be served within the hour or textures would be ruined.

Her son was getting thin. I wanted him to have a meal as much she did. After she left, I warmed the stew of barley, lentils, and beef, inhaling ginger and coriander as I brought it downstairs, but neither Tariq nor his bird noticed my arrival. Tulip was perched by the bay window, looking out at the illuminated yard in the last of the daylight. Tariq was sitting at the small table, hunched over some kind of project.

I put his mother's bowl on the counter.

"I can't eat any more haleem," he said without looking up.

"What are you doing?" I asked.

"I'm whittling."

"I didn't hear whistling."

"Whittling, Dawnjaan." He put his knife down, and straightened and rolled his shoulders. Then he started coughing and couldn't catch his breath. I got him a glass of water and sat with him.

Beside the knife was a set of roller skates so small you could hold them in the palm of your hand. Each wooden skate had four wheels and a T-shaped bar on top, sanded smooth.

I examined one under the lamp.

"She chews her footwear," Tariq said, wiping the sawdust away. Tulip flew over, landed on the chair, and cocked her head at her new toy. Then he dropped two books on the floor and stood on them and slid forward. "Left right left, like this," he showed her and pointed at the T-bars and said, "Step up."

She hopped onto the tabletop, picked a skate up with her foot, and flung it. They played that game for a while, her throwing the skates onto the floor and Tariq collecting them, until he walked away to do the dishes. Then she watched him a few more minutes, his back turned at the sink, before cautiously wrapping her toes around the T-bars.

"She's no ballerina but once she's on them, she cuts loose," he said with a quick glance.

Tulip inched forward, eventually taking bigger strides. She didn't roll along but walked the way a person on stilts would. Then she lifted one skate in the air and with a *tap tap tap*, set it down, and did the same with the other, going slowly forward.

Tariq gestured to a cardboard box at my feet. It was full of roller skates painted in different colours, some with race-car stripes. "She has enough there until she reaches seventy-five," he said, as his bird ran into a brick of paper at the corner of the table. I moved it out of the way and studied the cover, which read ONX-0801. "Did Ashraf bring this?" I asked, flipping through the document. "Is it helpful?"

"These are the ones that haven't been named yet," he said, taking it from me. "That's how many there are."

"That's a good thing," I said. "That there are so many trials."

"As many as there are stars." He tossed it on top of the stack of newsprint liners. "What would be helpful," he added, "is popcorn. Hand-popped without oil, salt, or butter. Not even if she begs."

"You're kidding, right?"

"I promised her *Downton Abbey*." He threw the dishtowel over his shoulder. "There won't be sleep for anyone until she gets it."

We went upstairs and Tariq and Tulip watched me make the popcorn, burning it twice before succeeding. Then we turned on the TV and turned off the light and I placed the bowl between us on the couch. As the theme music played, Tulip whistled a few barely discernible bars, stopping every time I glanced at her.

"It's her favourite show," Tariq said. But when I reached for some popcorn, she bit me, so we had to stop for minor first aid.

From the bathroom, I could hear Tariq talking to his bird. "You've got to quit being so confrontational, Tulip," he told her. "You have to learn to share."

When I returned to the living room, she wouldn't look at me but kept dunking her beak into the bowl, dropping kernels on the rug. Tariq apologized on her behalf.

"It's been a long winter," I told him. "We're all moody. Like pioneers in a cabin with that fever."

"I do feel feverish," he said.

I reached out and put my hand on his forehead, then jerked it away, saying he felt fine.

He sat back and his bird climbed his arm to his face, nudging his lips open with her beak, trying to push her head into his mouth. When he picked her up and raised her high, she made her *ah! ah! ah!* sounds of delight until he put her back down on the carpet.

"If she were a child, I could explain how it's natural for disease to weed some of us out," he said. "But how do animals understand mortality?" He watched Tulip pecking at the rug.

I stood abruptly and my foot did a stage stomp before I could stop my leg.

Tariq looked down at his bird. "Did you see that?" he asked her.

"Why can't you think positively?" I asked. "Instead of all this doom and gloom?"

"This isn't a production of *Faust*," he said. "The outcome is based on science. Not hope."

"I disagree," I told him, and my foot stomped again.

Then Tulip stomped a scaly foot into the rug twice, just like I had, and Tariq smiled. "You're right," he said. "I'm sure it will all be fine."

He stood and we were just a few inches apart, so close we could have danced. Then Tulip lunged at me again, going for my ankles.

"That's it," he said, scooping his bird up and taking her to the kitchen where he grabbed a banana, peeled it, and set it on the table. Once Tulip started mushing it with her feet, he returned to the living room.

"That's your mom's last banana," I told him.

"Oh well." He sat back down on the couch and I joined him, and we stared at the rug. After a few minutes, he asked, "Did you sleep in my bed?"

I busied myself tying my hair back. "I don't think so."

"The day I arrived. I thought I could smell you."

I untied my hair and smelled it, then raised an arm.

Tariq laughed and said that wasn't what he meant. "It was earthy. And savoury sweet."

"Do I still smell that way?" I asked.

He slid a hand to the nape of my neck and leaned in. I found I couldn't move, until he let my hair drop and looked away. "My taste buds and sense of smell are mixed up," he said. "But you don't seem as morose. As before."

"Without my cheating husband, you mean."

Tariq rubbed his head. "All I'm saying is, feel free to lie there if that's your spot. This is your home."

"That's not what I heard." I tried to read his face. "Did you make our down payment?"

"That's between Ashraf and I." His phone rang then, and he moved away. I understood some of what he was saying. Go. I'm fine, brother. We'll be fine. I'll look after Mom.

"What did he want?" I asked after he hung up.

"He's been asked to start sooner. But he's reluctant to leave until I'm done. I told him to go."

"Good riddance," I said, even though I knew it sounded childish.

"He also says he needs to speak with you."

"Is she still pregnant?"

"I assume so. Unless you put a hex on her like in *Rusalka*."

"Hexes are your mom's racket," I told him.

Tulip squawked from the kitchen. "Should we impress her with your acrobatics?" Tariq called out to his bird. I followed them to the staircase leading upstairs and Tariq put her on the banister.

Tulip shuffled sideways up it and slid down. Again and again and again.

"Definitely cabin fever," I said. Then, "I wish I could do that."

"You can," Tariq replied. So I did. And so did he.

21

I still had enough connections to book rehearsal time in at the House while the company was on tour. The theatre was less in demand during the day, and I thought it would help for when I sang again. Yet the second I stepped back on stage, I couldn't manage an even note, or get a full breath to properly support my voice. I pushed too hard and it wobbled.

After several failed solo attempts, I asked the Warblers if they wanted to visit a distinguished opera house, and they enthusiastically accepted. On the day we were to meet, I went in early. But when I arrived at the empty concert hall, I saw that Georgie was already there, seated at the grand piano in a bubblegum-pink tracksuit.

I listened from the wing. The melody of Chopin travelled upward, filling the theatre until she stopped suddenly, shook her hands out, and said, "Motherfucker." Then she saw me and frowned.

"How did you get past security?" I asked.

"Smoker's door," she replied.

"I didn't know you played," I added, approaching. "You have an interesting sound."

Georgie held her head high. "I was good," she told me. "I even met Glenn Gould. I had the top, meanest pedagogues in the country."

"What happened?"

"I lost my nerve." She made room on the bench. "Quit lording over me."

Staring at her gnarled hands on the keys, it occurred to me that she never complained. None of the Warblers did. At least not about their own misfortunes.

"I've got a new drug," she said, as if reading my mind. "It helps."

"Why aren't you the one teaching?" I asked.

"Because as I'm sure you've deduced, we're neophytes," she replied. "That's all we'll ever be. We get together out of loneliness. And for the laughs." She ran through a section of Ravel's *Concerto for the Left Hand* until her fingers were a blur of movement. Then she stopped and said, "Your turn. Sing me your comeback number." She bumped her hips against mine, pushing me off the bench.

I had no comeback number. But I moved downstage and readjusted my sheet music on its stand. Trying to relax my shoulders and neck, I took a breath in and sang Norma's "Casta diva" prayer. I had always loved Bellini's bel canto for its pure and ethereal melody, light yet penetrating, and full of passion. Playing the broken-hearted priestess of the Druids, I gazed upward, asking the moon to return things to the way they were. But I couldn't hold my notes for their full length, or keep a steady flow of air going. There was no legato. I could hear my voice shift gears as I changed registers.

"Yikes," Georgie said. "Didn't you warm up?" She grabbed my sheet music and went to the prompter's box, a small booth projecting from the floor at the front of the stage, opening toward the performers and accessible from the orchestra pit. "Is this thing safe?" she asked, kicking it.

I told her it wasn't used anymore. She got onto her stomach, grunting as she slid backwards into the box.

I sat on the protruding lid.

"Do you mind?" she asked.

"This was disguised as a seashell in *The Flying Dutchman*," I told her.

Her arm reached out and punched my calf. "That's nice," she said. "Now get your butt centre stage."

I did as Georgie instructed. But looking out at the empty seats lit by emergency lighting, I imagined only booing and laughter. Then I found myself thinking about Ashraf and the child he was having without me.

"Over here, stupid," Georgie called out. "Pay attention."

I could see her red bun and pink arms sticking out of the box.

"*Breeeeaaaaaathe*," she was saying.

I relaxed my shoulders and took a deep, grounding inhale and exhale. As I began once more, my thoughts turned to Tulip, and how free flying with her was like hitting high notes. I felt lighter inside and stopped thinking about my own limitations.

Georgie conducted and mouthed my cues as needed until we reached the end of the song, and I smiled down at her. "That felt pretty good," I said.

"Do it again," she told me. "Without that affected nasal tone."

"That's my voice," I told her.

"You didn't sound like that in *Cinderella*. You're overcompensating."

"You saw *Cinderella*?"

"Only the first half. My knees hurt and quite frankly I got bored, so I left. Your floor scrubbing aria was magnificent, though."

We did another run through after which Georgie tried heaving herself out of the box but couldn't, so I went around through the pit to assist her. But when she came out, she pushed me inside and closed the door, and a few minutes later her runners were kicking chalk into my face.

"How does it feel down there?" she asked.

"Claustrophobic," I told her.

"If you don't get over yourself, you'll be standing in an upright coffin for the rest of your life," she said. "I was too prideful. I felt overlooked and walked away and hid in the stacks for thirty years. I never got closure."

"I thought you said —"

She wiggled her bangles over her wristband. "Yes. Well." Her foot began tapping. "And another thing," she went on. "I'll tell you why your voice turned against you, because other than that irritating tick, it sounds the same now as then. You lost your confidence. What are you holding back for? Where did that wild abandon go? Although, I did find you lacked a smidge of depth."

"This is a physical injury," I reminded her.

"You mean your illustrious nodules?" She made a *pffftt* sound. "Those are every singer's excuse when they can't hack it, and nothing but a manifestation of stress. Your divorce should help move things along."

"Right. Maybe you can discuss this with my ENT specialist and tell them your expert —"

"Where you at, Phantom!" Ben interrupted my retort. The Warblers had arrived.

"How did you get in?" I called up from the prompter's box. "I was supposed to register everyone."

"I've got just the tune for you, Tariq," Walt was saying. "It's from *The Bridge on the River Kwai*."

"How does that go again?" Tariq asked.

Walt started whistling. I could hear Reno joining in, and the others as they filed on stage. I grabbed Georgie's foot. "Tell them to stop," I pleaded, "or we'll be cursed."

"Don't be preposterous, Dawn." She walked away, harmonizing with the group.

"Josephine!" I yelled, but Jo had headphones on and was cueing up songs.

"What a tremendous stage," Walt said. "I can see why these productions are so full of pomp and circumstance."

"It beats that sewage plant she took us to," Ben said.

Then I heard another familiar voice. "This is movie screen? Too small."

"It's for subtitles, Amiji," Tariq told his mother.

The whistling started up again.

"Surtitles," I said, but no one heard me.

I sank down in the box and thought back to *Tosca*.

The night I got the gig, I phoned Ash on the drive to the airport. When he promised to fly out, I pictured myself singing "Vissi" to my husband later in the evening, knowing it would move him deeply.

I'd been so self-assured, reaching the venue and meeting the artistic director, touring through what scene sets we could access. My vermillion dress fit superbly, the seamstress having adjusted it while I was en route. I felt luminous, chatting with my fellow singers and the conductor. I thought I had arrived.

My performance was called crude and disappointing by critics. Hours of hilarious hiccups, a comedy of errors, my new nickname Tumbling Tosca. One reviewer said the dog — a stagehand's, not meant to be there — didn't roll over. But Puccini did.

Judith never said a word about it when she informed me that, upon learning of my disastrous appearance, my own company had tried to cancel what was left of my contract. But she could do nothing when my vocal coach and singing teacher let me go, and tentative bookings vanished before agreements could be formalized.

By oversinging "Vissi," I had destroyed my vocal cords. They weren't moving properly and were covered in calluses. Specialists advised voice therapy and rest, but not surgery. My voice had become a whisper. I took my leave.

But the curtain would rise again. I knew now that I was probably never going to be a powerhouse. There were hundreds out there better than me, and younger. We would all be replaced, in turn. It didn't bother me anymore. Thinking back, what bothered me most was that Ash hadn't flown out on his week off. With no explanation other than that he was too tired to make the trip, after all. Replaying the catastrophic night in my mind, what upset me more than my wounded ego, more even than the despair that came with failing as an artist, was that my husband hadn't been there for me.

I stood up.

From inside the prompter's box, I could see the Warblers practicing, in their own world, not caring about having no audience. They didn't try to match each other either. They all sounded different, like notes from bottles at sea.

Eventually Reno spotted me. "What are you doing in that hole?"

Then Ben approached. "No disrespect but your mother-in-law's insane. She keeps asking me about Tariq's future. She thinks blind people are psychic."

Mina arrived behind him, red in the face. "Tell me," she pressed. "Tell me if my son —"

"I don't know," Ben said. "I'm sorry but I just don't."

She glanced over at me. "Done, why you are hiding?"

"I was thinking," I said. Then I had them take their places with the others, and from the box I clapped loudly and cued them up one by one.

I told Reno he was too fidgety but that I liked the stirring pause he'd inserted between stanzas to convey feeling. He replied that he hadn't been pausing so much as catching his breath. I asked Walt if he could stand straighter, which would help him to attack his first notes. I told Ben to soft-pedal his warbles, and Georgie to becalm her tremolos, and Jo told everyone they were making strides. As for Tariq, he kept busy trying to teach his mother how to whistle while she shushed away his bird.

By then we had run out of time. A jazz booking waited in the wings. Tariq and Reno approached and held their hands out. Going through the door would have been easier. But I reached up and they pulled me onto the stage, and I didn't bother wiping off the dust.

22

In the cold morning twilight, a chickadee woke me with its clear *fee-beee* call, so like the first notes of Debussy's "Clair de lune." I opened the curtain to the ending of a moon and patches of glowing snow but couldn't spot the chirping body anywhere.

After her son convinced her he'd regained his strength, Mina had finally returned to her condo. Despite the absence of her snoring, though, I hadn't slept well, and went downstairs to make coffee. There, I found Tariq at the living room window. "We're out of oatmeal," he said, nodding to Tulip on the table. "Hope you don't mind."

I went and stood with him.

"The steroids keep me up," he added.

"Did you hear the bird?" I asked.

"First sign of spring," he said. When he breathed in, I could hear wheezing.

We watched the light change and waited until it came again. Two notes an octave apart, a stillness, and a repeat. That was all.

"I think he's saying, 'Hello, darling.'"

"Really?" I asked.

He put his hand on my shoulder. "I have no idea."

I tried to come up with a clever response. But all I could think about was his hand touching my skin where my robe had slipped.

Then he pulled it away and his face changed, like he couldn't get enough air in. He started to choke and collapsed.

I called an ambulance. When Tariq came to, he searched around frantically for Tulip, frozen in place on the rim of her bowl. "Get her in the roost," he said, his voice barely audible as the first responders arrived.

Two men crouched beside Tariq and asked him questions while I rushed into the kitchen, Tulip hurrying away from me before flying up to the still ceiling fan.

"What a beautiful parrot," one of the men said.

Tulip flattened her feathers, growling and hissing.

Tariq tried to sit up, insisting that a stretcher wasn't necessary. But the paramedics made him lie back down. Then they gave him an oxygen mask. Once it was on his face, Tulip flew to the ground and charged across the room, lunging at the men. She tried to bite through their pant legs, assailing whatever she could get at with her beak. When Tariq reached his arm out to reassure her, she bit the hand before her. He gave a small cry as one of the paramedics shooed Tulip away with his boot, while the other bandaged his hand and said, "Let's get you out of here."

Tulip shrieked and paced circles. Tariq tried to talk to her but he was short of breath, and the mask muffled his words.

"They're here to help," I said, kneeling down, but in the confusion all she saw was intruders taking her companion away. She would not be appeased.

I grabbed my coat and ran outside as they lifted him into the ambulance. When he saw me, he pointed at the house. I would have to settle his bird down before joining him. The vehicle left with no lights or sirens.

Back inside, Tulip was fixed on the spot where Tariq lay minutes before, turning her head all around. She ran down the hallway, looking in every room.

"He's not here," I told her. "They took him away to fix him."

She checked the rooms a second time, and after a few squawks to which no response came, dropped her head and wobbled back under the kitchen table.

I called Walt and waited nearby until I could swaddle her, then took her downstairs and suggested a nap. But when I opened her roost door, Tulip pecked at my chest until I moved away from the cage. So we went back upstairs and sat on the couch, and she stayed perched there in my lap.

Even when I found a piece of popcorn between the cushions and offered it, she remained focused on the living room window. A crow flew past, then another. When I looked down at Tariq's bird again, I noticed faint lines across her charcoal feathers. I wondered if they were stress bars, which Tariq had warned me about.

Walt arrived in his old Cadillac. At the door I told him I'd changed my mind and would take Tulip to the hospital with me.

"So why am I here?" he asked.

I explained that Mina was stopping by. I didn't want her worrying and asked him to say that Tariq had an appointment.

"Lovely lady." He smiled. "Glad to stay."

I guided Tulip into my parka and kissed him on the cheek.

"Georgie's right. You need Chapstick," he told me, touching his face.

By the time we reached the hospital, they'd taken x-rays and admitted Tariq. I got to his room just as the nurse was leaving, and once we were alone I unzipped.

He gave a weak laugh as I put Tulip on the bed. Then she climbed onto his chest and crouched as close to his face as she could get, and they were quiet like that for some time. He checked her feathers, confirming the stress bars, and told me where her supplements were stored. When we heard Dr. Horne approaching, I put her back in my coat and stepped aside.

The doctor explained that Tariq's breathing problems were from fluid build-up around his lungs, and that they needed to insert a needle through his chest wall to drain him.

"Like a rain barrel," Tariq said, and Dr. H. nodded and told him that they would test the fluid to determine whether it was caused by an infection or new cancer cells. He also said he had the results of his midpoint scans, and unfortunately they indicated microscopic traces of the disease in his abdomen.

Tariq stared at his hands. Then he looked directly at the doctor and asked him if he thought he should continue. "If I were your son," he said, "what would you tell me to do?"

Dr. H. kept his gaze steady on Tariq. "My advice would be to stay the course."

"Because it's the last resort?" Tariq asked.

"There are always other options," Dr. Horne replied. "Clinical trials, or immunotherapy, for example."

Tulip pecked at my armpit. I started sweating. "What about more radiation?" I asked.

"We can't target a specific location anymore," he explained.

"Then do another surgery," I said.

Dr. H. turned to Tariq again before continuing. "We can't scrape this away," he told him. "It would only weaken your immune system and put you at risk of infection."

"I understand," Tariq said.

"I don't," I said loudly. "Mix up another kind of cocktail, then. Can you at least do that?"

With every question I asked, Dr. Horne's body seemed to slump. He brought up Tariq's allergic reactions, adding, "We're using what's been proven to be the most effective drug combination. I would advise you complete this course at an increased dosage before starting on another plan." He closed his tablet and stood. "Think it through. Get a second opinion if you'd like."

"We have a convention to get to," Tariq told him. "I don't want this interfering."

"Do the high dosage," I said, my voice projecting.

"I'm right beside you. There's no need to yell." Tariq turned to the doctor. "She's on vocal rest. But as you can hear, her voice is fine."

Dr. H. smiled, then became serious once more. "There may be additional side effects," he said. "Heart palpitations. Joint pain and sleeplessness. Nothing you can't handle."

Tariq looked at me, and then at my squirming chest.

"All right," he said.

I released my held breath and stepped out of the room while they discussed the new regimen. When Dr. Horne came out, he told me, "We'll keep him a few days. Go to your shindig and phone me if there are problems. Try to enjoy this time. And get that bird out of here."

He left down the hall in a hurry.

I returned Tulip to Tariq and threw my coat off, fanning myself with my shirt while they shared a soda cracker. They got crumbs everywhere. It took them a long time to eat it, so I went to the window and watched the goings-on in the parking lot below until I saw the doctor weaving through the parked cars, briefcase in one hand and coat in the other, rushing, dropping his keys, his shirt untucked. I realized then that Tariq's fate was out of his control and stifled a low sob.

He called me over. I wiped my face and returned to the chair by the bed.

Someone stood outside the door, talking. "Yogurt, pumpkin seeds, brazil nuts," she was saying, "work wonders. And those vitamins are two hundred a bottle for a reason. Placebo? No. I don't think so."

"That sounds like Cherry's daughter," Tariq said.

But I couldn't look at him. Instead I dumped the contents of my purse into my lap. Tulip's toys — including a rubber duck, a wine cork, a large button, and a wood dowel — came tumbling out. I found my Chapstick and put some on. Then Tulip stuck her tongue out, small and black and darting, and licked Tariq's chin. After she settled on his chest, he closed his eyes. "What's the opposite of an overture?" he asked.

"Finale," I replied.

"Not exit music?"

"People are already walking out with the exit music," I told him.

"What about requiem?"

"Requiems are death songs. They stand apart."

"Encore, then?"

"The finale is essential to the last scene. It's not an addition that follows it."

"So the finale is the part that stays with you."

Postlude, outro, coda, recessional, finale. All led to an ending. "I prefer overtures," I told him.

"That's because you're that black-capped bird," he said, "carrying on before any other living thing makes a sound."

I went back to the window. "Are you saying I practice too early?"

When I turned, Tariq was looking down at his bird, giving her a neck rub. Then he tickled her and said, "I love you," and held her out to me.

I put my parka on and tucked Tulip inside. "What do I tell Ashraf and your mother?" I asked.

"Nothing," he replied. "Nothing has changed yet."

And then, although it was midmorning, he said goodnight.

No one was there when we got home. I paced and so did Tulip, both of us unsure what to do. Eventually I put *Downton Abbey* on, and we watched it until Walt and Mina arrived, moving slowly through the door and leaning on each other.

"Where did you go?" I asked. "We were worried."

"She wanted to see her son," Walt said.

Mina stared at her rug.

"Would you like tea? Or something to eat?" I asked.

She shook her head without speaking, and Walt suggested she rest.

I put my arm around my mother-in-law and led her upstairs to the bedroom, expecting a fight. But she only breathed heavily, struggling with each step as she clutched the banister. After she removed her jewellery and sat on the bed, I offered her a glass of water and a sleeping pill and put a recording on low of Jessye Norman spirituals. Mina's dark eyes were already half-closed as she lay down and wiped her nose on her sleeve. Soon she was snoring. I covered her with a blanket, closed the door, and returned downstairs where Walt was entertaining Tulip with a gold exercise ball, knocking into things while she observed him from her perch.

"Thanks for nothing," I told him.

"She's a persuasive woman." He sat and stilled the ball. "We both know what it's like to lose someone too soon. I couldn't lie to her."

I rolled the ball away. "That was my husband's," I said. My throat tightened, thinking about Ash. "I don't even miss him."

Tulip flew to the ground, nudging the ball with the top of her head until she wedged it between the armchair and her play stand.

"Mieux vaut être seul que mal accompagné," Walt said.

"My French is rusty."

"Better to be alone than with someone who's no good for you," he translated.

"We were about to start a family."

"About to?"

I explained that we had waited because of my career.

"With the right one you wouldn't've waited," he replied. "Or thought it through." Tulip pooped, paced, and strategized, trying to scale the ball. Walt gave a lopsided smile. "Tariq says you're singing in the shower these days. And that it's a real soap opera."

My cheeks burned with embarrassment.

"You don't see it," he said.

"See what?"

"How you're in harmony with yourself. Around him."

Tulip took flight from a chair, landed on the ball, and gave a short scream as she struggled to not slip off.

"I've been working on a signature song for the group. It goes something like this." Walt stood with his hands on his hips. "We've gone astray, world . . . Deaf in the loud nothing day . . . Hear us whistle now." He pulled his pencil and pad from his pocket and made a note. "Then the refrain goes, hear us whistle now, hear us whistllllleeeee . . . boom, boom."

Tulip extended her wings upward, then her head, as far up as it would go.

"It's catchy," I told him.

"Much obliged." Walt bowed. "It's haiku."

He sat with me again.

"I didn't know he was no good," I finally said.

"You know how you know? It goes by too fast. With the one." He looked at Tulip balancing on her orb, and all around the room, then glanced up the darkening staircase. "It all goes by so fast," he said again.

23

There were complications. Tariq stayed in the hospital longer than expected. He would have to miss practice, he told me when I called. He wouldn't let us visit either, because he didn't want Tulip catching diseases, and his mother's around-the-clock company was more than enough.

While we spoke, Tulip stayed hooked on the living room curtain. There were birds building a nest in a fir tree beside the house. For close to a week, the male robin had been flying back and forth with his beak full of building materials, while the female wove twigs together and cemented them with mud, lining the inside with grasses.

"Do you want to talk to him?" I whispered to Tulip. She glanced at the phone and returned her gaze to the robins. Then I heard Mina berating one of the nurses. Tariq said he would see us soon, and we hung up.

After that my phone kept pinging. Ash was getting persistent. *We need to talk about selling*, the messages read. *We need to discuss our separation.* I typed and deleted until the Warblers rang the bell, then knocked as they tried opening the door. When I let them in they tromped through, protesting to Jo, who turned to me with "I bet Dawn doesn't wash her mouth before a concert."

They tossed their coats on the bench and watched me.

"Do you mean gargle?" I asked.

"She means neglecting our hygiene for the high art of whistling," Georgie said.

Jo rolled her sleeves. "I just don't think it's wise to brush your teeth on show day, is all."

"Why not?" I asked.

"Toothpaste numbs the mouth," Jo said. "It's no different than the rule of no kissing before performing. And keeping your lips out of the wind and sun."

"Makes sense," I told them.

Georgie crossed her arms. "We've got a half-day drive together. I'm not sitting with these dragon mouths for that long."

Then everyone wanted details on Tariq. I explained that he'd had an infection, and that his medications were being adjusted again.

"Do you have one of those horned helmets?" Walt asked. "Because now would be the time to wear it."

I told Walt I hadn't played the Wagnerian role of a Norse warrior maiden since my student years and would not re-enact one of the worst stereotypes of opera in popular culture solely for their pleasure.

"Fine. Be that way." Georgie dropped a page torn from a book into my lap. "That's my contribution to the time capsule."

It was a poem by Emily Dickinson. I tried reading it aloud but couldn't finish. After composing myself, I thanked her and said it was beautiful, and she rubbed her knuckles and nodded.

I put the poem in a shoebox and circulated it. Ben added birding binoculars, which got everyone asking questions. When Jo put in her framed photo of Ronnie Ronalde with her grandfather, Walt commented that she looked a lot like her grandad, only Jo said he was pointing at the wrong man. Then Walt rolled his beret and dropped it in, and Reno placed in his tin whistle, which he said had been particularly useful for learning "My Heart Will Go On." He passed the box to me. As Tulip flew from the curtain to Ben, one of her moulted feathers landed inside.

"Ah! The drift," Walt said.

"What drifted?" Ben asked.

"The way that there feather fell."

Petting Tulip, Ben kicked his feet up on the coffee table. "I would've become a plumologist. If I could see."

"I can't picture you as a lung doctor, Benny," Jo said.

"The plumologist studies feathers," he told her. "Flamingo, eagle, ostrich. Spangled cotinga, lyrebird, motmot . . ." As Ben described the feathers of exotic birds, everyone hunted around for Tulip's moults, holding them high and letting them fall until the box was blanketed.

"What about you, Missy," Georgie said. "What's your donation?"

I took my plastic bird from the mantle and placed it inside.

Reno grabbed his whistle from the box. As he began playing the theme from *Titanic*, Walt pulled his beret out and put it on and said, "That's better." Then Ben asked for his binoculars back, and Jo retrieved her framed photo, studied it, and said, "I don't look like Ronnie. Do I?" I reclaimed my bird, too. "On second thought, I'd like to keep this," I told them.

Georgie picked the box up off the coffee table. "So we're left with feathers and an old poem. Some capsule."

"And our arias," Ben said, fiddling with his phone. "Which I'll record tonight."

Jo struck her tuning fork against the table and held it until it resonated. "Time to hustle," she said.

We ran through our arias one last time. Afterwards Ben suggested videoing Tariq in so he could rehearse as well. Studying me with his watery blue eyes, Walt nudged me.

I went to the garage and sorted through my props. The Wagner box still gave off a whiff of the decade-old production when I sang proudly in the chorus. As students, we had celebrated every minor achievement as if we'd made it to La Scala. That year, I also had the sense that someone was out there for me and felt a guiding presence while performing in the campus theatre, as if everything in the universe was aligned. Then I met Ash.

I braided my hair and put the horned helmet on and reached for the rest of the battle gear. The mesh-like dress and breastplate, the knee-high leather sandals, the metal armbands and spear.

When I went back inside, Tulip screeched until she realized it was me. Then I took a bow and emitted the cry of the Valkyrie.

Walt and Jo fell off the couch arm in arm, Georgie said she'd peed herself and Ben insisted on a feel, then joined in with the laughter until Reno told them to knock it off. Then Jo dialled Tariq up. When he answered, Tulip flew from her perch to the arm of the couch and did her *tap tap tap* at the screen. Tariq waved.

"How are you, friend?" Walt asked.

"It's nice to be able to breathe again," Tariq told him.

"We thought you'd want to do your final run-through," Jo said.

Tariq was all for it. He asked for me, so I approached and he grinned with "Hello Brünnhilde." I felt my face flushing and removed the helmet. Then he told me he liked my braids. "I've decided on *The Marriage of Figaro* overture instead of *Pearl Fishers*," he added.

"That's too long." I looked to Jo for confirmation, but she said nothing.

"Nonsense. Let him do it." Georgie pushed her way in to the screen. "She's just sensitive about the theme," she told Tariq.

"Or it's not in her repertoire," Ben said.

I got up and retrieved a recording with myself on the cover, in a pear-coloured saque back gown, and showed it around.

"That's a sturdy-looking dress," Tariq said. "Are you Susanna disguised as the Countess there? Or the Countess disguised as Susanna?"

"How does he know so much about opera?" Georgie murmured to Walt.

Jo cued up the score and prompted Tariq. When he began, his rendition of the winds and strings was impressive. But he couldn't keep the fast tempo. Tulip stayed quiet with the rest of us while he stopped, gave an awkward laugh, then tried to continue. After he lost his breath again, Walt jumped in whistling and playing conductor, then Ben joined in, still recording it all, then the rest of us. Like so many operatic melodies, it was a piece no one knew they knew until they heard it. We continued and finished together.

"Bis! Bis!" Walt cried, even though it had sounded horrible.

"The first time I heard it," Tariq told us, "it made me feel so . . ." He looked at me, then over my shoulder to whatever lay beyond.

"So what?" Jo asked.

"Alive," he finally said.

He took a sip of water, licked his lips, and tried again. This time he had it. But before long, the person on the other side of the dividing curtain said, "Who the fuck's whistling!"

"It's me," Tariq replied.

"You do that again I'm gonna punch your head in," the other patient said.

"That sounds like one of my inmates," Jo said. "DC 49502. Hands big as skulls."

"It's my neighbour," Tariq explained. "He's in pain."

Then the nurse came in so he told us goodbye. When the screen went black, Tulip shrank into her feathers, emitting a small sound like a drawn-out *ooohh*.

Everyone looked at the rug then, studying its lines and curves, until Walt pulled a camera out and suggested a group picture to commemorate our last class before the Biennial. He set it on self-timer and we squeezed onto the couch. Instead of saying cheese, we puckered up like we were kissing the air, or ghosts. The Warblers went home after that.

Once they left Tulip waddled from the kitchen to the front door, scratching it with her foot.

"We can't go to the hospital," I told her. "But he'll be home soon."

She headed for the walkout, lethargically descending the stairs. I followed and made her nighttime oatmeal, which she pushed around in her bowl. Then she made her way to her cage without coaxing, tail feathers dragging on the ground. She climbed the bars, nudged the door open with her beak, and went inside.

While she sat on a low perch, I adjusted her stuffed animals and drew the cloak over the roost and turned her flashlight on. Then I crawled under my mother's quilt. "Goodnight, Tulip."

It had been a long time since I felt rested. But I was tired, and I was pretty sure she was, too, and after a lot of tossing and turning we both slept.

24

Jo had rented a van for the road trip. When she picked us up, Walt was next to her in the front, with Georgie and Ben behind them. I took the back seat with Tulip, who had the most luggage out of everyone, and Tariq, who'd been home a week. He looked better already; his face had lost its grey cast. He joked with Walt and seemed high on life.

Then Reno pulled up on a motorbike. Tariq plunked the carrier on my lap and got out, and the two of them spoke at length. Reno gave Tariq a helmet, showed him things on the dash, and called over that they would meet us halfway there. At that point Mina emerged. She was loaded up with bags, which she dropped in the grass to pull her son off the bike. Tariq held his mother's shoulders and spoke with her, until she put a hand to his chest and forehead, as if in blessing. Then she toted her bags to the van and poked her head in. "Of this foolery I am not approving," she said and went back into the house.

"I thought she moved out," Ben commented.

"She still has keys," I told him. "She goes back and forth a lot."

Georgie rummaged through the bags. "Does Tulip eat eggs?" she asked, squinting at the carrier. "Or would that be cannibalism?"

Watching Tariq ride away with Reno, I said I didn't know.

"She should be able to eat small amounts of meat, eggs, and cheese," Ben said. "Even though birds are lactose intolerant."

I unzipped the carrier and Tulip stepped onto my knee. Georgie glanced back again and they eyed each other. Then Tulip hopped onto Georgie's armrest. "Shoo," Georgie said. "Get back." But Tulip had already climbed into her lap and was doing her soldier stepping.

And then we all heard it. "Orgie," Tulip said.

Jo stopped pulling out of the driveway. I grabbed my notebook and wrote it down. First Ben, now Georgie. Her second word. Soon it would be my turn. Walt guffawed. "Hey, Orgie," Ben said. "Pass the chips."

Georgie held her arms in the air, waiting for Tulip to go. "Give me that cage," she told me.

"Tariq said she can stay out since it's a long drive," I replied. "You might as well get comfortable. When she wriggles her bum like that, it means she's settling in."

Georgie's arms dropped. "Little bastard," she told Tulip, who started preening.

I thought the Warblers would make a racket the whole way there. I had my noise-cancelling headphones ready. But once we left the city and got onto the highway, everyone quieted down.

For a while we played a game where Walt whistled and we had to guess the song. But after "White Cliffs of Dover" he got pensive and told us he needed to save his energy and tilted his chair back to rest. Georgie was too preoccupied with Tulip to talk, and Ben was busy dictating messages through his phone to his new girlfriend. I called up to Jo and asked how her son was doing. But she only replied with "We take each day as it comes" and kept focused on the road.

As we passed farmlands and patches of blue star-shaped flowers, and small French towns studded with spire churches, I looked for motorbikes. Then Ben played "Pretty Bird," which he said was one of Roger Whittaker's lesser-known songs. The lulling harp put me to sleep, and I didn't wake until we pulled in at a rest stop alongside a river.

Reno and Tariq were already there, sitting at a concrete table. There was still snow on the ground, through which wild crocuses grew. "Where are we?" I asked. Jo said that we had bypassed Montreal and were on the route along the Saint Lawrence, heading toward Quebec City.

Tulip flew from Georgie's lap to the dash where she could see Tariq. It looked cold out, and she didn't seem to have any desire to escape, settling on the heating vent instead.

When Jo turned her phone on, it pinged and pinged. She listened to some messages, shaking her head. "Well," she said, hanging up, "that's it."

Georgie looked over the top of her sunglasses. "What's it, Josephine?"

"Biennial's cancelled," Jo said.

Ben removed his earbuds.

"Come again?" Walt asked.

"The other regions made the decision without me. Early this morning."

"And you didn't bother checking your phone?" Georgie asked.

"I turn it off while driving." Jo rubbed her neck. "Joop got a gig with Cirque du Soleil. Once he pulled out everyone else did, too."

"All eight registrants, you mean," Georgie said.

"We were up to thirteen," Jo told her. "Plus us made twenty."

"Even Luella's out?" Walt asked.

"They're sleeping together," Georgie said. "Of course she'd follow him to the circus." She muttered something about amoral amateurs. Then she slid her door open, went around to the back of the van, opened a water jug, and brushed her teeth. She returned with the box of trophies and pushed them on us. "You win, you win, you win," she said, taking the largest for herself, every aspect of her face drooping downward.

Reno and Tariq approached then. "What's the holdup?" Reno asked, reaching for Mina's bags. "We're starving."

"Nature calls." Walt got out, taking rigid steps toward some trees.

Tariq took Walt's seat and greeted Tulip. Georgie rammed a trophy into Reno's chest, then Tariq's. She even put a small golden cup on the dash for his bird. "Honourable mention," she told her. "Let's go home."

"What's the deal?" Reno asked, taking the seat next to mine.

Jo explained. "I'm sorry," she told the group. "I know you worked hard for this."

Reno shrugged and bit into his sandwich. "It's not your fault."

"It most certainly is." Georgie took a sharp breath in.

Tariq stared out at the river and fed Tulip a carrot but said nothing. Walt came back and took his walker from the van and positioned it to face the water.

"Screw the convention," Ben said. "Let's still go."

Tulip looked up from the radiator.

"I agree," I told them.

"The committee cancelled the curling arena," Jo said. "We don't have a venue."

"What if we go on," Tariq said, "to the sea."

"Quebec's not on the ocean, hon," Georgie told him.

"But it's on the Saint Lawrence," Walt yelled, adjusting his hearing aid. Tariq brought the window further down.

"Which turns into the gulf," Ben said before murmuring questions into his phone.

"How far?" Jo asked.

"The river turns to saltwater at Tadoussac," Ben said. "Three hours north of Quebec." He listened some more. "There's whales there."

"I'm in," Reno said.

"Do you still want to see the sea?" Tariq asked his bird as she stared out at the beginnings of the river through the windshield.

Walt hit the side of the van. "Allons-y!"

Jo typed on her phone. "Our Quebec hotel's refundable." She put her glasses on, adjusting the rear-view mirror. "Now's your chance to practice that French, Walter," she told him. "You're in charge of booking rooms."

While Reno got out and helped Walt back into the van, Tariq came and sat next to me. "Can she eat eggs?" I asked.

"A taste of my mom's egg salad is fine," he said. "It's bland. Is she behaving?"

I nodded and asked if he was enjoying the scenery. I didn't know what else to say. Tariq looked out at the gleaming motorbike. "I get the whole Zen, meaning of life thing now."

A snort came from Georgie. Then Tariq went up front and gave Tulip a neck rub before returning to the bike, which swiftly carried them away.

Walt did research on his tablet and made some calls. "We're a month early. Everything's closed till May," he told us. "Except a roadside motel restaurant. They're busy since for now they're the only game in town. But la madame is holding our spots."

"Fantastic," Georgie said. "Reno can get pointers for his new property."

"Is it pet friendly?" Jo asked.

"Oh yes." Walt reached out to Tulip on the dash and offered her a nut. "They sounded very friendly."

I wanted to know if it was just me she wouldn't step up to. I asked Walt to try, and Tulip got right onto his outstretched hand. Then he brought her to his knee and she craned her neck toward Mina's bags. "She can sample the egg salad," I said, and Georgie distributed sandwiches and peppery cookies.

Back on the road, there was little traffic. We passed countless villages and farms backed by forested hills on one side, and the Saint Lawrence on the other, and eventually we were all yawning. Jo slapped her cheeks and emptied her coffee. "Tell us a story, Ben."

"Do you know the one about the nightingale and the rose?" Ben asked.

"Go on then," Walt said.

Ben turned in his seat. "So this student wants to dance with his professor's daughter. But she won't unless he gives her a red rose. The nightingale overhears the student weeping about this, so she checks every bush in the garden for a rose. But there's no red roses. Not a single one."

"How about trying another garden," Georgie said.

"They don't exist anywhere. Like, they're extinct." Ben emptied his juice box. "But this white rose tells the nightingale there's a way to make one. She'd have to sing with her heart pressing on a thorn. When she sees the student all devastated again, she impales herself and sings all night, till her heart's blood colours the flower."

"The nightingale dies?" Jo asked.

"Uh huh," Ben said between mouthfuls of chips. "Then the student presents the rose to his prof's daughter and she rejects him anyway. Because she got jewels from another guy in the meantime."

"Goddamn. Then what?" Georgie asked.

"He chucks the rose and goes back to studying metaphysics and stops believing in true love."

"That's one hell of a story, kid," Walt said as we took another turn on the high, winding road, and suddenly the ferry to Tadoussac came into view.

It was getting dark as we neared the dock line, but we could still see the bay with chunks of ice. Tulip was dozing in Walt's lap and missed it. But Ben asked us what we saw. So we did our best to describe the forested rocky landscape surrounding us and the otherworldly Saguenay fjord up ahead, scattered with long low boats like pieces from an immense chess game.

"I'll tell you what I don't see," Georgie added. "And that is a five-star resort."

When Jo opened her window, you could smell pine trees and salt in the air. I breathed it in, thinking how Tariq had been right. From international hotel rooms and buses, and guided tours and crowded walkways, I had seen the sea. But in all my years of travelling, I had never seen a coastline quite like this.

25

The motel was called Chantmarin, meaning sea shanty, song of sailors, sea song. It was situated on a hill overlooking the town and harbour, a white building with red awnings and small lighthouses beneath the numbers on each door.

As we pulled into the near-full lot, Reno was walking around taking pictures while Tariq sat resting on the bike, until he saw us and came over. "I feel like I'm still moving," he told us. Tulip was just waking up. "What do you think?" he asked her, but she dozed off again.

I went into the lobby with Walt. The lady at the desk told us about their restaurant specializing in seafood and pizza, and she said we were between seasons. Summer activities hadn't begun and the winter ones had ended. But we could still walk the board-walk and visit the dock, and one Zodiac tour was already running.

"Et les baleines?" I asked.

She replied that the whales were still mostly gone. "No hump-back," she said, shaking a finger. "No minke." Only the blue whales and belugas stayed through winter.

"C'est beau, Madame," Walt told her. Blues and belugas were enough.

Then she raised three fingers at us. "Trois chambres," she said.

Walt turned to me. "I did ask if she had room for seven."

"Yes. Fine. Three room pour sept personnes." She pushed the registration book at Walt. "Deux lits par chambre."

"Looks like we're doubling up." He wrote our names in, putting Tariq down with Ben. "He'll want privacy for his . . . rituals," he said, but then stopped writing. "Unless you two —"

"I'll go with the girls," I told him. "Tulip will be happy with Ben."

Walt nodded. "That leaves me with Reno. Up all night analyzing our pad."

The woman gave us key cards and wished us bonne nuit. Then we went outside and explained the sleeping arrangements. There were some grumbles but it was cold and everyone was worn out, so we split up the remainder of Mina's food and said goodnight.

The room I shared with Georgie and Jo was small but clean, with sky-blue walls and paintings of sailboats above the beds.

"I suppose the diva needs her own berth," Georgie said.

"I don't mind sharing," I told them.

"You have to rest," she replied. "Or god knows what will happen to that precarious voice. Jo and I have doubled up before. I'm used to her ugly feet in my face."

Jo threw her bag on the sofa. "I'll sleep here."

Then we shared Mina's dishes, eating them cold from the containers. "She's a good cook," Jo said.

Georgie sniffed. "These spices would have destroyed our performances."

"She was probably trying to sabotage us." I sliced an apple and passed it around.

"She's not so bad," Jo said. "She just seems lost. With her sons grown up and her husband gone." She fished around in the rice, adding, "No one needs her anymore."

While Jo was in the shower, Georgie took her tuning fork from the couch, removed her wraps, whacked the nightstand, and put the stem to her wrists. The steel vibrated with a crisp high pitch.

"Any better?" I asked.

"It's hogwash," she answered. But she struck the fork and pressed it to her knuckles again and again, tossing it back onto the couch only when Jo came out of the bathroom.

We watched TV, then put our pajamas on and got into bed.

The walls were thin. I thought I could hear whistling but couldn't tell whether it came from Tulip or Tariq or Ben. I put my hand on the blue dividing us, then slept.

In the morning, a light knocking woke me.

Jo and Georgie were still out with earplugs and eye masks. When I opened the door, Tariq stood there with a Thermos. "I want to show you something," he said and gave me a toque and gloves.

I quickly dressed and brushed my teeth and hair, and put on the winter wear adorned with whales, and went outside.

Tariq sat on the bench by the door. He looked wide awake, like he'd been up a long time already. When I asked if he'd gone jogging, he poured me coffee and said yes. It was so chilly I could see my breath. I suggested we take the van to wherever it was he wanted to go.

"It's only fifteen minutes away," he said and stood and took my empty cup.

"You're pushing yourself too much," I told him.

He zipped his coat, then mine. He walked so fast I could barely keep up. It was windy, and the hair outside my toque whipped my face as we continued down a hillside path, through some pines.

Aside from a few walkers with their dogs, we were alone. The path led to a long white building with a red tin roof topped with a steeple, overlooking the bay. It was the Grand Hotel, closed for the season, and gulls cried above us as we walked around it. Just below lay a tiny chapel like something from a storybook. It also had a red roof and its yard was filled with tombstones, enclosed by a miniature fence.

As we crossed the road, Tariq stopped to study the pavement and took a picture of seagull droppings whorling together like an abstract canvas, before we moved on to the boardwalk spanning the waterfront.

There he approached a telescope, fed it a coin, and told me, "Look."

He pointed to some ice floes in the distance. I put my eye to the lens while he stood behind me, his hand on my back. "See that other white, between the chunks of ice?" he asked.

All I saw was more ice surrounded by oily-dark choppy water but continued panning the seascape until I noticed something else.

There were three of them. They were small and blended in so well. Only their perfect arcs stood out from the angular blocks around them.

They didn't jump or offer a show of somersaults but glided gracefully just beneath the surface. Then I spotted another and another, at least ten, an ephemeral pod moving through the water like a chorus conveying a message.

One dove under, its tail fin coming into view like a white butterfly. Then the others dove, one and one and one into the depths, and the sea was black again.

I turned and grabbed Tariq's hand. "That was incredible," I said and looked down at our whale gloves, and let go.

He put his hands in his pockets, squinted toward the sea, and nodded. "They're the ones that look like they're smiling," he said. "Like birds, they have no vocal cords, but they still sing."

"You sound like Ben," I told him.

"They're known as the sea canary," he went on, "because of their whistles and trills."

Over the wind we listened for the music of the belugas, but they had gone.

We continued onto the rocky shoreline to the snow-encrusted sand. At the water's edge, we took our gloves off and dipped our fingers in to taste the foamy saltiness, glacial on our lips. After that we walked for some time without speaking, once in a while stopping and looking out.

Then I asked if he thought the new dosage was working.

He kicked at the sand and looked out at the water again. "Anything's possible," he said, and as he said it a white back resurfaced, then another. The pod was still with us, following our path closer to the shore, and this time we could hear them chirping as they splashed around.

"I wonder what they're saying," Tariq said. "I wonder what they're telling us to do."

We watched until the glistening figures vanished again. Then we waited a little longer. But this time the darkness of the water felt absolute and we returned unaccompanied along the bay.

Before ascending to the boardwalk, Tariq picked up a stick and carved script into the half-frozen sand, the lines of each character wavy.

I asked what he had written.

He discarded the stick and turned away from the water. "Your name," he said, taking in the historic hotel. "The red roofs are for the sailors," he added. "To guide them home."

26

There was a statue of a mermaid at the Chantmarin's restaurant entrance and pictures of fishermen and whalers on the walls. One of the few places open, it was bustling with tourists, but the Warblers had secured an orange booth and were tucked into it as if on a life raft.

We ordered pancakes and eggs and a breakfast wrap for Tulip, hidden from the other diners in her carrier. When the food came, Tariq discretely unzipped her door to feed her, but she was dozing. "It's not like her to nap through a meal," he said, looking concerned. Then our basket of deep-fried pork rinds arrived and her head popped up, her small grey face assessing her surroundings through the mesh. Tariq offered her a piece of wrap, then another, and once she finished, he gave a deep exhale.

"Remind me why we're here?" Georgie asked, covering her shoulders with her coat.

"Try to have a good time, my dear," Walt told her. "You might surprise yourself."

"This is my first vacation in twenty years," Jo said. "I plan on enjoying it."

"Lighten up, Orgie." Ben leaned into her shoulder.

Reno threw a rind in the air, catching it in his mouth. "What are you going to do with that?" he asked of the shoebox in her lap.

"Wouldn't you like to know." Georgie tapped her metallic nails on the lid.

Ben, in his swallow T-shirt, rubbed his stomach like he was full. Then he told us that he had added our recordings to the box.

"Give us the swallow, Benny," Jo said.

Ben made a swallow call. The Warblers concurred that it wasn't his strongest.

"They can't all sound amazing," Ben said. "Besides, that's not why birds sing."

"Why do they sing?" Reno asked.

"They sing to sing."

"They sing to signal and alert and show off," Walt said.

"Not all the time," Ben replied. "Not when they don't have to."

The Warblers pondered the restaurant ceiling as though it were filled with birds. Then Jo studied the placemat, which was a map. She chose a lookout point to visit and we got going.

When we pulled up at the site — the Saint Lawrence opening onto the Saguenay fjord — it really was ocean-like. The water was so wide you saw no shoreline, only a rippling endlessness dotted by great grey ships.

Tariq had taken the front seat with Tulip so she could get a proper first glimpse. Once Jo parked, he lifted her up to the dashboard and said, "We made it."

Tulip stared at the water and blinked. She took a step forward then looked away, as if it was too much. Then she shuffled closer to the windshield, staying quiet before emitting an *ooohh*, her chest quivering. She bowed at the seaway then turned to Tariq, flapping and hopping from one foot to the other, her wingspan taking up the entire dashboard.

"Sweet Jesus," Georgie muttered. "You're blocking our view."

After he tucked Tulip into his coat, we got out of the van. While Walt set up his walker and the others took in the surroundings, Ben quietly asked me for a description. I told him that the day was clear and the water went on beyond our field of vision.

The shoreline was a forest with big jutting rocks still covered in traces of white.

"Wild," he said and ran his hand along the branches of a pine. "Do you get outdoors much, in your industry?"

"Not really."

We went single file down the path to the lookout. As we approached, the air smelled like fish and wet stone. Then Walt pulled a tripod from his basket and set up his camera. Everyone gathered to fit the frame, a tight octet of "One sec!" and "Ouch!" and "Mercy!", arms tangling to secure each other's balance, while Tulip clicked her tongue. Walt set the timer, and we took a photo for posterity.

Then Walt rested on his seat, put a hand above his eyes, and looked around. "I'd say this is as good a place as any for an aria."

"What? Here?" Reno asked, turning.

"Had I known, I'd have worn my dress," Georgie commented, but Reno was already walking out onto the frosty rocks.

"I want to know what love is!" he yelled, raising his arms in the air.

"Don't slip!" Georgie yelled back.

"He's changed his song again," Jo said.

"To a power ballad." Walt adjusted his binoculars. "It's a doozy."

While Reno serenaded the sea, we caught fragments of his sound in the air, accompanied by the rhythmic slaps of the waves. He stood so close to the edge that it looked like he would fall off. "There's too much heart in that man," Georgie said. When he finished, he bowed to the blue expanse before returning to us and hooking his arm through Walt's.

They walked out slowly together. Once Walt chose a spot on the flat stones, he let go of Reno and removed his beret. The melody of his aria travelled through the thick surrounding forest, then drifted beyond the green, away from us. Afterwards he stayed out there on the rim, talking to the air. Or maybe to Mae. We didn't ask when he came back.

Then Jo went out with Ben who made a high clear call, and a trill resounded from the spray. When he finished, Jo put her hands on his shoulders. She seemed to be giving him a pep talk, the kind you'd give to your own child, and he nodded and she hugged him, and they returned.

Georgie took her bun out and unzipped her coat, exposing a wrinkly bosom as she stepped onto the rocks. When she whistled, she clutched her hands against her chest as she gazed out. She had picked a good key so she didn't go too high. She held back at the right moments, and all the while her hair lit up in the sun like a flare that said I'm still here.

"Will you go out?" I asked Tariq as she made her way back.

"Come with us," he said.

The three of us walked to the ridge. Mesmerized by the water, Tulip remained mute while Tariq whistled their overture. I went in on the refrain. Although we were far from symphonic, it was exhilarating to stand there with them. Then Tulip started squirming. Tariq scanned the sky for predators, released her from his coat, and extended his arm.

It was something, to see her perched majestically, ready for flight. Tariq watched her, then looked out to the horizon and waited, while Tulip glanced from Tariq to the air, until finally she shifted and crouched and extended her wings, her eyes on the sky.

Then Tariq coughed.

Tulip turned back to him.

He couldn't stop coughing. He leaned forward and bent his elbow, his other arm with Tulip on it still extended. He tried to shake her off. But she only flew a few feet up then landed on him again. I pulled a bottle from my bag. While he drank, his bird clutched his sleeve and gave the sky one last look before climbing his arm to the collar. He had no choice but to let her back in.

"What the hell was that?" Georgie asked as we rejoined the Warblers.

"A miscommunication," Tariq said. Tulip tucked her head into the coat, hiding against a gust of wind and the frigid *keows* of circling gulls.

"Anyone for a Zodiac expedition?" Ben asked.

Walt told Ben he would go with him. Georgie said she was going to track down a hot toddy, and Jo wanted to get a coffee at the marina and write to her son. Reno said he was taking a ride, and there was room for one more.

Tariq glanced at Reno and back at me. "Go with him," he said. "We'll meet for supper."

"I'd rather stay," I told him.

"We need some time," he said, looking down at Tulip. He was pale and seemed tired. So Jo drove back to the motel, and we all parted company for what remained of the day.

While Reno fuelled up, I waited at a picnic table. The wind came back then. Every so often a crackling emanated from within it, like a gorge of ice shattering. Or the rumbling of a beastly fish, calling from a mythic realm.

27

Our route followed the natural curve of the river. On the bike the midday sun felt strong, melting the snow around us. We passed sweeping vistas and dune-like hills and uninhabited terrain. We passed wet tidal beaches and forests of savage beauty, above which drifted sea birds and floater planes. For a good long while, we just rode, before stopping at a spot with a trail.

"Let's check it out," Reno said.

"I've walked enough today," I told him, as he hiked ahead.

The path was steep and icy and I wasn't in the mood. The wind made the trees creak and fifteen minutes turned into thirty, then an hour. My hips and knees ached. I started tripping over roots and my breathing quickened. Then I fell and slid a ways down the incline, losing sight of Reno.

I sat on a log until he reappeared, only to wave an arm. Eventually I forced myself to continue up the slope until I could see a clearing, and Reno looking out onto the bay. There, I leaned forward with my hands on my knees.

"How come you didn't do your aria this morning?" he asked, offering me water.

I said I had forgotten.

"How about now?" He nodded to the massive wall of rock plunging into the water, pinkish where it had been struck by tidal surge. "And maybe sing it, instead of whistling."

"Why wouldn't I whistle it?"

"I'm guessing you're better at singing."

I walked to the edge of the viewpoint. We were so high up. I had never felt so small. I did a few vocal warm-up exercises and massaged my jaw. Then I focused on the untouched wilderness and began, sensing the strength returning in my voice. And the person I thought about while singing was Tariq. I sang as though his life depended on it.

The setting sun turned the clouds deep amber, reflecting on the water. The light was different here. It held a sepia tint that made it seem we were living already in the past.

When I turned back to Reno, he was filming me. "Wow," he said and put his phone in his pocket and clapped.

"Let's get back," I told him.

We all wore our swallow T-shirts to the motel restaurant. Georgie had her dress on under hers and Walt's was paired with his un-wrinklable tux. Even Jo sported dangly earrings for the occasion. I slid into the booth next to Tariq. He seemed more relaxed, and when I peered under the table, I could see Tulip perched on his knee, taking sunflower seeds from his palm.

We ordered fishermen's platters. Then Ben told us about the blue whales that had swum near their inflatable boat. He knew immediately from their blowhole breathing that it wasn't just waves rocking them on the water.

"Did you encounter the belugas?" Tariq asked.

"Sadly not," Walt said. "But we could hear them."

Everyone was famished. When the platters arrived, we feasted as if it was our last meal. Even Tulip smacked down a bit of fish, and Tariq had more than I had seen him eat in a long time.

Then the waitress brought pie and coffee and asked about our shirts.

"Nous sommes des siffleurs," Walt told her.

"Ah ouaih?" She grinned then noticed Tulip. "Elle aussi?"

"Mais oui," Walt replied. "Her, too."

"So much for health and safety," Georgie said.

The waitress pointed to a guitar and mic in the far corner of the restaurant. "You come," she said, motioning for us to follow. "Sifflez pour nous."

Jo turned to Walt. "How about the mall set?"

Their gig had been replaced by an electronic hip-hop show. Walt nodded. "We can do that, right guys?"

"Isn't whistling taboo for sailors? Doesn't it bring storms?" Reno asked as the waitress left.

"That's one line of thinking," Jo told him. "The other is that it encourages the wind strength to increase."

Everyone hurriedly ate their deserts while Georgie tore her T-shirt off and stood, adjusting her wine-coloured gown and making her way to the front. The rest of us followed as the waitress spoke into the mic. "Salut," she told the diners. "Allô! We have special guest for you."

Walt picked up the guitar and stepped in. "Bonsoir, tout le monde," he said and strummed. Then we looked to Jo for our cue and began. The songs were crowd pleasers. We did "Super Trouper" and "Lean on Me." We did "God Only Knows" and "Ring of Fire," with Ben, Tariq, and Tulip acting as the trumpets while Walt, Georgie, and Reno carried the tune. People couldn't believe it. They stopped talking and eating to listen.

More groups came into the restaurant. The crowd got bigger. People joined in. By the time we performed "All You Need Is Love," it had turned into a kind of flash mob and Jo raised her arms up at the crowd to say come on, do this with us, and they did.

Then a girl called out "Viva la Vida!" so Walt told her to come up to perform her request.

"Where are you from?" he asked, and she told him Mexico. "We'll finish with 'Viva la Vida,' friends," Walt said. "Which is Spanish for . . ." He looked to the girl.

"Long live life," she said. Her English was good. She spoke into the microphone to explain that the title of the song came from Frida Kahlo. These were the words she wrote on her last painting before she died.

"Start us off," Walt then told her.

The girl whistled the first few bars alone.

Walt snapped his fingers, then motioned for the rest of us to join in, then the diners. It was a popular song, familiar to all. When we reached the refrain, everyone held their phones up like little flames and whistled *whoooaaaaaa*, *whoooaaaaaa*, and you heard all these people releasing everything they had from within. Tulip took off then, flying around above us. When the song ended, she came back down to Tariq's arm as if an invisible line tethered her to him. The clapping went on and on, every person in that room smiling and laughing, catching their breath.

"That's how you leave an audience. Wanting more," Jo told us.

Walt shook the girl's hand. "Thanks, folks, we're the Warblers," he spoke into the mic. "Merci, mes amis." We bowed and said adios to the girl and au revoir to the waitress, then paid our bill and walked out of the restaurant, leaving the diners to their dining.

Outside, Georgie suggested a toast. We went to our room while Reno ran to the dépanneur and came back with sparkling wine and cups.

"I guess that's a wrap," Walt said, pouring.

"We kicked ass," Ben said.

Georgie adjusted the strap of her dress with "Group gigs aren't so bad after all."

"We'll come back every summer. Like the whales," Reno said.

"No, we won't," Georgie told him.

"In that case, it's been a blast," Reno said, and we tapped cups.

"I am so proud of you all," Jo said.

I took a step forward. "It's been an honour."

"You're not rid of us yet." Georgie passed around pretzels. "You still owe us a class."

"Tchin, tchin to that." Walt raised his cup again.

"Santé," Tariq said, raising his.

I sat on the bed and opened the laptop. I wanted to see the painting that the Mexican girl had mentioned. I thought it would be skeletons in elaborate costumes, but it was a bright still life of watermelons, all reddish pinks and greens. On the melon's pulp was Kahlo's signature and in big letters was written *VIVA LA VIDA Coyoacán 1954 México*. A text accompanying the painting described how the fruit figured in a lot of Mexican art. It was associated with the Day of the Dead, and it was the dead who ate it.

Tariq sat beside me on the bed with Tulip and glanced at the picture on the screen. "We love watermelon," he said.

28

Tariq took a scenic detour home with Reno the next day, the rest of us reaching the city long before them. Jo dropped off Tulip and me first. As we turned onto our street, I noticed Judith waiting out front, pacing and talking on her phone.

"That's my agent," I told the Warblers as Jo pulled up.

"Maybe we can audition for her," Walt said.

"Is she hot?" Ben asked. "Do you want us to stay?"

I said I would be fine and got our things out of the van, and they drove away in slow motion. Judith finished her call and rushed up to hug me, stepping back when she saw the bird. "What in god's name . . ." she started.

"Would you mind getting us some donut holes?" I asked, dropping our bags at the door to find my keys. "It's to your left at the intersection. Anything without chocolate is fine."

Judith forced a smile. "I'm here on serious business, Dawn."

I explained that I had promised Tulip donuts as soon as we got home.

"Who is Tulip?" she asked as I handed her a bill, thanked her and closed the door. Then I rushed to tidy the place up. I was like Elektra in her mad scene, hurrying to toss ropes and toys and games under the furniture, pulling out my sheet music and scores.

When Judith returned, she handed me the bag with a raised pinky and glanced around. She didn't remove her coat and gave the couch a few quick swipes before sitting.

I offered Tulip a hole. She rolled it along the windowsill and eyed our visitor's discus pendant, while I went into the kitchen to make tea.

"Is Ashraf away?" Judith called out. "I heard about the merger on the news."

I replied that yes, he was away, but we had another house guest.

"You mean that creature?" She crinkled her nose at Tulip.

"She belongs to Ash's brother." I placed a mug before her. "He's staying with us."

When I told her that he had stomach cancer, Judith remained expressionless. "I'm sorry to hear that," she said. "My cousin had it. They gutted him."

"Is he okay?"

"Better than ever." She reached for the donuts, helping herself to one, then another. "Lost twenty pounds in the process, which did him a world of good." She pulled a compact from her purse and checked her face. "I suppose by now you know about Svetlana."

I told her that I hadn't been in touch with anyone in months.

"She's had some differences with Maestro Boom." Judith sighed. "More recently, she stopped turning up for rehearsals. On opening night of *La bohème,* she threw her stole into the pit and exited during the banquet scene because she claimed someone was trying to poison her. Katie Price had to go on in a slip. Surely you heard all this?"

"Did they fire her or did she quit?" I asked.

Judith looked down at the rug and ran a nylon toe across it. "This is new," she said. "Must be worth a fortune."

"She walked out and they need a stand-in," I answered for her. "So why not go with Katie? Isn't she one of yours?"

"Katie is moving on to the Met."

In other words, the company had not provided the up-and-coming singer with security, and on hearing of her stellar performance, the Met had offered her an audition, then a contract. "After she finishes the run, which she graciously agreed to complete," Judith added. "Leaving a vacancy for the summer tour."

Performing in the off-season to raise funds for a new concert hall had been Maestro Boom's initiative. The summer tour, which included guest performances by powerhouse voices, was the most popular show of the year. Tickets sold out in every city within hours.

"How is everything feeling here and here?" She put her hand on her chest, then her throat. "I spoke with your ENT specialist. He said your cords have healed nicely and that it's safe for you to sing."

"Why would they want me back?" I asked. "After what happened?"

"It's that video, clever girl." She nudged me. "It's gone viral. I'm sure it influenced the board's decision when they teleconferenced this morning."

"What video?"

"The one of you up on some rock. It's very risqué."

I silently cursed Reno and explained that a friend had recorded the performance without my knowledge.

"Whatever you say." She winked, then scrolled through her phone. "Rehearsals start in June."

"Mixed repertoire?" I asked.

Judith nodded, lifting my ponytail and studying the ends. "This could use a trim," she said. "Unless you plan on singing Isolde."

"And the aria?"

She let go of my hair, patting her twisted pin-up. "That's up to you," she replied. "Svetlana was going to do Wally. Obviously you'll go with a big costume number. Turandot or Dido on the pyre, if they can get the flame machine."

I stood and paced, letting that familiar rush from the pressure of a looming vocal deadline invade my body. What did it matter that I was third in line? There were hundreds snapping at my heels and I'd still been chosen. It was an invitation to return to the stage and possibly the last I would receive.

"I accept," I told her.

Judith pumped a fist in the air. "Excellent," she said. When she got up to go, she noticed white flecks on her cashmere coat. "What is this?" she asked, brushing it off.

"Fairy dust," I said.

"It better not stain." She walked to the door. "How did that whistling class turn out, by the way?"

Tulip looked up from her donut.

"It turned out well," I replied.

When Judith laughed, I noticed her pointed eyeteeth. "We can get you out of that now," she said. "Yayoi Oto can take over. She's on leave with a goiter."

"It's nearly finished," I told her.

She glanced back at the messy living room. "You seem to have a lot on your plate."

When I said that I would manage, she nodded, put her sunglasses on, and told me that she would be in touch with paperwork.

Once she was gone, I did a victory dance around the couch. Tariq came in then, and his bird flew to his outstretched arm.

"How was the ride?" I asked.

"Breathtaking." He rubbed his nose on Tulip's beak.

"And how are you feeling?"

"Fine," he replied. "Please stop asking."

I decided to share my news. "They're letting me sing again."

He brought Tulip back to the sill and took off his coat. "I didn't realize you needed permission," he said. Then he asked in what opera, and I said it was up to me. A solo of my choosing.

"You'd make a good consumptive Violetta. Or Carmen in that ruffle dress."

"I'm tired of playing long-suffering heroines," I told him. "I'm sick to death of death scenes."

Tariq smiled and nodded. "I hear you."

Near the window was a box I'd tossed some toys in. He tapped it with his foot, looking outside. "Cardboard," he said. "I forgot to put that in the binder, under what's critical to her happiness. She likes playing in boxes. If you cut holes and stack them, she'll explore for hours."

We watched Tulip hunt for crumbs. Every time she backed up too close to the edge of the sill, Tariq guided her forward.

"Did you and Anabelle want kids?" I asked.

He didn't answer right away. "We had other priorities," he eventually said.

"Walt says delaying means —"

"Wrong person, wrong time."

"Do you believe that?"

"I do," he said.

Standing on one foot, Tulip tucked her head under the leg that was in the air and preened. Tariq spotted her with his hand in case she tipped. "You'd make a good parent," I told him, and he looked up at me.

"You too," he said.

There was a small plastic bridge under the coffee table. A toy I had missed. I picked it up and set it on the sill and Tulip climbed the rungs.

"If you could show somebody a bridge," I asked, "what bridge would it be?"

"Congress Avenue," he replied. "In Austin."

I asked what was special about it.

"It's home to the world's largest urban bat colony," he replied. I shuddered.

"Unlike birds taking off from the ground," he continued, "bats only fall into flight. Every night they fly out from the structure's underside to forage. There are boat tours and observation decks. But the thing to do is just stand in the middle. And wait for them to fall."

29

As his brother neared the end of treatment, Ash would not stop calling. When the dividing door was open, I could hear Tariq constantly answering the same questions about cell counts and numbers, while my husband hunkered down with his gashti on the other side of the world. To me, Ash's messages were all the same. *We need to talk about the house*, they said. *We need to talk about assets.*

Then Tariq's last pill day came and went, with more tests and scans, and finally results day arrived. But he wouldn't let me go to the hospital. It was going to be a long process, he said, of mainly waiting around. "Stay with Tulip," he told me. "She's grimy and needs a bath."

After he left us, I watched him walk out to the car. He wore a pressed shirt and pants. Everything about him appeared healthier as the chemicals left his body. He'd regained weight. His eyes were more open. His complexion had a warm undertone, and his hair had grown the length of a buzz cut.

"Repeat after me," I told Tulip on the sill. "Hello robin, hello poppies, hello sun."

Tulip put her foot on the window and watched the car pass beneath the canopy of trees. Once he had gone, I tried enticing her to the sink with sweet potatoes. Instead she waddled to the dividing door and downstairs, where she scrambled into the bathroom. Tariq had installed a perch in the shower there.

I ran the water while she climbed a towel and flitted to the tub ledge. "Step up," I ventured, adjusting to a gentle stream and bending to offer my fingers. She stretched her foot out then pulled back, until I brought the showerhead down and she curled her feet around it, and I lifted her to her perch.

As the water misted her, Tulip craned her neck. Then she bowed her head and I reached out tentatively, stroking her between the eyes with my finger. She made a purring sound. And just like that, I knew she trusted me.

Once she'd had enough, she sidestepped to the end of the perch. I turned the water off and swaddled her, and took the emery board from the medicine cabinet.

When I sat with her, she rolled onto her back, wriggling as I inspected her feet. Her pressure point was almost gone. As I reached for her ankle, heart pounding, I told her she could watch *Downton* in exchange for a pedicure.

Her leg was the most delicate thing I'd ever held between my fingers. I worked on each toe carefully, and she reacted with mule kicks now and then. When we finished, I set her up on the bed and turned on the TV. As the theme song played, she whistled faint notes, while my mind wandered to Tariq.

I tried to distract myself by playacting my upcoming scene, but nothing felt right. So I cleaned the roost, changing Tulip's papers and bowls. Then I opened the French doors for air. Clouds drifted past, full and white. Petals from the apple tree carpeted the grass, and the beginnings of lilies grew along the fence through old mulch. When Tulip's show ended, we ate pasta, peas, and corn. "I should go," I told her. "I should be there."

She climbed off the table and down her chair, crossing the room to her roost. Inside, she started preening and seemed content. So I put on Barber's Adagio for Strings and drove to the hospital.

Once there, I was directed to a hall of meeting rooms. Tariq's door was ajar. I could see him examining scans on a wall monitor, with Dr. Horne pointing to darker darknesses. Suddenly it felt like I was intruding on an intensely private moment. So I stood outside and waited.

"I thought I'd be dead months ago," Tariq said. "Then I got Christmas. And a trip."

"We're all terminal. That's what I tell my patients when they get discouraged."

"Fair enough," Tariq replied.

I pushed the door open and it slammed against the wall. "There have to be other treatments," I said. "What *can* you do?"

Tariq and Dr. Horne stared at me, then the doctor turned to Tariq. "Would you like me to —"

Tariq nodded and called me over.

"How can you be smiling?" I asked.

He gave my sleeve a tug. "There's no more evidence of disease."

I looked at Dr. Horne. He gave a solemn nod, explaining that the increased dosage had worked. There were no further growths, and they could no longer detect any presence of cancer. "We can be cautiously optimistic," he said. "We'll continue monitoring closely. We'll adopt the watch-and-wait approach."

I threw my arms around the doctor.

"Am I free to go?" Tariq reached for his blazer.

"You're all done," he said and shook our hands and left.

I had more questions. But Dr. Horne was already hurrying down the corridor. I turned to Tariq, who sat staring out the window.

"Everyone's waiting for news," I told him. "Georgie wants to throw you a fête."

He promised to let the Warblers know once he'd spoken to his family.

"How do you want to celebrate?" I asked.

"By never coming back here."

"We need to do more than that."

He looked around the room and guided me out. "I'll think about it," he told me.

All week long I removed spent foliage from the earth. I cut back what would grow again and pulled out what wouldn't by the roots. I tore at weeds until my hands were raw and Tariq opened the French doors and said, "Come on, we're going to a game."

We drove to the royal park of the Canadian monarch. I hadn't ever been, but Tariq said he liked it there for Tulip because dogs weren't allowed. At the entrance gate stood the Warblers, who all congratulated Tariq. "You said party," Georgie poked him. "Outdoor exercise is not my idea of a bash."

In the park were commemorative trees planted by dignitaries, of all types and sizes identified by plaques. We followed a path to a small stone palace with a sparkling fountain and walked through a rockery with hundreds of rose species not yet blooming.

Then we made our way to a green field where a cricket game was in full swing. Jo laid out blankets. We sat under an oak tree and Tulip pecked in the clover as we watched the players in yellow-and-blue uniforms scatter on the field.

Tariq told us that it was one of the first matches of the season. I liked the sound the ball made on the bat, the click before it arced through the air. There was something hypnotic about the way the men moved in a kind of cosmic harmony.

After some time, the umpires removed their hats and the teams took a break at their clubhouse. There was music over the loudspeaker with a sitar and flute and drums. Women poured tea. Grandparents played with grandchildren. The men ran to their babies and held them up over their heads.

"Nothing much happens in this sport, does it," Georgie commented.

Tariq said that cricket was a thinking game. A metaphor for life, about the human condition and how it strengthened under duress. Matches could last for days, an action repeating itself until one team was crushed.

"So it's about patience," Jo said.

"And reaction," Walt added.

"And maintaining one's integrity," Tariq said. "Making the most of the hand we're dealt."

Ben asked what the bats were made from and Tariq said the handle was cane and the blade was willow. It was tough and light, absorbing shock without splintering. Close up, you could see the red streaks the ball made when it got struck.

"All-time favourite match?" Reno asked.

"The Ashes," Tariq told him. "Between England and Australia. Whoever loses gets their symbolic ashes put into a crystal cup."

"I know of an Ash I'd like to burn and put in a cup," I said.

Tariq lowered his head.

"The susurration of an ash tree," Ben said, "is a hiss."

"Is there any tree that has no susurration?" Tariq asked. "A tree that's just . . . an absence of sound?"

Ben thought it through. "The yew."

Tariq looked out at the clubhouse. "I'll get us some jalebiyan," he said and got up. But he moved uneasily as he crossed the field. Reno caught up with him and put a hand on his back as they walked.

"Did you seal the deal yet?" Ben asked, removing his sneakers and wriggling his toes for Tulip.

"What deal?" I squinted to see them mingling with the players.

"Have you two said what you have to say to each other? Now that your ex is in Japan."

"Very funny." I lay back, adding, "I never would have done something like this before."

"That's what they all say." Georgie smelled her sunblock before applying it.

"I think she means take time out for leisure," Jo said.

"I always had a full schedule," I explained.

Walt shook his head. "Quel malheur."

Reno and Tariq returned with syrupy knotted rings. We ate and watched Ben feed Tulip, who devoured her piece of the sticky dessert from his hand. Then Tariq sat next to me and pulled a red leather ball from his sweatshirt pocket, tossing it into the air and catching it before offering it to me like an apple. The ball had rows of white stitching around it and gold lettering on either side that said Test Match Special Edition. It was un-squishable. I thanked him.

The players took their positions. The game started up again. Tariq sat back on his elbows and said, "I need a plan B for Tulip."

"You're out of the woods, son," Walt told him.

"I know," he said. "But it's irresponsible not to have a plan."

"Just chuck her into the sky," Georgie said. "Like in the movies."

"She'd last five minutes." He reached toward his bird and she preened his fingers.

I looked out to the field. The game was in an intense hold, the players stock-still in their positions like ancient garden sculptures.

"What about a sanctuary?" Reno asked. "Like the one in Niagara Falls."

Tariq told him that the birds were only there to please tourists, who were encouraged to feed and touch them. They even had to perform in daily shows. He didn't want her going there. "The best would be what she's always known," he added. "A human home where someone devotes themselves to her."

Tulip climbed Ben's leg and watched us. "We shouldn't be discussing this with her here," Ben whispered.

In a low voice, Jo asked about a rescue with other parrots. Tariq rejected her suggestion, looking at me. "She only has the capacity to love one other person. And she needs their entire love back."

I felt light-headed and concentrated on the players as their shadows grew long in the sun. I told Tariq he was wasting his time thinking about such things, when he had beaten cancer.

He rubbed a blade of grass between his fingers. "I've always found that battle analogy inane."

I had a hard time swallowing. "You're here, aren't you?"

Tulip left Ben's leg and stopped at each one of us, pecking at our feet. "I'll come back as a tree," Ben said, lying down. "Probably a dogwood, where birds can rest and feed."

"Moving on to reincarnation, are we?" Georgie lay back, too.

Jo looked up at the branches shading us. "I'll be a beech," she said. "They make great tree houses."

"Redwood," Reno said decisively, like he'd long ago thought it through.

"Palm," Georgie rushed in, as if someone else would take her choice.

"Maple," Walt said.

"Willow, Tariq?" Jo asked.

"Sure," he said, turning to me. "What about you, Dawnjaan?"

"A prickly pear," Georgie said, and they laughed.

"I guess we're all in the woods then, after all," Tariq joked.

"Not the same one," Ben said. "Our varieties would never meet." He stood and gave a call of three triplets, full of longing. "White-throated sparrow," he told us. "Where've you gone, my lost love, my lost love, my lost love?"

"You know what's great about birdsong?" Walt said. "It doesn't need updating."

Ben gave another call and Tulip flew to him, while Tariq looked out at the field. "I used to come here all the time," he said. "With my father."

"Were you close?" Jo asked.

"Very," he replied. "I couldn't get through his funeral."

"Waste of time, those," Georgie said, and Tariq nodded.

The air was turning cool. The other visitors had left. As we stood and collected our things, Tariq told us about the secret gate behind the clubhouse. "A small part of the wrought iron opens there," he told us. "So players can get in after hours."

Important officials lived within the confines of the park. Walt asked how it was possible for anyone to come and go so freely. "It's always been there," Tariq said, latching his arm through Jo's and leaning against her to walk. "Someday, we'll pass through it."

At the park entrance, I said my goodbyes to the Warblers. I started rehearsals soon and wouldn't see them until after the tour.

"Did you decide on your number?" Jo asked.

"Probably 'Ritorna vincitor.'" Judith had suggested the aria from *Aida*, since it came with a transportable set including obelisks.

"Don't touch anything while you're up there," Georgie said.

I showed them the picture of my costume. It was gold with a long cloak and a tall Egyptian-style hat.

"Will there be elephants?" Walt asked.

"No. But I get a beacon."

"Coming back with a bang," Tariq said.

"What's that supposed to mean?" I asked.

He offered Tulip a dandelion. "It just sounds complicated."

"Cassandra Huntington is being bungeed on," I replied. "Victor Chen will be in a Rolls-Royce that gets shot at. And Diego Silvo's doing his song underwater."

There was an awkward silence until Georgie said, "You'll be grand."

Then the air filled with the cries of the cricketers, and we took a few steps back into the park. Only the match wasn't over. We wouldn't witness the final outcome. We watched them play on, an eternal back and forth across the spheres, until eventually we stopped lingering and said our goodbyes again while behind us on the green, the players clapped and cheered.

30

Once rehearsals began, I hardly saw Tariq. Early mornings I took to waiting by the living room window until he appeared around front, stretching in the half-light then jogging away, leaving me observing an empty street until I had to dress and go.

My days were filled with sessions. Sessions with the throat specialist. Sessions with my vocal coach and accompanist. Sessions singing and building strength and stamina. Sessions with administrators and Judith. With a divorce lawyer.

The odd time I got breaks and stopped in at the house, he and Tulip weren't there. When I arrived home late at night, it was always quiet. Occasionally I made noise in the kitchen on purpose. But he didn't come up to talk. Another time I sat in the garden with a bottle of wine, listening to Liszt, until I got cold and tired and went back in. This was the routine until the day before my departure, when I knocked on the dividing door and went downstairs.

Tariq was reading at the table. I sat across from him. He put his book down and we watched Tulip preening on top of her roost. Since I'd last been downstairs, he had created foraging toys from empty pill bottles and attached them to the rungs of the cage; they dangled beneath her like chimes.

"Does the gold hat fit in your suitcase?" he finally asked.

"Technically it's a cap-crown," I told him. "Wardrobe takes care of it."

Tulip dismounted to her tray, where she busied herself licking a piece of mango. "We'll be going soon, too," he said.

"Where to?" I asked.

"Back to work."

"But . . . where will you stay?"

"At a friend's; he's abroad." He glanced outside. "He has a big yard. She's always wanted an aviary."

"You can stay here as long as you want." I fidgeted with the hair elastic on my wrist. "I won't be around much anyway."

Tulip took a chunk of fruit in her foot and waved it at Tariq.

"No thanks," he said.

But she kept waving the mango until he took a piece, then she wrapped her toes around what was left and kept chewing.

I asked what his mother would do once he moved.

"I told her she can come stay with me awhile," he said.

"She must be overjoyed," I said. "For you."

He smiled, saying he'd never seen his mother joyful. "But we're all relieved," he added.

We heard the sound of a motorbike in the driveway. Then Reno was at the French doors, opening them.

"Do you lovebirds have plans?" I asked.

Tariq got up then. "Sorry, man. I'm tied up," he told Reno. "Take Dawn."

"Do you want to see the motel?" Reno asked me. "It's still pretty dingy."

"I have an early flight," I replied. "I need to pack."

Tariq pushed us together. "Go," he told me. "Live a little."

"I'll give you two a minute." Reno looked at his boots and left again through the garden.

I stared at my tree. Soon small apples would grow, and this year I would pick them and make preserves. "I have no desire to go," I told Tariq.

"You need to try new things," he said.

We heard the bike's engine again. "Why have you been avoiding me?" I finally asked.

He picked one of Tulip's ribbons up off the floor. "To let you focus."

"Yet you want me to get on a vehicle that's going to fill my mouth with silt."

He wrapped the ribbon around a finger. "We have a vet appointment," he said, nodding at Tulip. Turning my way again, he exhaled heavily, adding, "Humour him. He's a good man. And he did come all this way."

With a lump in my throat, I went upstairs and got a scarf to protect my face, then met Reno out front. Not making any small talk I got on and gave him a tap when I was ready.

First we rode through residential neighbourhoods, then down the highway, past factories and concrete buildings at city limits. I kept my hands on his waist as he accelerated. Then came that feeling of flight where we feathered slightly off the pavement, and my mind cleared, and my worries blew away like dust.

We took a secondary road, passing truck-stop diners, antique markets, and billboards for places that no longer existed. "People will take this route again," Reno yelled, "when they get tired of the fast-food highway." Soon after he pulled into a gravel parking lot by some harvested fields and killed the ignition.

The motel was a greyish two-storey building nestled in cedars, fronted by the shell of a pool. A diamond-shaped sign in the lot said Big's Motel. All around were open fields with grazing cattle and bird boxes along fence posts.

I scanned the never-ending openness. "So this is home."

"Jo suggested renaming it the Skylark," Reno said.

We got off the bike and he showed me what he envisioned as the lodge, which was more like a barn, and the main house where the retired owner had lived with his family. There was no doubt it was rundown. But it had a gable roof and a covered porch and big windows. Nearby, a tire swing hung from a tree. I told Reno I could see him there with a wife and kids and a dog.

"Tariq mentioned you want kids," he said.

As some clouds moved along, a low sun hit the house, bathing it in warm soft light. "Someday," I told him.

"Same," he said. "I just need to find a gal who blindsides me. And get her to fall for me."

Walking through the dry grass and breathing in the country air, I thought how Reno was brave to give up what he had and start over. "You're really taking a chance out here," I said.

The corners of his mouth turned up, and his eyes went from grey to greenish. He picked some trash up off the ground and looked out at the vast tract of land. "I figure it's important to change it up. Even after you've been on a path a long time."

We went back to the motel and opened the doors to air out the rooms. He showed me a few, explaining how he would remodel them. I sat on a bed in a room with a heart-shaped hot tub, the window onto the road gritty like an old photo. No cars passed. You only heard the wind and horses neighing.

"When's your first concert?" he asked and sat down beside me.

"The day after tomorrow."

A chrome bike flew past, then another, and a few minutes later several more, a shining pod flashing before our eyes. Reno grinned. "Told you," he said. Then he became serious again. "We've been taking rides. Don't know if he mentioned it."

"Will you check on him while I'm gone?"

"Course," he said.

I pointed to his neck tattoo, which I had thought was a design until then. Closer, I could see letters forming a phrase. "Were you in a gang?" I asked.

"Nothing that cool." He laughed. "Just a frat."

"Italian?" I asked.

"Latin," he replied. "While I breathe, I hope."

When I asked him what he had studied, he said only that he was the first in his family to go to university and that everyone was proud of him, even though he'd dropped out. "How did you end up —" I began.

"A lowly orderly?" he interjected. "I did it because night shifts paid well. Not because I cared. But then, you know, you get attached." He looked out at the empty road again. "Anyway. That's all there is to me."

He got up and I followed him outside, and we walked the length of the building and locked the doors. Then he turned to the large wood structure behind the motel. "Imagine a music school there," he said.

"In the barn?" I asked. "Who would come here?"

"There's a lake through those trees," he pointed. "To fish and swim. Would that lure you?"

I looked around and told him no.

"Give me a year," he said.

The sun had gone down. Red-orange remnants streaked the sky. Reno handed me my helmet and I looked back at the motel, the barn, and its accompanying home. "This place reminds me of somewhere," I said.

"Where's that?" he asked.

As the colour above us dimmed then burned away to something impenetrable, the fantasy farm picture from the chemo ward came back to me. "Nowhere," I told him.

We rode back to the city in the dark. When we pulled up at the house, we could see Tariq at the kitchen table. He saw us, too, and came to the window with Tulip, raising his hand in a wave.

"He looks good, don't you think?" I commented.

"Sure," Reno said. "Real good." He put my helmet away. "See you in a couple months."

"Good luck with the Skylark," I said.

He ran a hand across the night. "The Skylark Motor Inn. Yeah, that's it." He hesitated like he wanted to say something else. Then he shook his head at the ground, adjusted his gloves, saluted me, and rode off.

Inside, Tariq was emptying the dishwasher. Tulip scrambled off when I approached. "We're running low on supplies," he said. "We borrowed noodles."

"You might as well move up here," I told him. "Until you go."

I put water on to boil and helped with the dishes. The kettle emitted a scream. "That thing has a terrible whistle," Tariq said. "Right, Tulip?"

She was busy climbing the curtain but looked back and squawked.

"This kettle gives whistling a bad name." He poured the hot water into the pot as I dropped a teabag in. "We'll get you a new one before we leave."

We sat on the couch and drank in silence. Tulip reached the top of the curtain, and the cat across the street appeared at its window; beneath it pale flowers glowed like fireflies.

I glanced at Tariq, then down at the rug's deep colours interwoven with lighter threads. The more I studied its patterning, the more hidden images I saw. There was a fruit tree with half-open buds. There were dogs and peacocks.

"I hope to be here," he said, "when you next perform."

"It doesn't matter," I told him.

There was a white stone on the table among Tulip's things, perfect in its oval form. He picked it up and turned it around in his hand. "It's all about the egg, isn't it. Coming full circle and all that."

"Ask her." I nodded at his bird.

He pressed the stone into my hand. "To new beginnings," he said and emptied his cup. "You probably need to finish packing."

There were things I wanted to tell him. But all that came out was "I look forward to my kettle."

Tariq leaned forward and his lips brushed my cheek, then the other. "Alvida," he said, which meant goodbye, farewell, until next time, but which I always thought sounded like "All my life."

He stood and got Tulip. Once she settled on his hand, she fluffed her feathers and raised her beak, appearing almost regal. Then they were gone through the dividing door, which closed on its own behind them.

31

The tour began in Boston. There were twenty of us on the program and my colleagues had new headshots. They'd been made to look younger than they were. I also noticed that I was slated to sing early in the lineup with the unknown novice singers.

On performance day I didn't speak. Entering Aida's mind on the car service to the House, I arrived two hours before curtain. Walking in, I could already hear the others doing their vocal exercises. In my dressing room, I turned on the humidifier and made tea. I started warming up to release any tension in my jaw, neck, and shoulders and practiced my blocking in front of the mirror. Then there was a knock at the door and the makeup artist came in with her case on wheels, followed by Judith.

Soon after, Wardrobe arrived with my costume. They pinned my hair and slipped a long black mane over it, fastening the tall cap over the wig. "Give her more eyelashes," Judith told the women, glancing up from her phone. "And blush. She's too waxy." She returned to her scrolling. "They're all here," she said. "The influencers. The critics. This is it, Dawnsey. Make us proud." She stood to go and gave me an air kiss. "In bocca al lupo," she said. In the wolf's mouth.

"Crepi," I replied.

Alone again, I fine-tuned my resonance, overenunciating my Italian. Then I ran down the hall to the piano and gave myself a few notes, returning to the dressing room as the lights dimmed in the concert hall. At that point, Wardrobe passed through again to put my gown on, squeezing me into so many layers that I couldn't see myself. From then on, I walked around the small room and asked Verdi for his blessing, concentrating on Aida's raw emotion until I heard my loudspeaker cue, and someone knocking at the door.

I held my fabrics up and followed the assistant down narrow halls to the busy stage area. At the edge of the curtain, I focused on my breathing, while the Don Giovanni preceding me bellowed his final notes and got dragged off to hell. When the applause for the baritone ended and the stagehands rushed to replace his brimstone pit with my backdrop, someone shoved a sceptre in my hand and cued me to take my place.

I walked to my mark, temple and sphinxes flanking me on either side. Then the curtains rose and there was the audience, a faceless mass from under the lighting. The orchestra began, then I launched into Aida's ascending cries, projecting over the musicians and spectators, beyond the theatre walls.

With each phrase, my singing acquired power. I acted Aida's inner turmoil with perfection until the climax, where my vocal melody reached its pinnacle and nearly the entire orchestra joined in as Aida realized, with terror, what she had done. At the last crescendo, I deliberately held my line a fraction too long before releasing it, attaining my final sigh-like note as my temple transformed into a tomb. Then I took a reverent bow and floated away.

The applause subsided more quickly than I thought it would, as the next performer was heralded downstage. We were a factory of voices going on one after the other. An assembly line of arias.

I returned to the dressing room where Judith was waiting for me. "You nailed it," she said. "They'll be hard pressed to find faults." She stepped aside as Wardrobe helped me to undress.

"That's it?" I asked.

"It's a solid comeback." She spoke more to herself than to me. "I don't think we could ask for more."

My layers disappeared, and I was left looking at a version of myself I no longer recognized. Instead of feeling invigorated, I felt emptied. My performance had been flawless yet trained, my voice disconnected from me.

Judith waited, her hand on the door handle. She had more important headlining artists in the show. "Join me?" she asked.

She knew I never watched others sing. I told her no.

"Meet us at the reception, then," she said. "Mingle and network."

"I'm tired," I told her. "I think I'll rest."

"Optics, Dawn," she said, adjusting her brass choker.

I promised to attend the next after-party, and she nodded and left. I could hear her heels clicking down the hall, hurrying, hurrying.

I went back to the hotel and slept. And got on another plane. And performed the same song over and over again. And Judith was right. Any mention of my singing in reviews was positive. But most didn't mention me at all.

In the bigger centres we offered matinees, two performances in one day. We travelled to Philadelphia, Washington, and Chicago. After the Eastern cities, Judith returned home to other business. With her departure, I no longer felt the pressure to attend the nightly gatherings, instead leaving the theatres quickly for some air or a bite to eat or simply to go to bed.

We crossed the country and made our way back again, further south, through Los Angeles, Phoenix, and Santa Fe. Thrust back into placelessness, I went from one city to the next to the point where I forgot where I was and didn't care. By the time we reached the southern states, I was depleted. My throat was bothering me and the cortisone injections weren't helping. The more I sang, the more my vocal tract turned against me.

One night, after a gruelling performance involving acid reflux, I pushed my way out steel doors leading to trash bins at the back of the theatre and came out beneath a sky so pink, I reached into my bag for sunglasses.

By then I was a pro at undressing and working with Wardrobe, to return my outfit and escape in under ten minutes. It was still early evening. The sun was going down. The air was hot and humid and breathing it in felt good. Since the building was in a park, I decided to take a walk.

A lot of families were out enjoying the summer night. I looked at signage, reading this and that about Austin. This was Austin. I approached the next person I saw and told him what I was looking for, and he pointed, saying I was less than ten minutes away.

I hurried as the sky deepened to fuchsia. Soon I could see streams of people walking toward the downtown lake, so many it was like there wasn't even a bridge, only bodies holding each other up in an arc. I made my way through the crowd until I found a place to stand in the middle and waited there as the sky turned indigo. And then they came.

The bats emerged from crevices under the structure. First there were dozens, then hundreds and thousands. You could hear their wingbeats like a pulse, a heartbeat, an orchestral score of notes coming off a page, fluttering, swelling, the air alive with movement.

I heard someone say one and a half million each night at sundown. There was a smell and a high chirping. I stayed watching with the others on the bridge as the sky swirled black, and still they flew.

The surrounding park was full of life.

There were street performers and musicians and food trucks, acrobats and popcorn carts and magicians. I got a snow cone and found a bench. I would tell him what I had seen. And I had other things to say, too. I recited it all in my mind. There was no reason to hold off anymore. We were adults. These things happened. The scenario was banal compared to the messed-up tales of opera.

As if on cue, my phone rang. "Guess what I just did?" I told him, tilting my head back to a few stars, these points of falling light. "You were right. It was unbelievable."

Only it wasn't Tariq at the other end of the line. It was Ashraf, his voice flat. "I knew you wouldn't pick up if I used mine."

I stiffened, my throat tightening. "What do you want?"

"My brother has died," he said.

32

I took a night flight home. The house didn't look like ours in the morning twilight. I didn't want to go inside. When he heard the taxi pull up, Ash came out. I put my suitcase down, and my crying husband approached me on the driveway, and we hugged through the low hum of crickets.

Inside, Mina sat on her rug with her back against the couch, staring blankly ahead. She didn't respond when I crouched and touched her arm. "She hasn't moved since yesterday," Ash said.

The living room was covered in droppings and smeared banana. "Where's Tulip?" I asked.

The place was freezing. I turned the air conditioning off and draped Mina's shawl over her legs, positioning a cushion behind her back. Then I went to the dividing door and put my forehead on it a long time before opening it.

I heard a lot of scratching coming from the roost as I descended into the walkout. It was dark, the blinds drawn over the doors. When I turned a light on, Tulip tucked her head under her wing as if the sudden brightness hurt.

The newsprint beneath her was torn to shreds, her cage filthy, her bowls empty. When I unlatched her door and tried to coax her out, she turned away, plucking at her chest.

In contrast to Tulip's roost, the rest of the walkout was spotless. Her flowered suitcase was at the stairs as if ready to be transported, along with her other belongings stacked beside it. The bed was the way I had made it the day Tariq arrived, with decorative pillows over my mother's quilt. On the night table, a rose drooped in a vase, its colour more intense than I recalled. I set fallen petals on Tulip's tray then filled her bowls, but she still didn't move.

I opened the French doors, removed my shoes, and walked barefoot to the rosebush. The flowers had deepened almost to red and someone had been tending the garden. All through the yard the plants grew and bloomed, their sweet scents mixing into the warm air.

The sun was rising, the sky changing to orange. I stumbled to a sitting position in the grass. I wanted proof. But it had been three days already. As with Majid Khan, once Tariq was gone, Mina would have made sure his corpse was washed, shrouded, and buried before the following sunset.

Ash came out and lit a cigarette and sat beside me.

"Why didn't you tell me sooner?" I asked.

"It was an embolism. We didn't know."

"But the chemo worked. He was fine."

Ash shut his eyes. "Half the people on that shit die from blood clots. He'd started another round. He was on it again."

"Wait . . . but why?"

"Why do you think?"

The muscles between my ribs cramped and spasmed. "Did he —"

"Horne said he would have passed out. Knowing him, though, he probably suffered. Before it got to that point."

My husband blew smoke rings in the air. I glanced at the open doors to the shadow of Tulip's cage.

"Did she see his body?" I asked.

"I thought I told you," Ash replied. "She's the one who found him."

"I mean Tulip."

"The bird?" He stubbed his cigarette into the grass.

"Did she see your brother? Before they took him away."

"How should I know? I was on a fifteen-hour flight. Trying to get home before my mom put him in the ground."

"Where is Anabelle staying?"

"She left straight after the burial. Had a new man at her side. Hardly said a word to us." His phone rang then. Ash checked it and put it away.

"Don't you have to get that?" I asked.

He dropped his face in his hands. "I can't cope."

Watching my husband, I felt nothing for him. We had married too fast. Because I had to leave on a tour, and he wanted to prove his parents wrong, we had rushed things and failed.

He lay back in the grass and reached for my arm, to draw me down with him. "For old times?" he asked. In a minute he would sleep. I stood, left him in the garden, and drew the French doors closed.

When I tried coaxing Tulip out once more, she lunged at my hand. I found cranberries in the near-empty cupboards and placed the dried fruit on the chair and went upstairs again.

My mother-in-law hadn't moved. I sat beside her and put my hand over hers.

"I am alone," she said in a small voice.

I mentioned her other son who loved her very much. Soon, I reminded her, she would also have a new daughter-in-law to torment.

She sniffed. "And Burberry," she added. "This is baby."

"They're naming their child Burberry?"

Mina nodded.

"Are you sure it's not Barbara?"

"Ashraf say Burberry. Like barb wire."

Ash came up the stairs then. "I'll take you home, Amiji," he told his mother, speaking on in Urdu before turning to me in a hushed tone. "Roya's there preparing everything. She needs sleep."

We helped her to stand. Mina moved slowly, grimacing with each step. Ash collected her purse and some pills and a six pack from the fridge.

"I'll be back later," he said. "I have to get his things from storage. And contact the banks and our lawyer. There's so much to do. And I can't stay long. The baby's due —" He stopped himself and apologized. My husband had aged by a decade. He had new wrinkles. He'd put on weight around his middle, and his forehead was dotted with rash bumps.

"It's okay," I told him.

Once they left I went back downstairs.

Tulip had come out of her cage. She was perched on top of it and was looking out at the yard, Tariq's empty pill containers dangling beneath her.

Parts of her chest were bare again, like when she'd first arrived. But her tail was still a brilliant red, and her gold eyes glistened against her grey body. When I held my hand out level with her chest, she turned away.

"I don't know what you saw," I told her. "But he didn't abandon us. He died."

Her feathers flared like a porcupine raising its quills. Then she doubled back to the corner of the room and flew at me.

I shielded my face and crouched behind the table but she attacked me again, knifing my arms with her beak until I ran upstairs and slammed the door as she rapped against it.

There was a lot of blood, but the cuts weren't deep. I cleaned and bandaged them and went through the yard to the French doors.

Tulip had relocated to my chair and was pulling the stuffing out. I knocked on the glass. She eyed me and flattened her feathers.

When I stepped inside, she flew onto the kitchenette cupboards for a bomb dive, forcing me out again.

I heard the Warblers out front. I had called Ben from the airport, but instead of going to them I leaned against the side of the house and slid down the wall, until they came and found me.

As they circled around, I studied their faces in the harsh light of the sun. Ben kept his shades on. Walt looked ancient. Reno rubbed his forehead like it hurt, Jo's eyes were red, Georgie's chin wobbled. For once, no one had anything to say.

"She won't eat," I said as they examined my arms.

Jo accompanied Ben to the French doors and he went in alone. Soon we could hear him talking to Tulip. Then Georgie pulled scissors from her purse. "I'd like to go to the cemetery," she said and walked to the rosebush and clipped.

Reno blew his nose. Walt pulled out a handkerchief and dabbed his eyes. When Ben came outside with Tulip, everyone approached them. I got up then and stormed into the walkout.

I pushed shelves over and emptied drawers, dumping everything on the ground. I tossed Tulip's suitcase and turned her boxes upside down. I tore through the cupboards, searching for something left behind until Jo rushed in and held me down.

"What's gotten into you?" she asked.

Walt came in after her, bending with difficulty to pick a few things up. "I was the same when we found out about Mae," he said. "I was so full of rage."

Then Georgie appeared at the door with her jumbo bouquet. "Let's pay our respects," she said.

I directed Jo to the small cemetery in the suburbs and we pulled up next to the only other car, which was Ashraf's. "My husband is here," I told them. They craned their necks to see.

"That's him?" Georgie asked. Ben requested a description. "He's sporty," she said. "Not suited to Dawn at all."

I walked to the Khan plots, arriving at a mound of earth that looked too compact. A wood stake served as his marker. He would have had no coffin, his body positioned facing Mecca, his bones blending in with the soil. There were no ornaments or wreaths; the place held a simple dignity.

Ash stood behind his mother, who knelt in the space between her husband's grave and her son's. "She insisted on coming," he said, taking me aside. Then he leaned in and kissed me. "Do you think we're making a mistake?"

I looked into his eyes. "I think it's time to finalize our separation."

Ash stared up at the sky and nodded. Then he noticed the group waiting by the car. "Who are those people?" he asked.

I watched the Warblers huddled in their small circle. "My friends," I told him.

After a few minutes, Mina stood and we led her away from the graves. At the gate I introduced Ash, and he shook hands with everyone.

"Maybe one day I can show you Mae's stone," Walt told Mina as he helped her into her son's car.

Ash said he would stay the night at his mother's. Once he drove away, I led everyone to Tariq's plot.

It was getting warm out. Walt sat on his walker and the rest of us knelt. Ben put Tulip on his knee and reached out to feel the earth. Georgie distributed flowers, and Reno passed a bottle of water around. From a sole tree in the middle of the cemetery, a bird sang. Ben said it was an oriole.

"Let's share a memory," Jo said.

"We talked about the rainbow bridge," Ben told us. "Where you reunite with your pets when you die."

Walt whistled a slow, wistful melody. When I asked him what the song was, he said Sinatra. "'I'll Be Seeing You.' Tariq asked me to whistle it to you. I forgot."

"To me?" I asked.

"We were at Birchwood," Walt continued. "He wanted to see the hospice. We walked through the grove and I did that tune and he said, 'You should whistle that at Dawn.'"

"He meant sunrise," Georgie said.

"She is the sunrise." Reno stood. "Isn't there a saying," he asked Jo, "about whistling over someone's grave?"

"It's whistling past the graveyard," Jo replied. "Which means being courageous."

"Or clueless," Georgie said.

"Where is our box, Georgina?" Jo asked her.

"Buried in Tadoussac," Georgie said. "It was Tariq's idea. It's somewhere under the beach there. Or it washed away. That's what we discussed. How life has a way of washing away from us." She undid and redid her wristbands to a repeating tearing sound until Walt reached out and stilled her hands.

Reno crumpled the bottle of water. "We talked about how the cure for dying's often worse than dying."

I sensed my anger rising. "Are you saying he shouldn't have kept up with the treatments?"

Reno looked out at the tree. We couldn't hear the oriole anymore. "I've seen my share of people go through pain unnecessarily. For those they love."

"I think what you mean is, fifty years ago when it was time to go, you went," Walt said. "There wasn't all this interference. People suffered less and stayed home with family."

"We met for a beer and talked about Everett." Jo lay a rose down. Then everyone else did the same.

"We talked about requiems." I put my hands on the mound of earth and turned to Tulip. "This is him."

"Depending on what you believe," Jo said.

"Tariq was an existentialist," Georgie said. "Therefore all this" — she waved her hand about — "is for Mina."

Tulip stepped off Ben's lap and climbed the mound, her every step tentative. She walked the length of the small hill and looked around at the other graves. She went up to the wooden stake and pecked it and backed away. Then she started digging.

Ben wiped the soil off his legs as it flew. She wouldn't stop. She used her beak and feet, burrowing deeper.

"She's going to exhume him," Georgie said.

I reached out to bring her back, but she lunged and bit me. "I don't understand," I told them. "She regurgitated on me. I even gave her a shower."

"She probably blames you," Ben said.

When I offered her my hand again, Tulip shrieked and took on her warlike stance. As Reno stood in front of me to block her, I lost it. "This could be your fault," I yelled at Tariq's bird. "What if you gave him some kind of infection? What if your bumblefoot caused this?"

"Whoa now," Walt said.

My phone rang then. It was Judith. I moved away to take the call. "How much longer, do you think?" she asked.

The tour was almost over. I stared at the grave and began to explain that I wouldn't be able to return, until Georgie approached and grabbed the phone. "A few days max," she told her.

"That's fine," I heard Judith say while Georgie kicked at my shins to keep me away. "Just get a date to me asap."

Georgie hung up and handed my phone back.

"He'd be disappointed if you didn't finish." This came from Jo. They were all watching me from the graveside.

I looked at Tulip, still digging. "She needs a home," I told them.

"If I was younger . . ." Walt began and reached out to Tariq's bird. This snapped her out of her trance. She scurried off the mound and stepped onto his fingers. In her mourning she had nothing against anyone but me.

"I'd take her, if it weren't for all the construction," Reno said.

"How long's she got again?" Georgie asked.

"Another fifty." Jo said. "With the possibility of an additional ten."

"Sorry, love," Georgie said. "No can do."

"Tariq told me she can't tolerate commercial flights." Ben sighed. "And my new place is mini. It would be cruel."

"Mine, too," Jo said.

Walt rolled and unrolled his beret and cleared his throat. "I get the sense Mina could do with some company."

"You're certainly noticing a lot about Mina these days," Georgie commented.

"My mother-in-law isn't keen on animals," I told them.

"She'd have to be passed on again when Mina's time comes," Reno added.

Ben collected Tulip from Walt and put a finger to his lips and made the *sshh* sign. Then we readied ourselves to go. "We need to bring everything," I told them.

"Why?" Georgie asked.

"Look around you," Jo said. "It's not done here."

"You should have removed the thorns." Walt rubbed at his fingers.

"Up yours, Walter." Georgie gathered the flowers and we left the cemetery. Then I took a stem from her bundle, walked back to Tariq's grave, and lay the rose there.

33

That night I wanted to grieve him. But Tulip's furious vocalizations kept me downstairs. No matter how I tried reasoning with her, she wouldn't let up until morning, when I opened her door, and she silently refused to come out.

While I paced around her roost she paced within it, up and down the driftwood, pretending I didn't exist. When I approached to offer a slice of fruit, she hooked her beak onto the metal door and pulled it shut. When I turned the radio on, she screeched over the music until I turned it off again.

And when she did finally climb out of her cage, head bobbing as she raced to the kitchenette, I noticed the work she had accomplished there, where a good chunk of baseboard had been turned into woodchips. I kicked her suitcase. In retaliation she gnawed on the legs of the table. Then she sauntered over to my mother's quilt.

"Don't you dare," I told her.

She puffed her feathers out and pinned her eyes on me as she began mangling the soft fabric with her beak. As I tried pulling the quilt away, she became more combative, scratching and slashing. Then she whacked the vase off the nightstand and crossed over to my dilapidated chair, lacerating what remained of the fabric.

I held the quilt in my arms and put my face in it. But it smelled sterile, all trace of him washed away. Watching Tulip tear around the walkout just as I had, thinking about her long lifespan and mine, I suddenly felt exhausted. I couldn't look at her without thinking about Tariq.

I tossed a rope and she rushed after it, flinging it around in her jaw. I left her there like that and went upstairs to place an ad online.

An hour later a woman called. She was interested but had questions. Was the bird banded and did it have a hatching certificate? I went downstairs to confirm the tiny ring around Tulip's ankle, then looked in the box of paperwork by the stairs. Noticing Tariq's binder there, I felt a brief, sharp pain. Yes, I told her. She had her papers. She then asked if the bird was a plucker. From where I stood Tulip's feathers were still thick in places. I told her that there were no bald patches that I could see. Could she fly to save herself if she fell? she asked. I said her wings were fine. But when she asked me if she was a biter, I hesitated, and she hung up.

The second interested party was at the house soon after, a small woman who looked like a bird herself. When I brought her down to the walkout, she went straight for Tulip, cooing at her sweetly. "Hellooo, pretty. Aren't you a sight."

Tulip shuffled into a corner but the woman swooped her up and locked her in her arm, closing a hand over her beak and petting her like a cat. "This one's healthy," she said. Then she turned her around and upside down and took pictures.

When her phone rang, she passed Tulip to me before I could object. I drew back and extended my arms, waiting for the razor chomp, but instead all I felt was a light and trembling body.

"Congo grey. One grand, cage included," I heard the woman say outside. "I can drop it off in ten." Tulip flew from my arms to the ground and rushed forward, sideways, and in circles to the bathroom. The woman came back in. "You said no charge so long as I take the apparatuses, right?"

"Two thousand," I told her.

"Your ad said free."

"She's in demand."

After the woman swore and left, I crouched and approached the half-open bathroom door. But every time I tried going in, Tulip hissed and lunged.

I met our third potential adopter at the donut shop, a twenty-something ex-Marine who seemed to know a lot about parrots. He glanced at the bandages on my arms and asked if we were having trouble bonding, and I said that I had been left with her unexpectedly. He said he took animals in from people like me all the time. Then he told me how he had a game where Monty went around the apartment and the other animals ran and flew to exercise their natural instincts.

"Who's Monty?" I asked.

"My python." He nodded toward his sedan. "Do you want to meet him? He's domesticated."

I thanked him and said I had changed my mind.

"Your loss," he replied and pushed away from the table.

It was all new staff at the donut shop. I bought some holes and drove to a place called Bird Room next, a rescue on an acreage owned by a smiling young couple to whom I recounted the situation. "She won't last much longer with me," I said.

"We understand," they told me. "She's welcome here."

The woman named Leah gave me a tour. The Bird Room consisted of a heated building lined with hundreds of cages but it wasn't noisy, aside from a little chirping and squawking. Leah explained that most of the residents were quiet because they were rehabilitating from trauma. Then she talked about overcrowding. "We're doing our best," she said. "But there's hundreds of thousands of unwanted birds." As we walked, she pointed and named the species. Canaries and finches, cockatiels, lovebirds, parakeets, and parrotlets, all colourful and several to a cage. They hopped up to the bars as we passed by.

Then came the medium-sized parrots who moved around less animatedly, and at the end of the line were the large parrots who didn't share accommodations. Some were twice the size of Tulip. Leah said these were their difficult personalities and she introduced me to an emaciated macaw named Carl, who had been carving a hole through his chest with his beak. When he growled, her eyes teared up. "Euthanasia would be the humane approach," she said. "But folks would be appalled if we suggested it." I followed her gaze down the hall of half-dead bodies and thanked her for the tour, and she muttered a few words of encouragement.

But as I returned to the car, she ran out after me. "You could always try Sunnyside," she said. "Their ecletus just passed and they're looking for a replacement. They called me yesterday. But none of our guys are . . . suitable." She provided directions to the garden centre and I drove there right away.

Even from the parking lot Sunnyside held promise. The log building was surrounded by trees, greenhouses, and outdoor art. Inside was a jungle of lush plants and flowers.

I spoke with a rosy-faced manager named Bev and told her Leah had sent me. "We're all still grieving Sweetpea," Bev said, tucking a grey curl behind her ear before showing me pictures of a deep red bird with a stunning violet belly, whose feathers looked like fur. "We had her thirty years. Kids loved her. She brought customers in."

"Tulip has red plumage," I told her. "And a long life expectancy."

"Well, okay," she said. "Any recommendation from Leah works for us." We went over some paperwork. When she asked if Tulip was amiable, I told her yes, adding that she whistled opera beautifully.

"Amazing," Bev said as we walked through the gardens to the dead bird's dwelling area. There, among tropical plants and humungous blossoms were perches and toys, a colossal roost and a trickling fountain, and banana trees.

"Don't mind the mess," Bev said. "We're in the process of disinfecting."

"I think she'd be happy here," I told her.

"Bring her anytime." She smiled. "We'll see if we can get comfortable with each other and go from there."

I shook Bev's hand and sped home.

When I entered through the French doors, all was quiet inside. "It's just me," I said, glancing around. "Try not to lose your mind."

Tulip wasn't in the bathroom anymore. Her fruit remained untouched and I noticed feathers on the ground. I looked under the furniture and heard a tinkling bell. The sound came from the roost. She was on the cage floor plucking at her stomach, her tail tapping the bell as she bent forward.

"I've found your Eden," I told her.

She kept plucking while I put on Satie and gathered a few of her things. Her favourite stuffed animals and chew toys, her sketchbook, puzzles, and placemat. Her nesting blanket and beak-sharpening stone and her box of roller skates.

"It's a garden," I added. "Like where your ancestors came from."

She sidestepped to the tip of her driftwood and looked out at the apple tree. I prepared her carrier, placing a donut hole in it and positioning it near her roost. A minute later she went in, and we made our way back to Sunnyside.

Bev was surprised to see me again so soon. I gave her Tulip's papers and her box of belongings and Tariq's binder, and once we reached Sweetpea's roost, I unzipped the carrier door.

It took a long time for Tulip to come out, and when she did, she looked around and up at Bev and me, then went back into her carrier.

"I don't see any red," Bev said.

I told her that she liked oatmeal before bed and that she vocalized most at sunset. I told her that she might be standoffish at first, but that she had been fiercely loyal to her companion.

"Wait a sec," Bev said, "you can't just leave her here."

"Call me if there are problems," I said. Then I crouched down to Tulip. "Goodbye," I told her.

She blinked at me, her yellow eyes wild like tiny sunrises. She opened her beak as if to speak, then closed it again. And then she turned away.

I could hear Bev calling after me while trying to talk to her new acquaintance. I could hear her paging for assistance, then cooing, and I could hear the laughter of children arriving.

After brushing stray feathers from the car, I drove home.

Once downstairs, I dragged my ruined chair against the bay window, pushing the roost out of the way. Then I undressed, got under my mother's quilt, and wept.

34

Ash came back in the morning while I was packing. When he cast a wary glance across the bedroom before entering, I told him that his brother's bird had been adopted. He thanked me, saying it was one less thing to deal with. Then he asked if I was finishing the tour. He was catching his plane soon, too, and would return in a few weeks.

I looked around at everything we had accumulated. "I don't care what you do," I told him. "Just put my things in storage."

"We agree to sell, then?" he asked.

I nodded, knowing that I would accept contracts in other cities and countries, anywhere, to stay away.

After he left to make some calls, I brought my suitcase downstairs and walked through the house one last time, the dream home where I thought we would raise a family. Entering the living room, I found Mina on the couch with photo albums in her lap. She looked up like she didn't recognize me.

"You should go to Tokyo," I told her. "There's nothing here for us anymore."

While she wiped her eyes, I slid one of the albums into my handbag. Then Ashraf joined us, and I told my ex-husband and his mother goodbye. It was hard to believe we might not see each other again. But I had no grief to spare for my old life.

My car pulled away. They waved from the living room window, and I waved back.

I took an early flight to New York, the last venue of the tour.

When I got to the hotel, my room wasn't ready so I went for a walk, winding up at the Conservatory Water near 72nd Street. And there in Central Park, I saw him.

He was standing by the pond holding a radio control, manoeuvring a model boat on the water. I called out to him. Eventually Tariq looked up from the sails decorating the small lake. He didn't seem surprised to see me and smiled. But as I made my way over to him, I got tangled in a school group. Then a balloon man blocked my path, and by the time I reached the other side of the pond, he was gone. I looked everywhere for him. I walked in the park for hours, then watched from the lake's café terrace, hoping he would reappear, until one by one families and tourists removed their boats from the water.

Walking back to the hotel, I stopped in at an antique bookshop and asked the seller if he had anything by Agnes Woodward. The man typed the name into his computer. "Opera singer?" he asked.

"Whistler," I replied.

"Bio says opera plus birdsong plus whistling." He got up from his stool and went to the back of the store, returning with a small, thin volume. "Published right here," he said, leafing through it. I ran my hand along the russet cloth with gilt-titling and paid him.

At the hotel I lay down and stared at the wall a long time before pulling the album from my bag. There, on each page, were more apparitions of Tariq. Pictures from student gatherings, pictures of him in cosmopolitan cities and rural landscapes. Pictures of him standing on archways, suspended over water, valleys, and forests.

I started to hyperventilate and phoned Georgie. "I think I'm hallucinating," I told her.

"That's grief. Use it."

"I can't do this," I said.

"Get a grip," she replied. "Your show's being live-streamed. We're all watching. Okay? Okay." She hung up on me.

I slapped myself in the face and regained control of my anxiety. I took a hot bath and did inhalations over the steam. I got out, rubbed the mirror, and faced myself. Then I pulled my hair into a simple bun and put on the plain black evening gown meant for receptions, and took the car service to the House.

Judith was there already. She never missed New York premieres. When I found her in the cramped dressing area in one of her dazzling ensembles, I made my request. "Absolutely not," she said. "There's no time for sound checks. You'll throw everyone off." When I told her I wouldn't go on otherwise, she left to make a few calls. "You're going to ruin yourself over this," she said when she returned. "I've got five covers vying for your spot if it backfires."

Hair and makeup came and went, with nothing to do. Then the assistant arrived and led me backstage. I was still slotted in the first half of the show. When the baritone before me finished and the musicians lowered their instruments, the program change was announced and Maestro Boom bowed in my direction and stepped aside.

A piano was rolled onstage. I walked on after my accompanist took his place, poised and waiting. On the screen behind us was an evening sky with faint traces of cloud. At least they had minimized things at my request for no orchestra or set. No costume or lights.

I had experience singing in German. I would manage.

There was enough of a soft glow that the accompanist and I could see each other. I glanced at him and he nodded, fingers hovering over the keys. He played, then I sang, and in that darkness Schubert's devastating lied on night and dreams carried me beyond sorrow. I didn't hold back or care what tore and, by some miracle, made it to the end of "Nacht und Träume."

No one even coughed. With the last notes a quiet permeated the audience, and for the first time in a long time I felt I was part of that collective held breath, experiencing the great composer's music.

Then came the standing ovation, the applause and bravas and calls of encore. I felt my chest heaving. I could breathe again. I put my hand to my pounding heart, bowed, and left the stage.

In the dressing room, my phone rang in my bag. It was my parents, who rarely watched my performances anymore. "Well done, Dawney," my father said, his voice wavering. "Glorious!" my mother yelled behind him. After speaking with them, I called Jo, and the Warblers talked all at once. "Your phrasing was flawless," Jo said.

"Tragedy plus romance, that's the key to marvellous music," Georgie cut in.

"Would you perform at my funeral?" Walt asked.

"Nice job, Daybreak," I heard Reno in the background. "You went straight for the jugular."

"Maybe you could add in the call of the loon," Ben suggested, just as Judith knocked on the door, opening it and pulling me out. It was intermission and she led me to a room of people who couldn't wait until the end of the show to meet me, she explained. I didn't know who they were, but they looked rich.

"That was divine," one woman in a silk suit said.

"The most perfect rendition ever," a man in tortoise-rimmed glasses added, wiping his eyes.

"I could listen to you all day," a man wearing an ascot told me.

Bouquets were presented. I autographed programs and accepted business cards until the guests returned to their seats, and Judith accompanied me back to the dressing room. "You've got your new signature song," she said.

I told her that I would never sing it again.

She stopped and unlatched her arm from mine. "This will launch you. It's what you've been waiting for." She waved her phone at me. "Look. We already have asks."

"I'm retiring."

"All right, no props. We both know you're a disaster around those. But a solo career of recitals. That's your future."

I thought about her proposal. But my desire for the stage was gone. I took off my dress and put on my jeans and T-shirt. "I want a different kind of life," I said.

She shook her head. "Well," she finally replied. "That was one hell of a swan song."

I thanked Judith for everything she had done for me and told her that I was going home.

"Home." She repeated the word with a vague smile, as if foreign to her. Then she looked down at her phone and rushed away.

After leaving the House, I went back through Central Park.

I searched the dim paths that ran in all directions, lit by Victorian lamps. I looked on benches and in the passing horse carriages. I walked along the water once more, and under some trees where a few bats flew like a litany. I didn't know what I thought I would find.

35

When I landed the next morning, I directed the driver to Sunnyside. As soon as I walked into the garden centre, Bev rushed over. "You need to collect your parrot," she said, grabbing my arm. "She's terrorizing the kids. People are scared to walk past her. No one can get to the oleanders and she doesn't whistle or talk."

She followed me down the green path. From a distance, on her branch surrounded by exotic vegetation, Tulip seemed in her element. She almost looked wild and free. But as I got closer, I could see that she was raising her left foot every few seconds, as if it hurt again. Her plumage was lacklustre, her stance stiff, her eyes wide with fear.

When she saw me, she bobbed her head rapidly. I put my hand beside her on the branch. She waved a leg. I moved my hand in front of it. Then, lightning fast, she stretched her foot out and her toes curled tightly around my fingers. She used her other foot to push herself off and step up, and we were one.

I bent my arm a little, while Bev shoved her carrier into my free hand and picked up her box. "Let me help you," she said, ushering us down the path. When I stopped to comment on some fig trees, she grabbed one, with "It's on the house," as she hurried us outside, helping us into the car.

The driver said he didn't mind if I kept Tulip on my hand. So we rode like that, the both of us quiet, looking out the window at the passing scenery.

When we got home, no one was there. We checked all the rooms but Ash and Mina were gone, and Tulip wouldn't leave my hand. My arm ached and I was losing circulation in my fingers, so I took her to the kitchen for a snack. There I saw the new kettle on the stove, red like her undertail. I swallowed hard and filled it, retrieved her placemat, and set her up with applesauce.

While Tulip ate, I drank tea and flipped through her binder. There was a number on the inside flap for the vet. She was looking rough so I called to make an appointment. After providing the receptionist with our names, she asked me to hold. When she came back on the line, she said, "You can come now. She'll fit you in." So I coaxed Tulip into her carrier with coconut chips, and we drove to the animal clinic.

The vet's name was Paula. We shook hands and she took the carrier and put it on the examining table. Then she peered inside and said, "Hiya, flower."

Tulip stepped out and onto her fingers right away.

"I was sorry to hear about Tariq," Paula said, pulling an envelope from a file and handing it to me. "This is for you."

She told me there was green space beside the clinic, where people sometimes waited. "After her physical, we'll do x-rays and buffer her beak," she added, raising Tulip up to her face. "Right, Tu? Your favourite."

So I left them and went out to the small park and found a bench in the shade. The cicadas were buzzing. The summer heat dried my throat. I opened the envelope and read.

Dawnjaan. Meri jaan.

This morning I looked outside and saw an owl and I thought, Death. Here it comes. It's still dark. A band is forming across the sky, a purplish bridge of light. Maybe I'm wrong. I hope to retrieve this from Paula a decade from now and slip it to Tulip for shredding. But if you've opened it, then, well.

I could beat my chest and say it's not fair. I always exercised and got seven hours sleep. I took care of my health, ate salads, never smoked, and didn't drink too often. All I know is this whole time I've been getting better, I've had this sense. That I won't. So I'm putting my affairs in order.

I heard you sing. On campus years ago, when I was teaching. One morning near my building I saw you in the grass, voice flowing like a gold thread. In the weeks that followed I saw you again and opened my windows to listen, and your music made me want more than what I had.

Then one day Ash came by and told me about the siren he met on his walk over. I'd never seen him so happy. After that, I heard about you through him. Then winter came. I didn't see you in the park. I left my position and moved on. So, no, I didn't attend your ceremony. And the reception, only briefly. Your parents are great, by the way.

If you've just done your foot stomp, don't be mad. What you taught me about opera is that breath control is key. The hardest thing to do is to hold back. If I ask myself why I didn't approach you, the answer is I would have screwed it up. I was hotheaded and reckless then. And once my brother arrived on the scene, I was too late. It would have played out with no win. A draw in a cricket match.

Over the years, I followed your career. I have your recordings and read about Tosca in the papers. By then I was already sick. Then came the months of your name appearing nowhere. And I thought, What the hell, why not go there. To see how you were doing.

To die on stage takes one song and good acting. But this disease is anything but swift. And these poisonous treatments, making me feel worse and not myself. I can't keep the *pills down. I hear words like terminal and compassionate care and think, Not for me. All that to say I'm ready.*

Which is true and not true. I'd like more conversations together, more silences, more sightings off the sea. On the other hand, I've lived. My one regret is not getting closer to people. And you're reserved, like me. But you have family now.

Which leads me to Tulip. Thank you. For changing your mind about her. If you made it to Paula's, I hope you two will be stuck with each other a long time. Did I ever tell you how I came to name her? One spring I drove out for your hometown performance of Ariadne and went to buy a rose. But at the flower shop, I noticed a bouquet enchanting in its strangeness. The florist told me they were parrot tulips. And that the meaning of tulips is perfect love. And even once they're cut and in a vase, they grow.

Yours,
Tariq

I opened another smaller piece of paper folded in a diamond.

See you later, Tulip.

I've enjoyed this life with you very much. I'm sorry I have to go.

Don't hate Dawn. It's not her fault. Be good. Make her laugh. Hahaha have a grey day.

I dream of flight, my feathered friend. I guess this means I'm getting closer to — to what? I don't know. Something up there. Soaring.

I folded the letters. There was a breeze and gulls hovered over the park. I studied their wheeling flight, listening to their harsh keening. My vision blurred as they glided by and were gone, I wondered to where, maybe a faraway body of water. My bench was no longer in the shade. I closed my eyes and raised my face to the sun until Paula called me back into the clinic.

She told me that Tulip would be fine. She gave me vitamin drops, ointment for her feet, and a neck cone in case she kept plucking, and said to return in three months. Then she got her into her carrier, handed her to me, and wished me luck. "He prepaid her appointments," she added. "Bring her around anytime. And call me if her droppings get too runny."

We said farewell to Paula and drove home. When we reached the house, we found Mina kneeling on the rug in the living room, struggling to reorganize her suitcases filled with clothing, dishes, and frames while Ashraf was in the kitchen, head in hands, documents spread all around. He glanced up before he continued skimming through forms. "He's given you his portion," he said.

I unzipped Tulip's door. She scrambled out and climbed the curtain, taking her watch at the window.

"Portion of what?" I asked.

"The house," Ash said. "Everything he invested. If you want to buy me out. I never put much down." He stacked the papers, stood, and handed them to me. "We're on the red eye." He went outside for a cigarette.

I sat next to Mina. She was folding skirts and cardigans, slipping small breakable items inside them. Plumes of smoke drifted past the window. I ran my fingers along the pale green vines in the rug. "I hated you," I told her.

"I hate you, too," she replied, placing a blue-veined hand over mine.

Then I said it before I could change my mind. "There will always be a room here for you. If Japan doesn't agree with you. Or if you want to visit."

Her kohl-streaked eyes widened just as Tulip screeched and swept down from the curtain, aiming for my mother-in-law's head. Mina ducked.

"*Done*," she said, "do not be keeping this buzzard!"

"It's your jhumkey she's after," I said, as Tulip reassumed her position on the curtain.

I did not say, I want you to tell me about your son. Every detail, memory, and story. I did not say, I want to know all his life. With time and some distance, I hoped we would express ourselves more freely.

Ash came back in. I began moving furniture aside to roll their rug, but Mina stopped me and looked to her son who sighed, then nodded.

"Too heavy," she finally said. "We keep it here."

"Are you sure?" I asked.

But she had already moved away and occupied herself folding scarves before Ash helped her to close her luggage.

When they finished, my husband came over to me and I thanked him.

"For what?" he asked.

"Goodbye, Ashraf," I said and went up to bed in broad daylight. Soon after I had climbed the stairs, I heard a *click click click* behind me.

36

How to Build an Aviary was the last chapter in Tariq's binder.

Following instructions on materials and placement was a blueprint in a plastic sleeve. I pulled it out and we studied the picture together at the kitchen table, then Tulip walked all over it, tore at the edges and chewed them until I coaxed her to her perch with a cherry.

The aviary had a vaulted top, with plenty of space for flight. Plants, dispensers, swings, and a bridge were also sketched in.

When I wondered out loud where he expected us to put such a contraption, Tulip gazed out at the backyard, to my once-again overgrown plants. Watching her, I knew I didn't need my voice garden. No flowers or herbs would help me to sing, and never had.

I dug through the drawer for a tape measure. Reno was over, helping me get the walkout reorganized. I was supposed to be making lunch. When he came up to the kitchen for water, he stopped at the table. "It's beyond my skills," I told him.

He stood at the sink and looked out the window while he drank. Then he came back and gathered the drawings. "I'll take care of it," he said and returned downstairs.

A few days later he arrived in a pickup truck with two helpers. The vehicle was full of building supplies and the men cleared the yard while Tulip and I observed from inside.

It was a record-breaking September heat wave. It hadn't cooled down in a week, not even at night. It sapped any desire to move and the air was so thick that breathing didn't feel like breathing, but Reno and the men worked all day in the sun. Even when I brought pitchers of water with sliced oranges, they kept working.

Reno had pre-cut and measured every part, which they spread out on the ground like a puzzle. First they put concrete squares down for a floor. Then they set the metal structure up piece by piece.

The enclosure was the size of a double garage with a high ceiling. It took up the whole yard, except a small spot off to the side where the men dragged the patio set. Then Reno's friends left, and I walked around the exterior of the aviary with him while he tested the strength of the bars, which were thin and pale grey.

A cage would always be a cage. But this one was infused with light and air, silvery like a castle. The neighbouring trees would bring shade. And they'd retained my flowers around the circumference of the garden, so Tulip would be surrounded by lilacs and peonies. The apple tree and the rose bush.

We added dispensers, a large swing, and enormous driftwood perches. Then I went and got Tulip. She wouldn't step up — she had only done that the one time — but she followed behind at my feet.

"It's not the jungle," I told her. "But you'll have more room in here."

Leery of new things, she walked outside the structure and we followed her around while she studied it from different angles. When she paused to peck at some clover, Reno leaned against the aviary, glancing from me to the small head in the grass. "It can always be disassembled," he said. "If you decide to move."

"Why would we move?"

"I'm saying hypothetically." He reddened and looked away, asking if he could use the shower. I told him where everything was, and he went in.

Then the Warblers arrived for our final session. I could hear them chattering as they came around the side of the house. Jo carried two big plants. Walt had a tall basin in his walker basket. Ben held a stuffed toucan and Georgie some kind of tripod lighting.

"Nice digs," Ben said as he ran his hands along the bars and stepped in.

Jo went in after him and put the plants in place. "It's not prison-like at all," she told me, looking around.

Georgie handed me the lighting she said was for potluck parties, then helped Walt roll in the basin. They put it in a corner and I brought the hose over, and we filled it. "She'll adore our sweltering summers out here," Walt said. "Or will she?" He reconsidered. "If she wasn't born in the tropics, how does that work?"

"The tropical climate's in her DNA," Ben told him.

We all stood inside the aviary then, admiring the handiwork while Tulip observed us from outside. "Reno did this?" Georgie asked.

"Pretty much," I told her.

"He must really have a thing for you," she said.

"Or for Tulip," Walt added.

We tried coaxing her in, but not even Ben could convince her. When she crossed the yard and climbed the table, we joined her. Then Reno came out and sat with us.

You could tell no one felt like practicing. Jo poured the glycerine water. Georgie pulled a battery-operated fan from her purse and aimed it at her face.

"I got us a gig at Birchwood," Walt said.

"Yippee," Georgie mumbled.

"Are you taking her free flying soon?" Ben asked me, while Tulip sidestepped up his arm to his shoulder. "Can I come?"

"Speaking of flight, when's yours?" Walt asked.

"I'm not going to L.A.," Ben replied. "I'm going to be an ornithologist."

Reno high-fived him. "Smart move."

"Why the change of plans?" Georgie asked.

"Look where entertainment got Dawn. No offence. I just don't want to be trapped in some dumb studio. I want to be in nature."

Jo nodded like she already knew about Ben's new aspirations.

"So you're sticking around?" Reno asked.

Ben shook his head. "I'm going to volunteer in the Rockies. With Parks."

"When?" Georgie asked.

"Next week," Ben said, and we were all quiet again.

"That's thrush country," Walt commented. "Land of mountain bluebirds. And Townsend's solitaire."

"And the veery," Ben added.

Georgie blew her nose, tucking the tissue into her lime band. "Allergies," she said.

"Let's warm up." Jo cleared her throat, puckered her lips, and made kissing sounds. I followed along but no one else did.

"We're warm enough, Josephine," Georgie told her. I could see sweat marks on her top.

Walt pulled his handkerchief out and patted his face. "This humdinger's too much for me, too."

"This is going nowhere," Jo said. "Tulip, none of these lazybones want to sing today. Do you?"

Tulip didn't react. She was watching Georgie's fan, approaching it then running away.

"It's pretty much ready," I told them. "If you'd like to see."

We finished our drinks and I led them through the French doors into the walkout.

Georgie ran her fingers along the keys of the piano we'd positioned by the bay window. "I hope you plan on soundproofing," she said. "Or you'll have angry neighbours. That big blanket might help."

My mother's quilt hung on the wall. All the furniture, including the bed and roosting cage, were gone. But my shelf of librettos remained, and we'd added more shelving, with enough space for an impressive library. I had kept Tulip's favourite tattered chair, too, for when she wanted to stay indoors and listen. Maybe we would reupholster it, maybe not. She also had a perch by the music stands.

In the kitchenette we would stock healthy snacks and drinks. Students could look out at the apple tree as they practiced, and at Tulip on warmer days. With the doors open, they would hear the wrens, sparrows, and chickadees. They would hear jays and crows and woodpeckers. They would hear cardinals.

"It was Reno's idea," I told them.

"Actually I wanted her in the barn," he said.

"Where will Tutu sleep?" Walt asked.

"My room."

"Big mistake," Georgie said. "Did I ever tell you about Luciano?"

"Only a thousand times," Ben told her.

I pulled *Whistling as an Art* from the shelf.

"Is that a first edition?" Walt reached a shaky hand out. Carefully he opened it and read Agnes Woodward's words. "The foremost essentials of a good whistler are: pleasing tone quality, flexibility of tongue, adequate range, correct breath control, and bird imitations with an intelligent understanding of their use. Personality is also an important factor in the making of a successful public whistler."

"That leaves us all out," Georgie said. "Aside from Ben."

Walt re-shelved the book. "You're off the hook, young lady. We're grateful you taught us what you know. I speak for us all when I say we have a new appreciation for opera. Which is about seeing the world differently."

I nodded. Although more than anything, I knew now that opera was about tragedy from great misunderstandings. But this was not opera. In this life, we didn't die from broken hearts. And it wasn't opera that had shown me a new way.

"You're my peeps," I told the small group before me. "Get it?"

Georgie did her motorboat lips.

"How long've you been saving that one for?" Ben asked.

"Maybe we can host the next Biennial in your barn," I suggested to Reno.

"The convention's defunct," Georgie said. "We all know it."

"I'll probably be dead in two years," Walt said. "And I'm thinking of a trip to Japan."

"I don't know where I'll be," Ben said.

"I'll be too busy with the motel," Reno said. "But it goes without saying, free accommodations anytime."

"This is it for me, too," Jo told us. "I've got a cabin. My dad's old place. I've decided to move there and restore it for Everett. It's going to be his one day."

"Good for you, Jojo," Walt said. "You've served your sentence."

"If I were you, I'd focus on genealogical research." Georgie plunked herself down in Tulip's chair. "I guess I'll try something new, too," she added. "Maybe an erotic novels club."

"I'll need an accompanist," I told her, and turned to Walt. "And a whistling teacher."

Georgie reached for the wishbone prongs around Jo's neck. "In that case, I'd better get myself one of these."

Jo swatted her hand away. "What will you call it?" she asked me.

"Tulip's," I said.

"Two lips. Awesome," Ben said.

Walt put his beret on. "The lost art of whistling. Might be your most popular class."

Then I showed them the picture on the wall. No one had seen it yet. It was the one of us all in Tadoussac. These are the eminent Warblers, I would tell my students. Here was Reno who helped build the school. Here was Walt, their masterful instructor, and Georgie, their strict accompanist. Here was our renowned birder Ben, and Josephine, possible granddaughter of one of the greatest siffleurs ever to live.

Here was a man I once knew, with his Congo African grey.

Tulip clamped onto my shoulder, nails digging in, and made a funny, repetitive sound.

"Did she just call you Mum?" Jo asked.

"I heard ma'am," Walt said.

"I heard hum," Ben said.

"I heard yum," Reno said.

"I heard Yo-Yo Ma," Georgie said.

We kept listening.

An orchestra of finches appeared in a nearby tree. It was dusk and one by one they drifted to the aviary. There they danced before they flew off again, vanishing through a secret gate in the air.

Together we did "Finnish Whistler." After our last note, Ben continued on. "I can never figure out when the song's done," he said.

"Not ever," Walt told him, and the Warblers agreed.

There would be no finale or requiem. We were here to find our music.

Acknowledgements

Thank you to my agents, Samantha Haywood and Stephanie Sinclair, for their unwavering commitment to this book. Thank you to Jen Knoch, whose editorial talents transformed the story, and to everyone at ECW Press who helped bring it to life. I am also grateful to Crissy Calhoun, Courtney Evans, Joey Gao, Linda Hamilton, and Tariq Maqbool. Thank you to my first and final readers, Farhad Kazemzadeh and Denise, Hans, and Nadine Berkhout, and most especially thank you to the whistlers.

NINA BERKHOUT is the author of two previous novels: *The Mosaic*, which was nominated for the White Pine Award and the Ottawa Book Awards and named an Indigo Best Teen Book, and *The Gallery of Lost Species*, an Indigo and Kobo Best Book and a *Harper's Bazaar* Hottest Breakout Novel. Berkhout is also the author of five poetry collections, including *Elseworlds*, which won the Archibald Lampman Award. Originally from Calgary, Alberta, she now lives in Ottawa, Ontario.